BEAUTIFUL ILLUSIONS DUET BOOK ONE

EIGHTY-ONE *Nights*

GEORGIA CATES

Imprint: Georgia Cates Books, LLC

ISBN-13: 978-1-948113-12-0

ISBN-10: 1-948113-12-0

Editing services provided by Lisa Aurello

Formatting by Jeff Senter of Indie Formatting Services

Cover design by Georgia Cates

1

CAITRIONA LOUDEN

I HATE MATH.

Column one is my net income. Column two is my half of the rent, general expenses, tuition, etcetera, etcetera, etcetera. Column two exceeds column one. It exceeds it by a lot.

Dammit, I'm going to have to unfasten an extra button on my blouse to get better tips at the bar.

Rachel, my roommate and BFF, comes through the door, her arms weighted down by shopping bags. It's not the first time this week. Hell, it's not even the second time.

"Another shopping spree?" My comment comes off a little bitchier than intended.

She drops all of the shopping bags on the floor. "Ohhh, Cait. I have something grand to show you."

She rummages through the bags, removing a shoebox. She takes out a Christian Louboutin pump and holds it up. Wow, it's the real deal. There's no mistaking that with the signature red leather outsole. And the bottom is completely unscathed, meaning that these shoes didn't come from a consignment shop or thrift store.

"They're to die for, aye?"

Black paisley lace. Peep toe. Black leather trim. They could possibly be the most gorgeous shoes that I've ever seen. "They're stunners for sure."

She slips her feet into them and stretches one leg outward, admiring the way it looks on her foot. "I'm so in love with them."

Christian Louboutin shoes today. Louis Vuitton handbag and Clive Christian perfume three days ago. Unless Rachel has a long-lost aunt who died and left her a fortune, she can't possibly afford luxury brands like these. "How are you paying for all of these things you're buying?"

She stands tall and places her hands on her hips. "I have this month's rent if that's what you're getting at."

I've clearly pissed her off, but I think that my concern is a legitimate one. "I'm not implying that you'd stiff me on the rent. It's just that these shopping sprees are expensive. Very expensive. And I'm wondering how you're paying for them."

"In case you forgot, I have a job."

We have the same job. I know how much money she makes. "Waitresses at The Last Drop can't afford Christian Louboutin and Louis Vuitton and Clive Christian."

She takes off the shoes and stuffs them back into their box. "Don't worry about how I'm paying. I've got it covered, and that's all you need to know."

Rachel doesn't talk to me like this. Ever. Not even when she's angry with me. I don't care for it at all.

"I don't want you to get yourself into financial trouble because you had a weak moment and charged some things you can't afford."

"I didn't charge anything."

None of this makes sense. "Some months we are literally scraping together every pound that we have to make rent."

"It's okay. I got a second job."

She hasn't mentioned a word about another job. "Where at? And when do you go to this job?"

Rachel inhales deeply and her cheeks expand when she exhales. "You can't judge, and you can't jump to conclusions when I tell you."

"I don't like the sound of that at all."

"I'm serious, Cait. You know that you can be judgy."

Okay. I admit that I'm a little critical at times but only because Rachel has a spectacular talent for making really dumb decisions. "I won't judge." Maybe, depending upon how bad it is.

"A fancy businesswoman came into The Last Drop a few months ago. When she got up to leave, she handed a small envelope to me. There was £200 inside along with a business card."

"Two hundred pounds?" Holy shit.

"The card was for a business called Inamorata."

Inamorata. "I've never heard of that."

"Me either, but I called her because I was dying to know more. She refused to discuss anything over the phone, which I thought was a wee bit weird at the time, but I was too intrigued to question it."

I can see that. I'm sucked into the mystery of it right now.

"We met for dinner in Old Town at a swanky restaurant by the castle. We had a few drinks, enough that I was feeling pretty damn good, and she began to explain what her company is about. She calls herself a chatelaine."

Maybe I'm just a dumbass American, but I've never heard of that. "What is a chatelaine?"

"Sounds fancy, right? By definition, it's a mistress of a

household or large establishment. Cora's organization, Inamorata, is a business that introduces women and men."

"Inamorata is a dating service?"

"Sort of." Rachel bites her bottom lip and squeezes one of her eyes together, peeking at me through the open one. "But not really."

That face. I know it well and it's never good when it makes an appearance. "Sort of but not really means what exactly?"

"Cora is a businesswoman, a very savvy one who has made a career out of connecting people—very successful men and attractive women—for mutually beneficial relationships."

Ah, the pieces are coming together now. "Sounds like a fancy way of saying that she's a madam."

"I'm not saying that sex isn't an offered service at Inamorata. It definitely is, but a large portion of the connections are for companionship-only, without sex."

"Men are men and I understand what drives them to buy sex, but I'm not sure that I understand why they'd pay for a woman's company when that's all they'll be getting."

"You'd be surprised by how many men want a woman's company without sex."

Money seems like an unnecessary part of the equation. "Why not ask a woman out on a date then?"

"Some of the men are too shy or intimidated to approach a beautiful woman. They may be widowed and want company for a single evening without the complications of going out on a real date. They all have different motives for booking an inamorata. No single reason fits all of them."

"Are they looking for girlfriends or wives?"

"I guess some are, but most are only interested in

readily available women for a set duration. And they don't care about the price tag."

"What kind of money are we talking about?"

"I make £200 an hour."

"Holy shit, Rachel."

"My pay scale is at the bottom because I'm companionship-only. The girls who have sex make around £400 an hour."

These women are making bank, sex or not. "Why would any man fork over that kind of money when he could get laid by a regular prostitute for so much cheaper?"

"Inamorata clients don't book dates because they want a quick shag. They want the whole package: beauty, brains, intelligent conversation, arm candy they can take out in public or to a corporate event."

"If these women are so beautiful and intelligent, then why aren't they doing something else?"

"They all have an end goal but not the money to obtain it. Being an inamorata is a stepping-stone to bridge the gap."

"Is your chatelaine choosy about who she'll hire?"

"Very. Every woman brought on board is a huge upfront expense for Cora. She transforms them from head to toe, and it doesn't stop there. Each woman who represents Inamorata must learn etiquette, be articulate, and have the ability to converse about a wide range of topics."

Rachel is so well-spoken. I hadn't noticed that change in her until now.

"Has any woman at Inamorata ever been hurt by a client?"

"Not that I'm aware of, but I assume that it's happened at some point. Nature of the beast, I guess. We're obviously at higher risk because we are alone with men whom we don't know. That's why we all go through a class and learn how to defend ourselves. I'm confident in my ability to fight off a client if need be."

"I don't doubt that for a second, even without a class." Rachel has three older brothers. She's a natural-born scrapper.

"You mentioned upfront costs. I assume that Cora is reimbursed for that?"

"Oh yeah. She takes 50 percent of the earnings until her investment is repaid. After that, she takes 25 percent off of the top. But we keep 100 percent of any tips or gifts from a client."

"What's a typical tip or gift?"

"Jewelry, designer clothes, handbags, cash. Maybe even a predetermined monthly allowance if it's an ongoing relationship. Some of the lasses get college tuition."

Whoa! Someone could pay for my education?

Two more semesters—that's all I need to earn the credits that I require to graduate with my degree. Where things stand now, I'm going to have to take out a student loan to pay for tuition. Not the end of the world but I'd rather not come out of college with a mountain of debt if I can help it.

Dammit, I can't believe that my stepmonster talked Dad into cutting me off when I'm only two semesters away from getting my degree. I was so close to living my best life. I could almost taste it.

Heidi loves to watch me bleed. She enjoys holding me down and her latest farce proves it.

God, I hate that woman. And I hate the way she manipulates my dad. Not that he ever won any father-of-the-year awards anyway. He was a deadbeat long before Heidi came along.

"Is Cora looking for more girls?"

"Possibly."

"Do you think that she could be interested in a girl like me?"

"Absolutely. You're already beautiful without any effort at all. I'm happy to put you in touch with her if you like."

Let's be brutally honest about this. What I'm contemplating is a form of prostitution, sex or not. It doesn't matter what kind of label we put on it.

"I can see that you're hesitant, but she'd never ask you to do anything that you didn't want to. She's always looking for companionship-only inamoratas: dinner and drinks and discussion. That's it."

I inhale deeply and blow out slowly. "All of this scares me."

"Talking with Cora isn't an obligation. It's only a conversation."

Only a conversation. It sounds so much more enticing when she puts it like that. "All right. Set it up."

I'M STANDING ON A PLATFORM, THE WALL IN FRONT OF ME covered with a floor-to-ceiling mirror. I feel like I should be trying on wedding dresses in a bridal boutique, waiting to say yes to the dress so that I can be jacked up with a veil and jewelry.

Cora taps the center of my back directly between my shoulder blades. "Stop slouching."

She walks down the steps of the platform and looks up at me. "What is your European shoe size?"

"Thirty-six."

"Valerie, bring the seventy-five-millimeter black peep toes in her size."

Good Lord. This woman has an assistant for everything, even shoe fetching.

"We'll begin your stride training with lower heels and work our way up to the higher ones."

Cora is short like me, but you don't notice until you look at her tall heels and see that four inches of her height can be attributed to her shoes.

Valerie returns and places the black pumps on the floor in front of me.

"Louboutins." I didn't intend for that to come out. And I definitely didn't mean for it to sound so covetous.

"I understand. You've never had shoes like these, but your closet is about to be filled with countless pairs like them along with designer clothing and handbags. You represent Inamorata. You represent me. It's crucial that you always look your best, but your job right now is to be my student. Listen to me and you'll learn how to entertain some of the wealthiest and most influential men in Scotland."

That's a frightening thought.

"You aren't at all concerned that your clients won't like me?"

"You're going to be a polished gem when I finish with you. No part of you will be unlikable."

I'm pretty sure that she's wrong about that.

"Not everyone loves Americans." I've lived in Scotland for six years, but I still consider myself American—my first sixteen years were spent there.

"Inamorata clients are going to love that about you. You're a different flavor from my other girls."

I hear what she's saying, but I look at myself in the mirror and can't imagine any high-class Scotsman who would be willing to pay big bucks for my company. I'm nobody.

"What's wrong, Caitriona?"

"I'm afraid."

"Don't be. I do background checks on every man before accepting him as a client. I reject anyone with even a hint of a questionable past."

"That's not the kind of afraid that I'm talking about."

"Well, I need you to explain what that means before we go any further."

It's embarrassing to admit my fears. "What if they don't think I'm pretty enough? Or smart enough? Or interesting enough?"

Cora claps her palms together twice, making a high-pitched slapping sound. "Everyone out. Now."

Her three assistants scramble to get through the door, nearly running each other down. I truly believe that if Cora told them to jump, they would ask how high.

She comes up on the platform, standing behind me. She grasps my upper arms and looks over my shoulder at my reflection in the mirror. "Look at the woman staring back at you. Who is she?"

"Caitriona Louden."

"You're stating the obvious and it's a waste of my time. Look deep inside of the woman in front of you, and find the wee lass beneath her surface."

Find the wee lass beneath my surface? No way. That's stupid.

I shake my head. "I don't want to do that."

"I don't care if you want to do it or not. You're going to if you want to work for me. The choice is yours."

I contemplate walking out. I want to so badly, but I can't. I need money.

"What do you want from me?"

"Start by taking a long hard look at yourself in the mirror and think about what you see."

Long brown hair, thick and often unruly. Hazel eyes, more green than brown after I've had a good cry. Fair skin, a few scattered freckles across my nose and cheeks. Short and small-framed.

"Are you pretty?" Cora asks.

"According to others, I am. But I never was in my mother's eyes."

"What did your mother say to you about the way you look?"

God, you look just like that Scottish bastard. I heard that from her so many times that it became as much a part of my DNA as the X chromosome that he gave me. "She said that I looked like my father."

"Did she hate him?"

"She did eventually." His marriage to Heidi changed everything. My mother couldn't take his being happy with another woman.

"She saw him when she looked at you?"

"Yes."

"We grow up and become women, but no matter how old we get, we always have a wee lass living inside of us."

I've never heard anyone say anything like that, but I suppose it's true at least to some degree.

"Tell me about the wee lass inside of you."

Little Caity Louden. She's not someone that I like to think about. Her story isn't a happily-ever-after fairy tale. "Her father abandoned her before she was born. She was raised by a single mom in the trashiest part of New Orleans. Her mother worked at a bar on Bourbon Street, but she drank more cocktails than she served."

"Keep going."

"She learned at a very early age how to fend for herself because no one took care of her." No one loved her. It's hard to admit, even to myself only in my head, that the one person in this world who was supposed to love me unconditionally didn't.

"And?" Cora says.

"Her tears ran dry and her delicate, soft heart hardened. It turned to stone."

Cora nods. "Stone is strong and resilient."

My eyes move to hers. "Stone is cold and resistant to penetration without being broken."

"Also true."

I look back at myself. "I'm damaged. Something's missing inside of me. A piece of me is not here."

Cora walks around and stands in front of me so that we're face-to-face. "Strong people don't have easy pasts, and the scars they carry prove that they are stronger than whatever tried to hurt them. You're a warrior and a beautiful young woman who is deserving of good things and happiness. You're special, Caitriona, whether you realize it or not. Our pasts aren't all that different; I understand you far better than you can ever imagine."

Cora's words are… empowering and soothing at the same time.

She crouches, unnecessarily repositioning the shoes in front of me, and I see the act for what it truly is. She's lowering herself and elevating me. "Toes go in first, beautiful warrior."

I grow three inches when I step into the shoes. She stands upright, and it feels good to look this powerful, independent woman in the eyes. She makes me want to be stronger.

"Diamonds are beautiful. And they're also flawed. They don't crack but they do cut." Cora places a finger beneath my chin, lifting it slightly, and looks directly into my eyes. "Be a diamond, Caitriona."

2

MAXWELL HUTCHESON

I'M SITTING IN THE DARK CORNER, SCANNING THE SEA OF women. Blondes, brunettes, redheads. Tall, average, short. Slim, fit, curvy. The choices are endless.

The men at this gala are swarming around the women like bees to honey. Or dicks to pussy. Aye, definitely dicks to pussy. Every man here is hoping to take a bonnie lass into his bed tonight. And they will for the right price.

I like to think of myself and my circumstances as different from the other men at this event, but I'm kidding myself. I'm going to pay for a woman just like all of them.

"I'm glad you came tonight. This is exactly what you need."

"Well, I have you to blame if it's not."

Brady, my best mate, is the one who is introducing me into the Inamorata world. He began using their services right after his divorce and has continued to be a regular client. There is a rigorous selection process for clients and he's my foot in the door.

"The redhead in the black dress is hot."

"Aye, she is." But I don't want a redhead. I'm afraid that she would remind me of Mina.

"You don't sound enthused. What do you think of the blonde in the green dress?"

That would also be a no. "I think that her plastic surgeon did her a disservice with those implants."

"Really? I think that her diddies look great."

He would. Brady is a diddies man. Always has been.

"I like a more natural look." Ones that almost fit inside my hands. And won't smother me to death.

A lovely brunette approaches our table. White blouse. Black pants. Obviously, a server for the event and not one of the Inamorata women. "Good evening, gentlemen. May I bring you something to drink?"

"I'll have a Tomatin," Brady says.

"Same for me."

"Coming right up."

Brady watches the server's arse as she walks away. "Tell me what kind of lass that you're looking for and maybe I can help you find her."

"I don't have any particular physical characteristics in mind. I just want to look at her and… feel something."

"Feel what? A stauner?" Brady can be such a dobber sometimes.

"I can get a hard-on by myself. I'm talking about a connection. I want to be drawn to her."

"Answer this for me, Max. Do you want to hold her hand or fuck her?"

"I'd like to do both actually."

Brady twists in his chair. "There are two kinds of Inamorata women—those who fuck and those who don't. Look around. Some of the women have a pink rosebud pinned to their left shoulder. It's a symbol meaning that they are willing to fuck and don't mind being asked to do so. No pink rosebud, no pussy."

I hadn't considered that possibility. I guess that I thought they'd all be willing to have sex for money.

"You might want to keep an eye out for a rosebud while you're looking for this lass that you want to connect with. Because your cock won't be making any kind of connection with her if she's not wearing a rosebud."

I believe that my choices were just narrowed down significantly; many of these women are missing a rosebud.

"Two Tomatins," the server says as she places our drinks on the table. "Can I bring you anything else?"

"That's all for now. Thank you."

Brady holds up his glass. "Here's to you finally getting out again. And getting shagged."

"I'll drink to that."

We toss back our whiskies and I look around, searching for that special woman who catches my eye. I quickly realize that I'll never find what I'm looking for by sitting in the dark corner all night. "Come on, let's do this."

Brady and I talk to many women over the next two hours and I become discouraged. This gala is my only chance at finding a woman who will be agreeable to my terms, but no one stands out as a contender.

With each passing minute, tonight's search is looking more and more like a failure. What a fucking disappointment. I was so sure that I was going to find what I was looking for.

"Now here is the woman that you must meet." Brady takes her hand, kissing the top. "You're looking lovely as always."

The woman looks at me and smiles. "Always such a charmer."

"Max, it's my pleasure to introduce you to Cora, the beauty and brains behind Inamorata."

Long blond hair. Brown eyes. Flawless teeth and smile. Perfect cosmetics. She looks midforties, but I'd bet that she's older and does a great job of pulling off the look of a much younger woman.

"This is my best mate, Maxwell Hutcheson."

She holds out her hand and I choose to go with a simple handshake, leaving off the kiss. "It's a pleasure."

"How very nice it is to meet you, Mr. Hutcheson. I hope that you're finding everything to your liking this evening."

"I'm enjoying the gala very much. Thank you for extending an invitation for me through Brady."

"It was my pleasure, but your arm is empty, Mr. Hutcheson. Have you not found an inamorata to suit your taste?"

I should choose my words wisely; I don't want to insult this woman. "Brady and I have spoken to many beautiful and interesting women tonight. I've found it difficult to choose one."

"I'd like the opportunity to change that. Would you be willing to tell me what you're interested in? I'm certain that I can assist you in finding the perfect inamorata for your needs."

I don't see the point. Not a single woman in this room stands out to me but if she wants to try, then let her. "I'm looking for a three-month arrangement with a woman who is willing to remain completely innominate to everyone within my world except me."

"Obscurity is my specialty, Mr. Hutcheson. I have someone in mind, but she's fresh out of training. Is that something that you'd be open to trying?"

"Actually, inexperienced is preferable." I want a true girlfriend experience with this woman. It would be a turnoff if her actions were robotic, as though she's simply going through the motions like so many times before.

"I have the perfect inamorata for you. She's brand new so you'd be her first client. The girl is beautiful, intelligent, interesting—the whole package. How does that sound to you?"

Sounds like a definite contender if she lives up to what Cora promises. "I'd like to meet her."

Cora gestures to the back of the room. "Right this way."

Brady takes a step to follow and Cora lifts her hand, placing it against his chest. "Only Mr. Hutcheson."

"Come on, Cora. I'm one of your best clients. I want to meet her too, in case she's not for Max."

"All of this is new to her. She doesn't need to be overwhelmed on her first night."

Brady frowns and holds up his empty glass. "I guess that means that I'm getting another drink."

I slap Brady on the back and chuckle. "Sorry, mate."

"Aye, sure you are."

I follow Cora through the crowd and eye the pair of women that we're approaching. One is blond, the other brunette, and it's the darker of the two who catches my attention. She's an absolute beauty, and I somehow overlooked her when Brady and I were making our rounds.

Please be the one that Cora was telling me about.

She's wearing a short black dress, and it fits her body like a glove. Her heels are tall, just the kind that I love. Her chestnut hair is in loose curls, but I can't yet tell how long it is. I hope that it at least reaches midway down her back. I love long hair. Always have.

She looks up as we approach, and I'm not sure if it's because I'm so hard up, but I swear that her smile is the sweetest damn thing that I've ever seen.

"Doll, I'd like to introduce you to a new client. This is Mr. Maxwell Hutcheson."

The brunette beauty offers her hand and the corners of her mouth curl upward, exposing a pair of dimples in her cheeks. "Hello. I'm Lou. It's lovely to make your acquaintance."

The woman is American. Or at least I think she is. Her accent sounds different—not like what I've heard in the past.

"The pleasure is all mine."

Lou. I wonder if that's her real name or an alias. I know that I would use an alias in this kind of business if I were her.

"Mr. Hutcheson was on his way out the door, and I couldn't let him slip away without meeting you. Perhaps the two of you could have a drink together and talk about what he's looking for."

I've spent the entire evening looking for a woman who made me feel something, and now I've found her. "I would love to discuss that with you if you're interested."

Her arm loops through mine, and fuck me, just her simple touch sends a jolt to my cock, giving it life. "Lead the way, Mr. Hutcheson."

3

CAITRIONA LOUDEN

Maxwell Hutcheson.

He's tall and fit. Very fit. And the suit that he's wearing looks killer on him. He's nothing like what I had pictured in my head when I imagined my first client. This is not what I was dreading.

Dark hair. Light eyes, pale blue I think, but it's dark in here so I can't tell for sure. What I do know is that he is one of the handsomest men that I've ever seen. And I don't understand what he's doing at an Inamorata gala.

I snap back into the present and realize that I'm sitting across from him, staring at his face. It's as though I've forgotten all of my training.

I lower my eyes and face, hoping that he won't see the heat in my cheeks. I should probably apologize for staring, but there's no tactful way of telling him that I'm dumbfounded because he isn't a troll or old enough to be my grandfather.

I don't get it. Why in the world would this man need a paid companion? Surely women flock to him.

I recall the reasons why many of our clients use our

services. They're busy businessmen, often too engaged in their jobs to have time for dating. That must be it because there's no way this man would have a hard time finding a woman who was interested in him.

"Cora tells me that you're brand new. You've never had a client?"

His accent is heavily Scottish. You'd think that I would have gotten over hearing it after living in Edinburgh for six years, but the truth is that I still find it sexy as sin.

I look up and smile when my eyes meet his. Yes, I've decided that they are pale blue. And kind. I don't see judgment in them as I am certain that he is analyzing me and my decision to be an inamorata.

I believe that you can see into the soul of a person through his or her eyes. Thoughts. Intent. Opinion. The simplicity in their expression tells a story. It says more than any words they could possibly speak.

The lines around the corners of his eyes. The creases around his mouth beneath his facial scruff. The furrows across his forehead. All of these distinct contours mean that he smiles often, and when he does, it spreads over his entire face.

"Tonight is my coming out, I guess you could say."

"Then I've met you at the perfect time."

"The perfect time for…?"

He hesitates and his uneasiness is a visible mask upon his face. "I want to be transparent with you about what has happened in my life. I need you to understand why I have specific… needs."

I thought that I was going to be the uneasy one, but this man is stressed out. For some unknown reason he makes me want to bring calm to his storm. "I want to hear everything that you have to say, but please understand that I'm not owed any kind of explanation about your needs.

Your desires are what they are, and that's all that I must be told."

"But I want to explain. It'll make me feel better if I do."

Oh, I get it now. He needs to clear his conscience. "I'm listening."

"I'm a widower."

Many of the Inamorata clients are. There's nothing surprising about that.

"I'm sorry. How long has your wife been gone?"

"Three months."

Only three months and he's out cruising for a woman? What a dick. It's no wonder that he needs to clear his conscience.

"Was your wife ill?"

"No, she was killed in a car accident."

"I'm sure that must have been very difficult losing your wife without any kind of warning. Do you have children?"

"I don't have children, but my wife had a daughter."

"Poor girl. It's a painful thing to lose your mother." Even if she is a shitty mother who mistreats you.

"You must think that I'm selfish for being here so soon after my wife's death."

I sure do.

Come on, Cait. I mean Lou. Remember your training. You can't let him see you forming a negative opinion of him. "It's not my job to judge or question your reason for being here."

"Things aren't as they sound."

"I'm sure they're not." Okay. That might have come out sounding a little judgy. I need to watch my tone.

"My wife was cheating on me."

Well, I guess that explains why he doesn't feel obligated

to wait longer before seeking the company of another woman. "I get it now."

"The marriage was over. I was in the early stages of filing for divorce, but our friends and family didn't know. And since everyone was still under the impression that we were happy, I was thrown into the role of being the devastated, grieving husband."

Ohhh. "I see how that could happen and how it would be a problem for you."

"I stopped loving her some time ago, but I still grieved losing her."

"Of course, you did. Anyone would."

"I chose to not tell our friends and family the truth about our marriage. It felt pointless to put them through more pain when no good could come from it."

What a selfless and compassionate act it was to keep his wife's secret because he didn't want to put others through more pain. "That was very considerate."

"That consideration has bitten me in the arse. Everyone treats me as though my life is at a standstill without my wife. They coddle me, making it impossible for me to move forward. I'm fucking miserable. I need companionship, but they would not keep their heids if I brought a new woman into my life so soon after Mina's death."

I understand his situation, but I don't think that I can help him. He wants more than I'm willing to give. "I see what you want but that's not what I do." I point to my left shoulder. "No pink rosebud."

One corner of his mouth tugs downward. "Aye, I noticed after we sat down."

"I'm sorry that I'm not what you're looking for, but Cora will find another inamorata for you, one who meets your needs."

He reaches across the table and cups his hand over mine. "Wait. Please don't go."

I still and look at him. He lets go of my hand and sits taller in his seat. "I don't want another inamorata. I want you."

Ah, man. It's more than a little flattering to hear those words come from him, but the flattery doesn't lessen my integrity. "I can't give what you want."

"Just hear me out before you say no."

I hesitate a moment and nod. "All right, I'm listening."

"Give me three months. Let me be your only client during that time. Get to know me like you would if we were dating. Begin by forming an emotional connection with me and let it grow. If it progresses into a physical relationship, don't fight it. Let it happen."

He makes it sound way less jaded than it is, as though our relationship would be something real. But I know it wouldn't be. That isn't what this is about. "I'm the wrong inamorata for you."

"I can't lie; I want the girlfriend experience. All of it. But only if our relationship grows into a place where that's what you want also."

He doesn't understand. "I can't be intimate with someone outside of a committed relationship. That's not who I am."

"We'll have a relationship, and it's going to be within the realms of a commitment. It'll actually be more of a commitment than you've ever known before because we will have a binding contract."

He has this way of spinning his words and making me see the flip side of the coin without even turning it over. "You negotiate like an attorney."

"No. I'm an investment fund manager at a large firm."

He deals with money. Probably big money. I bet he's rich as sin. Most of the Inamorata clients are.

"You've made some good arguments, but I need time to think about this."

His smile widens. "Thank you for not saying no."

"Don't thank me yet."

"When will you give me your answer?"

Anxious much? "In three days."

He nods, his smile fading. I'm amused by the way he doesn't even try to disguise his impatience. Reminds me of a child but this man must be in his thirties. I can tell by the small patches in his facial scruff occasionally catching the light, casting a glint.

"How old are you?"

"Thirty-three." Eleven years older than me. "And you?"

"Twenty-two."

He groans under his breath. "That's young."

"My circumstances forced me to grow up quickly. I'm mature for my age, Mr. Hutcheson."

"You cannot call me Mr. Hutcheson."

I don't suppose that he would want me to be so formal since he's hoping to fuck me. "Maxwell?"

"My friends call me Max."

Cora insists that we maintain formality with a client in the early stages. She says that becoming too friendly, too quickly can initiate problems. Some men will perceive friendly and informal behavior as an invitation to treat the inamorata as though their relationship isn't a business transaction.

"May I call you Hutch?" Yes, it's a little friendly sounding but still a distinction from the shortened name used by his friends and loved ones.

"Hutch?" He smiles and nods. "Hutch. I like it."

"I do too." It fits him.

"Will you let me take you out tomorrow night? I don't think it's fair to ask you to make a decision like this without spending time with me."

Cora has been very clear about seeing Inamorata clients. Every date must be authorized by her. Break the rule even once and you're out. "I'm happy to go out with you if Cora approves."

"No worries. She'll agree."

I hope. I'd like to discuss in more detail what the girlfriend experience means to him.

When I'm home and in bed for the night, Maxwell Hutcheson is the only thing on my mind, making it difficult to drift off to sleep. But I finally do. I'm dreaming of him when the bed shifts beside me and I jolt awake. The instant that the adrenaline surges through my veins, my heart takes off like a helicopter. Boom, boom, boom, it beats against the inside of my chest.

"Rachel!"

"Yeah, it's me."

I'm relieved to hear her voice, but I'm annoyed as fuck when I look at the clock on the nightstand: 2:54 in the morning. "You scared the shit out of me. What are you doing climbing into my bed at this hour of the morning?"

"I'm dying to hear what happened with the client you met tonight."

She's not going to believe this. "He'd like to book me for three months, which is fine by me except that he also wants the girlfriend experience. All of it."

"Did you tell him that you don't have sex with clients?"

"Yes, but he wants to move forward anyway with the hope that sex will fall into place after we get to know each other. I told him that I needed to think about it."

"You're actually considering it?"

I know. I know. I know. I said that I'd never have sex with a client, but that was when I thought they were all trolls. "I guess that I'm not *not* considering it."

"You'd really have sex with this guy?"

"I don't know. Maybe, if we got to know each other and if the chemistry was right."

"He's fit. You should totally have sex with him."

"He is sooo good-looking, right?" I would have never dreamed in a million years that I'd land a client like him on my first night. How lucky am I?

"Cora's onboard?"

"She told me that it was going to cost him big time. So yeah, if the money is right then she's all for it."

"Will you see him again before making a decision?"

"He's taking me out tomorrow night. Well, technically, I guess tonight. He's sending his driver to pick me up because he has an early evening meeting with a client."

"He must make some serious money if he has a driver. What does he do for work?"

"Investment fund manager."

"I bet that he's really smart. And ultra-rich."

"Those are my thoughts exactly."

"If you do this, you have to be careful."

"Cora told me that she'd run an in-depth background check since the duration is so long."

"Not what I mean. I'm talking about spending three months with this guy. That kind of time together would make it so much easier to fall in love with him."

"I would never fall in love with a client." He's hot but I'm not stupid.

"It happens, Cait. It happens more easily than you think."

"That's not me. I have plans for my life, and they don't

include falling for a man who would pay a woman to be with him."

"Three months is a long time. You'll become close even if you don't mean to."

"We'll have to agree to disagree on that."

Rachel is wrong. To become close to a man, you must be able to let him into your heart. And that's something that I never learned how to do.

The truth is that I like the wall that I've built around myself. It makes me feel good. It makes me feel safe. It makes me feel strong. I don't think that I could let it down if I tried.

4

MAXWELL HUTCHESON

CALVIN SENDS A TEXT TO MY MOBILE AFTER HE AND LOU arrive at the entrance of the Waldorf Astoria. I'm instantly on my feet, taking a final look at myself in the mirror. Tie straight. Vest smooth. Sleeves loosely rolled up so this will feel more casual and less business.

I wish that I could go down and properly receive Lou. I consider doing so but I know how unwise that would be. I can't take the chance of being seen with a woman in a hotel by anyone who knows me.

Looking through the peephole, I watch her approach the suite. I decide that I'll let her ring the bell and then wait a few seconds before opening the door.

Damn, she looks gorgeous. Maybe even more beautiful than last night.

Hair hanging in loose curls. Mile-high heels stretching her legs. A one-shouldered black dress belted at the waist. I ache to reach out my hand and touch the exposed skin on her shoulder.

"Hello."

Her weight shifts to one leg and she puts her hand on her hip. "Seriously? You had your driver bring me to a hotel with instructions to meet you in a room?"

Okay. I clearly didn't consider how this might look to her. "My business meeting was in this hotel and since I can't take you to a restaurant, I thought it would be nice to have in-room dining so we could talk over dinner."

Her cheeks pinken and she reaches up, cupping her hand over her forehead. "Oh my God. I'm so embarrassed."

"It's all right. I can see why you would have jumped to that conclusion." I open the door wide. "Will you come in?"

She follows me into the open living-kitchen-dining area. "I wasn't sure what you might want to eat, so I took the liberty of ordering several of the best items from the menu. And I hope that sauvignon blanc is all right. It seemed like a safe choice."

"It's perfect. Thank you."

I pull out her chair and slide it under her as she sits. "I hope you're hungry."

"I am." Her dimples make a return, and I find myself wanting to know all of the secrets that she hides behind that angelic smile. "I should probably warn you that I'm a foodie, not one of those silly girls who acts as though she doesn't have to eat to survive."

"I'm glad to hear it." Mina was forever on some kind of diet and exercise plan. She inventoried every bite that she consumed.

I remove the lid over our starter. "Cured foie gras. Have you had it before?"

"No, but it looks good. How is it served?"

"Spread it on the brioche and enjoy. It's that simple."

She does as I instruct and takes a bite. "It's rich and buttery, but I can't put my finger on what I think it might be."

"Do you want me to tell you?"

No hesitation. "Yes."

"Duck liver."

"That's some fancy duck liver. I would have never guessed that."

"The thought of eating liver bothers some people."

She laughs. "I'm from New Orleans. We eat frog legs and alligator and suck out the insides of crawfish heads. I'm not squeamish about a little duck liver."

"You're a NOLA girl? I've never been to New Orleans. I hope that I get the opportunity to learn more about it from you."

"Everyone loves the party scene, but the food and history are what I love. It's amazing. I miss living there."

"Why did you leave?"

She lowers her fork and sits back in her chair. "My mom died when I was sixteen. I came here to live with my father."

"You're half-Scottish?"

"I am."

That's unexpected. "Do you still live with your father?"

"I did until I was twenty-one. That's when they stopped paying for my education and cut me off. And as if that weren't enough, they kicked me out of their house. My stepmother hates me."

"Why?"

"Because I breathe? Because my father had a child with another woman? Because he had a life before her and I'm the proof? Take your pick. Your guess is as good as mine."

"That's how you ended up at Inamorata?"

"Yes. I can graduate with my degree in two more semesters, but I can't afford tuition on a waitress's wages. When I found out that I could earn enough money over the summer to pay for school and avoid a student loan, I jumped at the chance."

Beautiful and intelligent. "What is your major?"

"English language and literature. I want to be a writer."

"What kind of writer?"

"I haven't decided yet."

I get the impression that she's holding back the truth. But I ignore the feeling and let it go.

Her eyes are on mine and for the first time I notice her unusual eye color. I thought they were brown, but I see that I was only partially right. They're more green than brown and there is a ring of gold around her pupil. And I also notice that her hair isn't a single shade of brown; it's full of honey-colored streaks, especially around her face.

"Is Lou your real name?"

She grins. "No."

"I didn't think so. You don't look like a Lou to me."

"What do I look like?"

"Emily?"

"No."

"Isabelle?"

"No."

"Are you going to tell me your real name?"

"No."

That's a lot of noes. "You know my real name. I would like to know yours."

"We don't tell clients our real names. It's for our protection."

"I understand why you wouldn't tell a typical client, but

I'm not going to be like the other men who seek the services of Inamorata. You're going to be with me for three months. We'll come to know each other well."

"I haven't said yes."

"No, but you're going to."

One of her brows lifts. "Cocky much?"

"Confident. There's a difference."

"It's better if you know me as Lou."

I'm going to let this name thing go for now, but I intend on finding out her real name before this relationship is over.

"Will you tell me about yourself or will that be a secret too?"

"I'll continue to tell you things about my life as long as it's nothing specific that would identify me."

She's a mystery and, damn, if that's not a fucking turn-on.

"Tell me what your idea of the girlfriend experience is." She nibbles her bottom lip and somehow manages to look both innocent and seductive at the same time.

"Our time together would be spent having conversations, sharing our passions and dreams, laughing, enjoying dinner or a movie. Forgetting the world around us."

"What about the physical aspect?"

"I'd like to begin with simple contact, swapping subtle touches back and forth."

"Open-mouthed kissing?"

"Aye. And when you're comfortable enough for things to progress, I'd like our intimate time in the bedroom to be romantic and intense and passionate."

"With eye contact?"

That question makes it sound as though she has already given this much thought.

"Only when it feels natural. I wouldn't want it to be forced."

I know next to nothing about her. But I know that when I look at her, I feel alive again. This woman has bewitched me. I want her. She has to say yes. I won't take no for an answer.

5

CAITRIONA LOUDEN

Rachel is out with a client. I have no idea when she'll be back, but I'm relieved to be alone. I need peace and quiet after tonight's meeting with Maxwell Hutcheson. My thoughts are running in a million different directions at once.

Sleep doesn't come easily. I stare at the ceiling for hours because I can't stop thinking about the man with pale blue eyes and what he wants from me.

The girlfriend experience. It's an intriguing proposal, almost as though our relationship would be scripted. No surprises. No fear of being hurt. No heartbreak. Most importantly, I would already know the terms of when and how things would end.

Being with a stranger is frightening, but Hutch somehow manages to put me at ease. What is it about him that I find comforting? His kind eyes and facial expressions? His soft voice? His dry sense of humor? All of it combined?

I eventually fall asleep, only to be awakened by Rachel sneaking into my bedroom again. I look at the clock: 8:27

a.m. This shit is getting old, but at least she made it to a reasonable hour this time. "Please tell me that this is the last time you're going to wake me up like this."

She collapses on my bed beside me. "I make no promises."

Placing my pillow over my head, I groan. "Go away."

"No. I want to hear all about your date with Mr. Girlfriend Experience."

"He had his driver bring me to the Waldorf, and I was instructed to go up and meet him in his room."

"Wow. He wasted no time trying to get you into bed."

It's only natural that she'd draw that conclusion. "The room wasn't for sex. It was for in-room dining because he can't take me to a restaurant or any other place where we could be seen together."

"Oh. Well, that part of the arrangement sucks, but I guess it goes along with his MO."

"I was pissed off about being summoned to a hotel room until he explained why he had me come there."

"I assume that you spoke more in-depth about his proposal? What are your thoughts about it now?"

"We used the time to become better acquainted with one another, and I must admit that I'm leaning toward the idea of saying yes. But having sex with someone I don't love? I'm not sure I can do that."

"You slept with Cameron and look at how much you hate him now." No truer words have ever been spoken.

"Valid point."

"You're overthinking this. The guy's rich and he promises you what could be the best three months of your life. I wish a client would make me an offer like that."

Rachel and I look at one another when we hear the knock on our flat's door.

"Who the fuck is here this time of morning?" she says.

She just got home from a date, which is a little worrisome. "Do you think your client followed you home?"

"I don't think so. He's a really nice guy."

"Well, you're presentable and I'm not, so you're going to the door." Perfect excuse for me to make her answer the door while I stay in bed.

"All right but you better come running if I scream."

I roll to my side, closing my eyes and snuggling against my pillow. I didn't get much sleep last night, and I could seriously catch some more Zs if Rachel would pipe down and leave me alone.

My mind is going, drifting into that restful place, until Rachel shouts my name. "Get up. You have to come and see this."

Shit. I should have known that she wouldn't let me go back to sleep. "Okay, but give me a minute."

With hair and teeth freshly brushed, I go to the living room and Rachel is all smiles. "Raith brought this by. He said that it was delivered to the office this morning with instructions to be forwarded to you."

There's a huge floral arrangement and basket of fresh fruit, pastries and champagne on the kitchen counter. And a thought occurs to me: no one has ever sent flowers to me before. Ever. How sad is that?

"Mimosas for breakfast. Can you believe that? And this isn't cheap champagne. It's expensive. Very expensive." Rachel holds out a small white envelope. "Here's the card, but I think we can already guess who these things are from."

You won't regret saying yes.

—Hutch

I rub my thumb over the words and smile, biting my bottom lip in an attempt to suppress my pleasure.

"Come on, I'm dying to hear what the card says."

"Just one line. 'You won't regret saying yes. Hutch.'"

"I don't know this guy, but I have to agree with him. I don't think that you'll regret doing it." Rachel takes out the bottle of champagne and lifts her brow. "It's still cold. Shall I pop the top and mix up some mimosas?"

"Go for it."

The cork shoots upward and hits the ceiling. "Well, that old bag upstairs will be bitching about that."

"No doubt." Mrs. Whitten is by far the grumpiest old lady that I've ever had the displeasure of knowing. She's forever complaining to the landlord about Rachel and me for one reason or another.

"I'm seeing him again tonight." I don't admit it but I'm excited. I like spending time with him.

"Where is he taking you?"

"Don't have a clue."

"The whole staying-out-of-the-public-eye thing limits your options."

"No kidding." Hiding. Seems like that will become a hassle after a while.

"I bet he takes you to a hotel again."

"That would be okay. I didn't mind." It was a suite, so it didn't feel a lot different from being in someone's living room for the first time.

"You should wear the black Dolce & Gabbana lace shift dress with your strappy Louboutins."

"I love that dress." There's no telling how much Cora paid for it.

"You should. You look amazing in it."

I feel ultra-sexy in it. "Yeah, I'm wearing it."

"And do your hair up in a vintage roll. You look so pretty with it like that."

"Ah, thanks."

We hold up our mimosas. "What do we toast to?"

"To your arrangement with Hutch. May it be the best three months of your life."

The thought is exciting and terrifying at the same time. "I'll drink to that."

~

THE COSMETICS, THE HAIR, THE DRESS, THE SHOES. I LOOK like someone other than Caitriona Louden.

I study the petite brunette's reflection in the mirror and decide that she passes for something she's never been—elegant and graceful and classy. I don't just look like another person—I am another person.

I am Lou.

The girl looking back at me can pretend all she likes but she's only different on the outside. Discomfort. Distrust. Doubt. She's filled to the brim with those emotions, yet she feels overwhelmingly empty inside. And she's held captive by that void.

Enough of that, Cait. You'd better get moving before you miss the train. Being late isn't an option.

Rachel surveys me when I come into the living room. "Do a spin and let me see all of you."

I twirl with the grace of a ballerina despite the high-as-hell heels that I'm wearing. "I look okay?"

"You look stunning."

Rachel is my best friend. It's her job to say stuff like that. "It's the dress and shoes."

"Hell no, it's not. It's all you, and Mr. Maxwell Hutcheson is going to beg you to give him that yes."

He can beg all he likes, but I'm not ready to give him an answer.

"I need to go if I'm going to make the six o'clock train."

"Are you going to allow him to pick you up here if this arrangement goes through?"

"I have no idea. How would you feel about his knowing where we live?"

"I trust you to make that decision. If you're all right with his knowing, then I'm okay with it."

I can already tell that catching the train to Inamorata's office for a pickup and drop-off is going to become a hassle. But this is a job and I'm getting paid for it. That's the only way to look at this.

Rachel stretches out on the couch and covers herself with our fluffy pink throw blanket. "I'll be right here binge-watching Game of Thrones while you're out."

"Again?"

"You know how much I love Jon Snow." Yes, I certainly do. "Be a doll and text if you're going to be late or decide to stay the night with him."

Is she serious? "You know better than that."

"It could happen if things go really well."

"I'll text if I'm running late but you can expect me home; there will be no staying over with him."

"Either way, have a great evening."

I see the familiar black luxury sedan parked in front of Inamorata as I approach. Shit, I'm breaking one of the first rules that Cora taught me. *Never be late. It conveys to the client that his time isn't important, and these men don't like to be made to feel like they're less than the most important thing in your life at the moment. Their egos need to be stroked.*

Hutch looks up as I approach the car and gets out. His

gaze follows my body, beginning at my feet and ending at my eyes. And then he smiles.

Damn. Just damn.

"Hello, beautiful."

"I'm so sorry if I'm late."

"You aren't late. I'm early."

I look at my watch and see that I've arrived eight minutes earlier than our designated time. "Well, that's a relief. I wouldn't want to be the reason that you're waiting for me."

"Do you need to go inside or are we free to go?"

This date has already been approved by Cora. "We can go."

I get into the car and slide across the seat, making room for Hutch. "Thank you for the flowers and breakfast basket. It was delicious. And unexpected."

"I'm glad that you enjoyed it."

"We did. Mimosas are the perfect excuse to have alcohol in the morning."

"Aye, they certainly are."

I fold my hands over my clutch so that I'm not tempted to fidget.

"You look lovely."

"Thank you." I smooth my hands down my dress. "I hope that my outfit is okay. I wasn't sure what I should wear since I didn't know where we were going."

"My apologies. I should have told you that I'm taking you to my house."

"Oh." That's surprising since it seems so important to him to keep me away from the people in his life.

"Perhaps I should have asked if that's all right?"

"No, your house is fine."

"I'd like for you to see where we'll spend the majority of our time. I mean, if you say yes."

"That's very thoughtful."

"I'm trying to be mindful of what this must feel like for you. I want you to say yes."

I'm surprised to find that Maxwell Hutcheson is so considerate of my feelings. "I can tell. Thank you."

Of course, he lives in a home that is more of a castle than a house, complete with the turreted tower. I almost believe that he has brought me here because he knows how much I'd love his renovated castle.

What can I say? I'm still American at heart, and we have a love for and fascination with the castles of Scotland.

"Your home is beautiful."

"We're on thirty-two acres so there's plenty of privacy. And only a mile from Kirkliston. You can get almost anything you need in the village without trekking into Edinburgh, which makes life much easier."

"Yes, I'm sure that is convenient. How far are we from Edinburgh?"

"Twelve miles."

We've been driving for a while. "It feels much farther."

"You can blame it on the traffic. It's brutal this time in the evening."

Hutch gives me a tour of his house and I'm caught off guard when he introduces me to the housekeeper and cook during our walk-through. I thought that I was supposed to remain unseen by everyone within his world.

"It's seven. Sonny should have dinner on the table for us."

How convenient that must be to have dinner prepared and placed on the table for you each night.

Hutch leads me into the dining room and pulls out my chair, pushing under me when I sit. "Is this jambalaya?"

"I asked Sonny to prepare a typical New Orleans dish

since it's probably been a while since you've had a taste of home."

Another display of thoughtfulness from Hutch. "It's been a really long time since I've had Cajun food."

"Sonny has traveled the world learning how to prepare a lot of different cuisines. Cajun wasn't one of them but I'm confident that he did a great job. He's a talented chef."

"It looks and smells delicious."

The Cajun holy trinity: celery, onion, and green pepper. The perfect Cajun seasonings and heat. Chicken, shrimp, and sausage. Tomatoes and rice. It only takes one bite to instantly transport me back to New Orleans. "He nailed it."

"I knew that he wouldn't disappoint. He also recommended pairing it with this light-bodied French Burgundy."

I was only sixteen when I left New Orleans. I have no idea what kind of wine complements Cajun food, but this works for me. "His wine choice is perfect."

We eat without speaking for several minutes, and then Hutch interrupts the silence. "You've had some time to think about my proposal. Is there any part of it that you'd like to discuss?"

I'd like to discuss every part of it. "I don't know where to begin."

"You can ask me anything. Don't be afraid."

I hope that he truly means that. "The sex part. I'm struggling with it."

"What part of it bothers you?"

All of it. "To begin with, you're a stranger to me."

He reaches across the table and places his hand on top of mine. "I won't feel like a stranger to you for long. You'll come to know me quickly."

He seems so certain but how can he know that for

sure? I'm attracted to this man, but I don't know that I can ever be comfortable enough to have sex with him.

"This will never be a real relationship, so being with you on an intimate level feels wrong."

I wasn't raised by a mother with the highest of standards, but I was somehow instilled with morals regarding the sexual relationship between a man and woman.

"It feels wrong because we aren't well acquainted, but we will be. I'm confident that our relationship will progress to a place of comfort quickly because there are no pretenses between us. Our honesty and known expectations will make everything easier and more relaxed. Our time together will be more satisfying because our only motives are to enjoy each other's company. There's zero pressure on either of us to be anything other than what we truly are."

No pretenses. No pressure. No pretending. I must admit that I don't mind that.

"Are you on birth control?"

Did he just go there with me? Yep. He sure did.

Birth control. Is that a conversation that I'm going to have with this man? Am I going to tell him those kinds of intimate details about myself?

I have to if I'm considering his proposition.

"I take the pill. I have for years."

"I'm not a fan of condoms."

"I'm not a fan of the diseases you can catch when you don't use them."

"I'm clean."

"So am I." And I have the documentation to prove it. "But there are two things that I won't allow you to give me: a disease or a baby." I'll never be that stupid.

"Your birth control pills eliminate the possibility of a baby. Would you be open to the option of having sex without condoms given that I provide you with a physician's report that I'm disease-free?"

"My list of sexual partners is a short one—very short—but I've never had sex without a condom. Ever. If I say yes to your proposal, that won't change."

One side of his mouth tugs upward. So damn smug. Like he knows something that I don't. "You can think it over and we'll revisit this conversation later."

We can revisit it as many times as he likes, but I won't change my mind about not using condoms.

Casual sex. That's what this is going to be between us. Can I go through with it? Can I give my body to a man who doesn't love me?

I've done it before. But of course, I didn't know it at the time. I thought that Cameron loved me.

"Sex changes everything between a man and woman. It complicates things. Do you really believe that we'll do this for three months and then simply walk away from each other without any kind of difficulty?"

"It won't be a problem if we go into it with the same expectations and are both aware of how things will end."

A built-in expiration date. A daily countdown to the end. Literally.

Am I really thinking of agreeing to this madness?

"Are you accepting my proposal?"

I shake my head. "I need to spend more time with you and become better acquainted before I can make that kind of decision."

"What would you like to know about me?"

Everything. I want to know everything. "Tell me about your family."

"My family lives in Glasgow."

"Is that where you grew up?"

"Aye."

I thought so. His burr is heavier than what I'm accustomed to hearing.

"Are your parents still married?"

"Aye. Still together after thirty-six years of marriage."

I can't imagine what that must feel like. My parents never married, so I have no idea what it's like to have your mom and dad living in the same house. Hell, I never so much as saw my parents in the same room together. Not once.

"Do you have siblings?"

"I have a sister who is three years younger than I am. Sara. She and her husband Adam have two sons. Leo is four and Mason is one. I also have a younger brother, Ian, who is twenty-two. He'll be starting his final year of study at uni in the fall."

"At Edinburgh?"

"Aye."

Ian Hutcheson. The name doesn't ring a bell but that doesn't mean anything. "The campus isn't that large. It's possible that my path has crossed your brother's. We could run into each other later down the road since I'll be returning to school in the fall. Would that cause a problem for you?"

"Ian will never know about our relationship. I don't see why it would be a problem."

Right. Because I'll be Hutch's secret. Unseen and unheard by everyone within his world.

"What about your late wife's family? Do you still have contact with them?"

"Aye, more than I'd like. They hover. Especially Mina's sisters. Her youngest sister is the worst."

"Were they like that before your wife died?"

"Aye, they stuck their noses into our lives and marriage, giving Mina a lot of unwanted advice."

Sounds like she was close to her sisters. "Do you really think that they didn't know about her affair?"

"Definitely not. Mina wanted people to believe that our marriage was perfect. She'd have never admitted to infidelity; it would have shattered her flawless image."

What a bitch. "Your wife left you in one hell of a predicament."

"You don't know the half of it."

HUTCH AND I GET INTO THE BACK SEAT OF THE CAR. I glide across the seat, stopping in the middle so that we're sitting next to each other, our legs touching. The only thing separating our skin is the fabric of his trousers, and the simple touch sends a thrill of excitement through my body.

Calvin peers at Hutch through the rearview mirror. "Where to, sir?"

"Back to the Inamorata office."

I'm feeling the effects of tonight's wine. Yes, I drank more than I should have, and Cora wouldn't approve, but Hutch and I were having some intense conversations tonight. I needed something to help me loosen up. And loosen up, I have. Liquid courage pulsates through my veins, making me feel brave. And flirty.

I rest my hand on Hutch's thigh, feeling the muscle beneath my palm grow taut. I can't make out his facial expression, but his breathing becomes louder, his scent stronger and oh so masculine. I'm suddenly hypersensitive to everything about this man.

Hutch places his hand on my knee and heat radiates up my thigh, gaining my full attention.

"I want to know what you're thinking," he says.

So many things are racing through my head right now.

If I do this, something will go wrong, and this man will hurt me. I know it as surely as I'm sitting here next to him, feeling how much he makes me want to say yes. "I'm not fool enough to believe that a fire like this won't burn one of us."

I'm not an idiot. *One of us* = me. I'll be the one to get burned.

Even in the dark back seat, I see him grin. "You think this thing between us is fire?"

Fire isn't a good enough word to describe what's happening between us. Inferno is a better word. But I don't reply to his question; it would be stupid to throw fuel on flames already blazing out of control.

I'm relieved when Calvin stops in front of Inamorata's office. I need to get away from Hutch. Now, before this conversation goes any further.

We get out of the car and walk up the sidewalk to the building's entrance. He shocks me by reaching for my hand. Such a sweet, intimate thing to do.

We're standing at the entrance of the building, and security is nowhere to be seen. It's not that late. Raith must be on break. And I'm glad because I sense something coming.

Hutch grips my hips and walks me backward until my back is against the stone of the building, a cage of muscular arms entrapping me. His eyes dart from mine to my mouth, then back up to my eyes. His mouth is so close to mine that I feel his warm breath on my lips. "I want to kiss you, but I won't without your permission."

My chest heaves up and down. I can see it moving in my peripheral vision, and my breathing is loud. So damn loud. I'm taken aback by the sudden and unexpected urgency that I feel for him.

Don't do this, Cait. It's a mistake. Maxwell Hutcheson is a mistake. He will hurt you.

Shut up, stupid gut feeling. I want this. I want him. To hell with the consequences.

"Kiss me." Make my fantasies come true.

Half of a heartbeat later, his lips collide against my mouth, and I open to invite his tongue inside to meet mine. The two share their first waltz and it's a slow, seductive dance.

Our first kiss. He tastes like residual Burgundy and man. All man.

His hands move from my hips, one to the nape of my neck and the other to my lower back, pulling me hard against his body. Through the fabric of our clothing, I can feel how hard he is, and it weakens my knees.

His mouth leaves mine and drags across my face, hovering over my ear. "Say yes and you'll have the summer of a lifetime with me."

"The summer of a lifetime, huh? That makes the offer very tempting."

"Tell me what it will take to make my tempting offer become irresistible."

"I need a little longer."

"You said that you'd give me an answer in three days. That's tomorrow night."

"I'm aware. And I will give you an answer, as promised."

"How will this work?"

"Cora will contact you after I've made my decision. If I decide to accept your offer, she'll ask you to come in for a consult. That's the first meeting. After that, she'll draw up the paperwork, and we'll have a second meeting to finalize the agreement."

"When can I see you again?"

"You won't see me again… unless we move forward with the agreement." I like the little wave of panic that I see in his eyes.

"If you say yes, when is the earliest that we can move forward?"

"That's all dependent upon Cora's schedule."

"I'm eager to move on this as soon as possible."

"I see that."

"I'm clearing my schedule for the entire weekend. I want you to spend it with me at my house."

"You're already asking me to stay over?"

"I understand that overnights will cost extra. Cora has been clear about that and I'm prepared to pay."

He's failing to see that my hesitancy has nothing to do with money. "We hardly know each other."

"I want to change that. I'm ready to get this stranger anxiety behind us so we can move on to the fun stuff."

Fun stuff. We both know what he means by that.

"I'll think about staying over. That's all that I'm promising."

"I had a lovely evening with you, Lou." He kisses my forehead, instantly changing my mood. The sweet, intimate action is completely unexpected and feels as though it has no place in the arranged-relationship discussion that we're having.

I watch him walk to his car, stopping midway to turn around and call out, "I hope you say yes to my proposition and to staying the weekend."

This beautiful man has a dark side that draws me in yet makes me want to run. But I know I won't run. I've never been more certain of anything in my life, and I wonder how in the world that I've allowed myself to be sucked in.

And there it is. I admit it. Even if Hutch doesn't yet know, he has me.

I take out my phone and choose Cora's contact. "Hello?"

"Cora. It's Caitriona. I'm calling to tell you that I want to move forward with Mr. Hutcheson's proposition."

"That's wonderful news. I'll contact him tomorrow for the consultation. Welcome aboard, Caitriona."

There. It's done.

I'm an inamorata. Officially.

~

"THIS IS CUTE." RACHEL HOLDS UP A G-STRING, THE BACK made entirely of stringed pearls. "You should buy this for your date this weekend."

I take the G-string from her and hold it up by the waistband. "Pearls in the crack of your ass? What do you think that would feel like?"

"Dinnae ken but I think that I'll buy it just to find out."

Nothing about that statement surprises me.

I pass the near-nothing scrap of fabric back to her. "Let me know how that works out for you."

We browse through the lingerie store and Rachel stops, turning to look at me. "Are you ready to sleep with him?"

I look around the store. "Could you say that a little louder? I don't think that old lady at the front of the shop heard you."

"Fine." She lowers her voice. "Are you ready to sleep with this guy?"

"No, of course not. I've only known him for a few days."

"You'll sleep with him if you stay at his place this weekend."

Rachel knows that I'm not a girl who sleeps around. "Why would you say that?"

"It's what he's going to expect. It's what I would expect if I were him."

"He can expect it all he likes, but I'm not going to have sex with him because of expectations."

"How much is he paying for you?"

God, those words make me cringe inside. "I don't know yet."

"You like this guy, don't you?"

"I like Hutch as much as I can like someone that I've only interacted with a few times."

Rachel shrugs. "Maybe you should go into it with an open mind and see what happens."

"Are you saying that I should sleep with him this weekend?"

"I'm saying that you don't have to rule it out completely." She chooses a silk cami-and-shorts set from the rack and holds it up to herself. "And it might be a good idea to show up prepared, just in case."

Prepared, just in case. Translation: pack lingerie in case there's some sexy time.

She holds out the silky pajama set for me to take. "Purple is a great color on you. It always makes your eyes look greener."

I take the set from her and hold it up to myself, imagining the way it would look on me. "This is sexy, yet it doesn't imply that I'm wearing it because I came to his house planning to have sex with him."

"Exactly. It could go either way."

I pluck a similar set in ivory and black from the rack, holding it up to myself as well. "I guess I would need a second outfit if I decide to stay both nights. A man like Hutch would expect me to wear something different on night two."

"Absolutely, but I also think you should buy something a wee bit sexier too."

I look up at Rachel's reflection in the mirror. "Something sexier?"

"Aye, in the event that you hit it off and want to go all the way with a bang."

"Buying lingerie for sex is premeditated. It'll be like going in with the mindset that I'm going to do it."

"Not really. It's no different than buying condoms. Doesn't mean that you're ever going to use them, but you always need them on hand for the what if."

Funny that she should bring up condoms. "He asked me to do it bare."

Rachel's eyes widen. "Are you fucking kidding me?"

"Not even a little. He wants the full girlfriend experience. No condoms."

"No fucking way. I'm putting my foot down on that one."

"He says that he'll provide medical documentation regarding his health. Proof that he's clean."

"Are you considering it?"

"No."

"Good, because yer aff yer heid if you do."

"You don't have to tell me."

I never even had sex with Cameron without a condom. And thank God for that.

Cheating fuck.

We migrate over to the section of sexier lingerie, and I pick up a pale pink baby-doll set trimmed with black lace. "This is sweet with a side of sexy."

"It's very cute. And it would look awesome on you. Well, hell. Anything would look great on you."

I look at the price tag. "It's cute and also very expensive."

"Think of it as an investment. If he likes the way you look in it, he'll be more inclined to spoil you with gifts."

I couldn't care less about purses and clothes and jewelry. "I'm doing this for tuition. For my future. As long as that's covered, I'm good. I don't need that other stuff."

"Tuition is a brill goal but carrying a new Louis Vuitton handbag never killed anyone."

I love Rachel but we have different objectives in life.

"If I decide to have sex with Hutch, it'll be because I want to have sex. Not because he's paying me for it."

A wide grin spreads across Rachel's face.

"What's that shit-eating smile about?"

"I wasn't going to tell you but…"

I wait for her to finish the sentence, but she doesn't. "Tell me what?"

She giggles and smiles even wider. "I slept with my client last night."

Oh wow. I wasn't expecting to hear that. "Really?"

"He's a repeat client. It wasn't about the money at all. I did it because I wanted to. I like him."

"What's his name?"

"Claud."

"Is he cute?"

"I didn't think so at first, but the more time we spend together, the more attractive he becomes to me."

She takes out her phone and thumbs through her photos until she finds a picture of them together. "What do you think of him? Honest truth."

I wouldn't classify him as good-looking, but I definitely see some sexy qualities about him. "He has pretty eyes."

"He does, right?"

"I like his facial scruff."

"Me too. I like the way it feels."

"How old is he?"

"Forty-four."

Yikes. Twice her age. "You're okay with him being twenty-two years older than you?"

"Aye, I actually love that he's in his forties. I've always had a thing for older men."

"Rachel, have you landed your whale?"

"I don't know. Maybe." She smiles and shrugs. "I'm the only inamorata that he sees. And our dates have become regular. We see each other at least four times a week. I haven't been out with another client in over a month because he books me out weeks in advance."

"Sounds as though he has a thing for you too."

"I think he does."

"Was the sex good?"

Rachel bites her bottom lip and rolls her eyes. "It was really good. He was very… *attentive*, which was truly surprising. I expected it to be all about his wants and needs."

Rachel's client sounds thoughtful and considerate. Sounds like someone that I know. I suppose that it makes sense. A selfless person is more likely to be a giving lover.

Hmm. That could definitely sweeten Hutch's offer. Who knows? Maybe it could take it from tempting to irresistible.

6

MAXWELL HUTCHESON

I'VE HARDLY SLEPT SINCE MEETING LOU. I'M FINE DURING the day while I'm busy at work, but she invades my head when I'm home, especially in the evenings. The worst is when I'm alone in my bed in the dark. And my hand always seems to find its way to my cock while I picture her beneath me, legs spread wide, hair splayed wildly on the pillow under her head, mouth forming a perfect O when she orgasms.

Damn.

My life has become a tragic circle of desperation to move on but plagued by the inability to do so because of the expectations of friends and family. I know that they love me and want only the best for me, but they're making me miserable.

So fucking miserable.

Am I wrong for wanting a woman in my life? I don't think so. At least not when I consider the circumstances that led to this place that I'm in.

"Lovely to see you again, Mr. Hutcheson. Please come in."

"Thank you."

Cora sits behind her desk and I take the chair across from her. Someone on the outside looking in might mistake our interaction for a meeting between an investment fund manager and his client. But this meeting is about something entirely different.

I'm here to pay for Lou's time. Pay for the use of her body.

I'm buying Lou. I'm not proud that it's come to this.

Cora laces her fingers together and places them on her desk. "I'm keen to hear what you think of Lou."

Her smile screams self-satisfaction. And it should. This woman is good at what she does.

"Lou is everything that you promised." And more. So much more.

"I knew that she would be, but the real question remains to be answered: is she everything that you're looking for in a companion or would you like to meet another girl before making your final decision?"

I don't care for the way that I feel when I consider the possibility of never seeing Lou again. "I don't need to meet other inamoratas. Lou is my choice. We clicked." Or at least I think that we did. It could all be an act, her playing the role of an inamorata.

Cora winks at me. "Lou feels the same. She's happy with your pairing." I'm relieved to hear the affirmation even if it does come secondhand. "She accepts your proposal and has agreed to move forward with the companionship agreement."

I'm soaring above the clouds. "Grand."

"I thought that you might feel that way."

"What's the next step in the process?" I want the formalities out of the way as soon as possible.

"I need a list of boundaries and expectations from each

of you. Every single one of them must be made known upfront so that you're both clear about what the other wants in the relationship. It's a tedious process but necessary. After we have each of your lists, we'll meet again and discuss your requests. Once the two of you reach an understanding, you're ready to move forward."

She says that it's a tedious process, but it sounds simple enough.

"Payment will be banknotes, in full and upfront."

"Understood."

"You told me that you were interested in booking for three months when we spoke last week. Is that still the case?"

"Aye, through August 31."

Cora takes out a calendar and counts the weeks beneath her breath. "Three days a week over the next twelve weeks. That's thirty-six dates. We'll estimate five hours per date at a rate of £200 per hour." She stops and looks up at me. "You understand that £200 per hour doesn't cover sex?"

"I need you to allow for sex. And I want Lou to be available to me twenty-four-seven for the full duration. Not for five hours, three days a week."

Cora's mouth parts but no words come out.

"And I'd like to pay for sex without condoms."

"That's not a service that we offer. I'm sure that you can understand why Inamorata wouldn't encourage unsafe sexual practices."

"Of course." Makes sense.

But Lou and I won't have the typical inamorata-client relationship. I will be her only client. Condom-free sex would be a safe practice as long as neither of us were having sex with anyone else. And I know that I won't be.

Cora counts beneath her breath again. "August 31

places us at eighty-five days from today. Availability twenty-four-seven for the duration is a lot of hours."

"Aye, I'm aware but it's what I want."

"All right. Let's start over with our calculations."

Cora taps numbers on her keyboard and jots down a number before doing it all over again. "By the way, I'm calculating from today since we aren't certain when this will be finalized. Her time between now and then must be accounted for."

Which means that I'm paying for days that I might not spend with her. But by paying, I'll be assuring that she won't be with other clients. I'm all right with that.

"Eighty-five days is 2040 hours." She blows her breath out between pursed lips and slowly shakes her head. "Each hour at £200 equals £408,000. Now let's allow for eighty-five of those hours to cover sex at a rate of £400 per hour." She circles a six-digit number and turns it around for me to see. "That brings your grand total to £425,000."

Lou and everything that I want from her is going to cost me close to a half-million pounds.

Do I want this? Is she worth that kind of money?

There's only one answer: abso-fucking-lutely.

"How much will Lou get?"

Cora's expression is deadpan. "I don't disclose that kind of information to clients."

"You will disclose it to me if you want my money."

Cora breathes in deeply, releasing the breath slowly. "I take 50 percent of their earnings until my investment is recouped. After that, I keep 25 percent. The girls retain 100 percent of any monies or gifts outside of the brokered agreement. I'm more than fair with my girls."

Lou is the one who will be playing the role of girlfriend to me for the next eighty-something days. I think that we can do better than 75 percent.

"This is a one-time broker deal. Your work will be finished as soon as our arrangement is finalized. I'd like to encourage you to take your investment in Lou off the top and allow her to retain 85 percent of the remaining balance."

"You're negotiating on her behalf instead of your own?"

"Aye."

"Well, Mr. Hutcheson. I can't say that I've ever encountered a client quite like you. I don't typically entertain the idea of negotiation, but I like Lou, and I like you, so I'll agree to your proposal."

"I expected a counter from a savvy businesswoman like you. Perhaps I should have asked for ninety."

She smiles. "I think that you've pushed your luck enough, Mr. Hutcheson."

Fair enough.

"When can we finalize everything?"

"Are you available Friday evening? Say five o'clock?"

Five is a wee tight for me. "Can we schedule for six?"

"Six o'clock works for me."

Another hurdle behind me. One more to go and Lou will be mine for the next three months.

7

CAITRIONA LOUDEN

"Maxwell Hutcheson negotiated on your behalf. You'll be receiving 85 percent after I recoup my investment."

Wait… what? "Why would he do that?"

"I learned a long time ago to not ask why, Cait. Simply say thank you and move on when a man does something nice for you."

"Is 85 percent all right with you?" Our agreement is seventy-five.

"Your arrangement with Mr. Hutcheson is a one-time broker deal. I get the return of my investment in you plus a very nice incentive for a few hours of my time. I'm more than all right with that, doll."

"I didn't know that you negotiate with clients."

"I don't. This is a first for me. And the only reason that I agreed was because his requests benefit you and not him."

Hutch is too good to be true. Men aren't this selfless.

Cora picks up a stack of papers lying on her desk. "Mr. Hutcheson has many expectations. That's to be expected for the premium price that he's paying, but if there are any terms that you don't wish to fulfill, this is your chance to speak up and amend the agreement."

"I understand."

I jump when Cora's office phone rings. "Yes, Raith. Send Mr. Hutcheson back."

I hear that Hutch is here and I instantly have butterflies in my stomach. I hold out my hand and look at it trembling. I try to steady it, but I'm unsuccessful.

"It's normal to be nervous—the first client is always the most daunting."

Hutch is my first and last. There'll be no need to continue working as an inamorata when this job is over. I'll have plenty of money to pay for college. Or at least I think I will.

"How much money will I be getting when this job is done?" I can't believe that I haven't asked that question before now.

Cora picks up a notepad from her desk and looks at it. "Your portion will be £340,000."

Three hundred, forty thousand and what the actual fuck?

Shit.

Shit.

Shit.

Did I hear that number correctly?

Cora smiles when Hutch comes through her office door. "Mr. Hutcheson. So good to see you again. Come in and join Lou and me."

I turn and smile at Hutch. "Hi."

"Hello. How are you?"

"I'm fine." Nervous as fuck, actually. "And you?"

"I'm well, thank you."

"Lovely. Everyone is well. Shall we begin?" Cora hands

over a printed copy of our agreement to each of us. "This part is somewhat uncomfortable, but trust me when I say that it will prevent problems down the road."

Cora pushes her reading glasses up her nose. "Now is the time that we make any amendments, so stop me if there is something that you don't understand or wish to change. The hard copy of your companion agreement will include formal terminology, but we'll use lay terms during this meeting."

We simultaneously voice our understanding.

"This arrangement, also known as the girlfriend experience, is between Maxwell Hutcheson and the inamorata known as *Lou*. The duration of this arrangement will end on August 31. Because the initial meeting was on Monday, he has paid for the duration of eighty-five days, although technically we're at eighty-one remaining days."

Eighty-one days.

Eighty-one nights.

Let me say that again. Eighty-one nights.

Cora looks up and we both nod.

"During the duration of your arrangement, Maxwell Hutcheson will be your only client. You will make yourself available to him at all times during the eighty-one-day period with these limited exceptions: severe illness or injury, death of an immediate family member or friend, or predetermined personal time off. Do you understand and agree to those terms?"

I turn to Hutch. "Can you expand a little more on predetermined personal time off?"

"There will be periods of time when I won't require your availability. An example would be when I'm tied up at the office or I've gone out of town. You'd be free to do as you wish during those times."

That's such a relief. The thought of making myself available to anyone twenty-four-seven is intimidating.

"Next are Mr. Hutcheson's expectations in regard to sex."

I squirm in my seat, my fingers fidgeting on my lap. I'm so damn uncomfortable having this conversation.

"Mr. Hutcheson has paid in advance for sex."

What the actual fuck?

"That isn't what we discussed."

"I don't expect to have sex every day for the next eighty-whatever days. Please get that thought out of your head right now."

That thought is in my head because that's what you've paid for. "I'm confused."

"After today, I don't want to talk about money again. The only way to ensure that is to pay upfront for everything that might happen. The money changes nothing. I still want to pursue an emotional connection with you, and if the physical connection happens, great. If it doesn't, I'll be disappointed, but I'll understand."

He says that the money changes nothing. I hope he means that because I won't sleep with him out of obligation.

"Do you accept Mr. Hutcheson's terms regarding sex?"

I nod. "Yes."

"Moving on to the time you will spend at the Hutcheson estate. You will have your own private chambers across the hall from Mr. Hutcheson's bedroom whenever you stay over."

"It's a wee bit masculine as is, but I have a decorator who can come in and change it to your liking."

"That's very kind but not necessary. I'm sure it's fine the way it is." It's not as though I've ever had accommodations to my liking. No reason for him to start changing his interiors to suit me.

Cora draws a line across the paper she's using as a checklist. "Sleeping arrangements on the nights that Lou spends the night will be as follows: Mr. Hutcheson will sleep in his bedroom, and Lou will sleep in hers unless both parties agree to share a bed."

We voice our agreement at the same time.

We spend the next hour going down a checklist of proposed circumstances. We voice our consent or rejection of everything from hand-holding to sexual acts that make my jaw drop. Hutch doesn't reject anything but for me, it's a hard no on quite a few things.

"Lastly, the termination of the companionship. Lou, you are entrusted to Mr. Hutcheson's care for a period of eighty-one days. At the end of those eighty-one days, your relationship will cease. Do you agree to those terms?"

Wow. Talk about finality. "I agree."

"All right. I think we've covered everything," Cora says.

Cora was right. This process was a pain in the ass, but I see why it's necessary. I have no questions about Hutch's expectations, and I believe that he understands mine.

Time to begin the girlfriend experience.

I MET HUTCH A WEEK AGO, DREW UP A FORMAL companionship agreement with him this evening, and now I'm going to his house to stay the weekend. Whose life am I living?

The last seven days have been a whirlwind. I have no real way of knowing, but I think that my companionship with Maxwell Hutcheson is going to be good. It feels right. Much better than seeing random men three times a week.

"Let's take your bag to your room and let you have a look at it."

Hutch leads me up the grand winding staircase. So typical for a nineteenth-century castle like this. Although it's a young home in comparison to many of the other castles in Scotland, it has tons of character. I love it.

We enter the last door at the end of the hallway. "I think you'll like this room. It's the largest guest room and has its own sitting area and en suite bath."

After living in that tiny flat with Rachel, it's hard for me to believe that I'll occasionally get to sleep in this beautiful room. "It's wonderful and far more than I am accustomed to. Thank you."

I grew up in a tiny run-down apartment in New Orleans. I didn't even have a clean bed. I slept on a nasty mattress on an old set of rusty bed rails, but look at me now. I've come a long way from that mice-infested apartment in New Orleans. And I'm not done yet.

8

MAXWELL HUTCHESON

My hands are in my pockets when we walk out of the house and Lou loops her arm through mine. The affectionate contact takes me by surprise, but I welcome it. I welcome it a lot, in fact. It's been too long since I've been touched by a woman.

"Where are you taking me?"

"I want to show you the barn and horses."

Her eyes widen and her voice is a wee bit higher than usual. "You have horses?"

"Aye, three Thoroughbreds. A stallion, a mare, and their new foal, all chestnut. Would you like to meet them?"

"Are you kidding me? I would love to meet them." She stops. "But shouldn't I change my dress and shoes?"

"I think you'll be fine for a quick visit. We won't stay long."

I hold Lou's hand, assisting her up onto the ATV. "Up you go, lass."

"Thank you."

I grab the seatbelt and lean across her body, buckling her in. Not that I don't believe she's capable of doing it herself. I do it because it gives me an excuse to be closer to her even if only for a moment. And fuck, she smells divine.

"All buckled in."

"Is the barn far from here?"

"No, but it's not a walk you'd enjoy while wearing those heels. Plus, I wouldn't want you to ruin your shoes."

Yes, I could have her change her clothes and shoes, but then she wouldn't be wearing this sexy wee black dress or those mile-high fuck-me pumps. And I very much like the way that she looks in both. I'd like to look at her in them for a while longer.

Lou reaches out and grasps the handle on the roll bar when I hit a bump a wee too hard. "Sorry about that. I'll slow down."

"I'm all right. I can handle a few bumps along the way. I'm pretty good at that actually."

"I'd like to hear more about that sometime. The bumps that you've encountered, I mean."

"Yeah, maybe when you're bored out of your mind and have nothing else to do."

I offer my hand, helping her down from the ATV. "Careful. The ground isn't level in this area."

She loops her arm through mine and her hand grasps my bicep. "I'm sorry you're having to hold me up like a drunkard."

"I'm not sorry. It's the perfect excuse for you to hold on to me."

She smiles and lowers her head. Is she trying to hide her grin from me? Or trying to appear coy because it's how she was trained to be by Cora? I wonder how much of her personality is actually her true self and how much is the woman that she has been trained to be in order to please clients.

I don't know but I want to find out.

"I haven't been around a lot of horses. Only the ones at Jackson Square who pull the carriages around the French Quarter. When I was a child, the drivers would sometimes let me feed them carrots."

"I'm glad to hear that you aren't afraid of them."

"So far, they haven't given me a reason to be afraid."

We stop in front of the first stall, and Lou places her hands on top of the gates.

"This is my stallion, Absolom."

Lou's eyes widen and a smile spreads across her face. "Oh, Hutch. He's beautiful."

The horses aren't the only beautiful thing in this stable.

Sol comes to the gate of his stall and pushes his head forward. "Can I pet him?"

"How could you not? It's what he expects."

Lou drags her hand down his snout a few times. "His hair feels different than the horses I use to feed."

"I make sure that my horses receive the best of care."

"I can easily see that. Most people's homes aren't as nice as this barn or even this stall."

"I didn't build the barn. It was here when I bought the property."

"Maybe so, but you've kept it in top-notch shape."

"Colin has. He's my stable hand who tends to the horses."

"He takes his job seriously."

"All part of his job; I'm the one putting him through veterinarian school."

Lou turns to look at me. "You're paying for your stable hand to go to college?"

"Aye."

"That is very generous."

"I'm not that generous. He's the son of family friends. It's more of a favor to his parents."

"Maybe so but it's still very generous. Vet school isn't cheap."

"Cheap it is not."

"Do you ride them much?"

"I do when my schedule allows." Which isn't often enough. "Would you care to ride with me sometime?"

"I would love to, but I would need you to show me how to ride. I've never been on a horse."

"I'd be happy to teach you."

It'll be nice to have a riding partner for once. Mina wouldn't so much as set foot in this barn. I've always had to ride alone.

Lou steps over to the next stall. "Aw… Hutch." She looks up at me and smiles. "A mama and her baby. That's so precious."

Mama. Not mum, which reminds me of her American roots. Not that I ever forget with that accent of hers.

"That's my special lass, Pristine, and her new foal, Nevan."

"Pristine and Nevan," she repeats. "I love their names. Where did you come up with them?"

"My mum names all of the horses in our family."

"Sounds like your family has a lot of horses."

"We've had quite a few over the years. My dad and I are polo players."

"Polo?" She smiles and nods. "I must admit that I've never known anyone who plays polo."

"Well, now you do."

"You play polo on these horses?"

"I do but more so on Sol."

"Sol?"

"Sol, short for Absolom."

"Oh."

"His speed and stamina are absolutely unparalleled.

Prissy is smaller and more agile, but she's easily intimidated in ride-offs."

"Which is better? Speed and stamina or agility?"

"It all depends on the game."

Lou watches my face and appears to be truly interested, even mesmerized, by everything that I'm telling her about my horses and favorite pastime. My new companion has no idea how good it feels to have all of her attention focused solely upon me.

So unlike Mina. My own wife never had any interest in hearing about one of the biggest passions of my life.

"I would love to see you play sometime." The smile fades, and she turns back to look at Prissy and Nevan. "But of course, I understand that will never happen given the circumstances of our arrangement. I just meant that it would fun to watch you play."

She extends her hand to pet Prissy and the warm yellow glow of the wall-mounted lanterns dances on her skin. I ache to reach out and touch her.

Would it be wrong to do so? She is my paid companion.

Lou is staring straight ahead when I move behind her. "Is Nevan Prissy's first…" Her voice is soft, and I believe that I might even detect a wee bit of unsteadiness.

"He's her first foal."

I slide one of my arms around her waist and pull her body against me. With my free hand, I push her hair over one shoulder and press my lips to the exposed skin on her neck, trailing kisses toward her ear. "I can't stand it any longer. I need to touch you. Is that all right?"

"Yes," she whispers, and her voice breaks halfway through the single word.

I glide my hand across her chest and push it down the top of her dress until my palm finds her lace-clad tit. I can feel her nipple growing hard through the lace as I slowly thumb it, but it's not enough. This is only a small taste of what I truly want, so I push my hand inside the cup of her bra from the top, forcing her breast to topple out of her bra. "Do you want me to stop?"

"I should. I don't even know you." Her voice is barely audible.

"But you don't want me to stop?"

Her head turns from side to side, the back of her hair rubbing against my chest. "No."

She moans when I pinch her nipple between my thumb and index finger and leans against me, lacing her fingers through my hand on her waist and tilting her head to the side. Her breath increases and her bum grinds against my groin when I squeeze and release her breast.

Her invitation to continue. But we shouldn't do this in the open. We could be seen.

"Come with me." I slip my hand inside of hers and lead her into the tack room, closing the door behind us. "We can never be seen together that way. We must always be hidden from the view of others."

She releases my hand and slowly backs away, stopping when her bum hits the table behind her.

Is she rethinking the situation? Thinking of telling me that I can't touch her that way?

She grips the edge of the table and watches me move toward her. "Hutch…"

I grip her waist and lift her to sit on the table, bringing us face-to-face. "Yes, Lou?"

Her throat bobs when she swallows, and I wait to hear what she has to say. But nothing comes out. And before it can, I close my fingers over hers, gripping her hand inside of mine. That's all it takes. Within two heartbeats she's inside my arms, and we're wrapped up in each other.

Her lips are pressing against mine, her hands roaming my chest. It's been almost two years since I felt this—a woman's kiss and fiery touch. And fuck me. Having a woman's body pressed against mine has never felt so good.

I want to do so many things to her all at once, but I can't stop kissing her. Her lips are so soft, and she has the faintest taste of wine on her tongue.

Her arms drape over my shoulders and I pull her body against mine until there's not a single bit of space between us. And I don't want any space between us. I want to feel her against me, her body tangled up in mine, even though we're fully clothed and making out like a pair of teen lovers in the tack room of my barn.

She breaks the kiss and breathes in deeply. "Whoa."

"I'm sorry but I've been wanting to do that all night."

"You have?"

"Aye. Very much so. I'm sorry if I was a wee bit overkeen."

"It was intense." She smiles. "But that doesn't mean that I didn't like it."

"I think that kind of kiss is confirmation that you don't still see me as a stranger."

"No, you're not a *complete* stranger to me anymore."

I push my fingers through hers, lacing them together. "You won't regret saying yes to this. To me. The next three months are going to be fab."

"I think so too."

9

CAITRIONA LOUDEN

HUTCH IS QUIET DURING THE ATV RIDE BACK TO THE house. Discomfort usually accompanies a lack of conversation, but I feel none. My mind isn't flipping through a mental Rolodex of discussion topics, searching for what we can talk about next. Not talking is okay. The quiet is peaceful and being next to him is enough to satisfy me.

Epiphany.

Hutch is right about this. Despite our lack of acquaintance, we're at ease with one another because there are no pretenses between us. Our expectations and boundaries are clear. And that eliminates the worry and anxiety that I would typically have at this point.

I'm his companion until the end of August, and I feel prepared for what that will involve. "I understand everything that you said about our relationship. It makes sense to me now."

He stops the ATV and turns to look at me. "Tell me why it makes sense to you."

"I don't feel pressured to impress you. I can be myself without the fear of rejection. I have no worries about what today, tomorrow, or next month means for us because I already know."

He reaches for my face and strokes his thumb over my cheek. "You can be whoever you want to be with me. Lou the inamorata or the true you… I'll happily take either of you. But if there's ever a time when you feel comfortable enough, I'd very much like to know your real name. Lou doesn't fit you at all."

I like Lou. I think it fits me perfectly. And if he knew that my real last name was Louden, he would agree.

I see how much Hutch wants to know the real me. A part of me wants to tell him who I really am, but my gut reminds me how unwise that would be.

"Maybe one day." That should pacify him for now.

"'Maybe one day' isn't a no. I'll take it."

We return to the house, and Hutch parks the ATV in the attached garage instead of returning it to its previous parking spot. I'm guessing that's on account of my shoes, and I'm not mad about that. Walking in these heels on uneven ground without scratching them is no easy task.

"Will you have another glass of wine with me?"

I strongly suspect that Hutch has something in mind for us later tonight, especially after our little sexy romp in the barn's tack room. I'd welcome a little bit of wine-induced bravery for whatever that may be.

"Yeah, I'd love another glass." Or two or three.

I take the glass of red wine that he offers, and we go into the living room. We sit close to one another on the couch, close enough that his leg is touching mine, and damn, I feel like a silly teenage girl sitting next to her crush. The simple touch of his leg against mine thrills me beyond belief.

Hutch rests his free hand on my leg and gently kneads

the muscle of my thigh. "I've sent the staff away for the weekend."

"Then who just prepared and served dinner?"

"Sonny left after cleanup. It's just you and me at the house until everyone returns on Sunday night."

We're alone and I'm no fool. He definitely intends on at least trying to see how far he can go with me.

"If the staff is gone, why were you so worried about someone seeing us in the barn?"

"You never know when someone could pop in for a visit."

An unannounced drop-in introduces all kinds of potential problems. "It's inevitable that one of your friends or family members is going to see me here at some point. What are you going to tell them about me?"

He takes his hand away from my leg and runs it through the top of his hair, making it fluff up. "I've been thinking about that. A lot, actually."

"And?"

He chuckles. "You could be the dog walker."

The dog walker? Is he serious? "Do you even have a dog?"

"No, but I can get one if it gives you a legitimate reason for being here."

I love animals but I'm not going to pick up dog shit for anyone. "I need you to be more creative."

"Such as?" He stares at me while I draw a blank. "Go ahead. I'm open to suggestions."

"Interior designer?"

"Mina hired a designer to redo the entire house a couple of years ago."

That's not surprising. The decor is new and beautiful. Come on, Cait. You're a smart girl. Come up with something.

"Got it. Event organizer for a party that you're planning?"

He frowns. "It's not a terrible story but it has holes."

"What kind of holes?"

"An event planner wouldn't make multiple visits to my house so that explanation feels more like a one-shot deal. And I also don't think it would come off as the truth if you were seen wearing anything other than professional clothing."

I have no intentions of walking around here in a pantsuit. "All valid points. What about housekeeper?"

"I've had the same housekeeper for years. Everyone knows that I wouldn't replace her."

I've met his housekeeper. She's no spring chicken. "Maybe you could say that she needs a little help with the housework because she's getting older and can't handle all of it by herself? This is a big house."

A line forms over Hutch's brow and he rubs his thumb back and forth over his bottom lip. "That would cover any questions about your frequent presence in the house."

I think that we have an ace in the hole. "Housekeeper beats dog walker, hands down."

"I like it. And it's one less thing that I have to figure out about this arrangement."

Hutch has so many people to answer to. He's a grown man with incredible success. He should be able to do what he likes without everyone else's input.

"Does your friend, the one who brought you to the Inamorata gala, know about me?"

"Aye, but not near as much as he'd like to know. He's eager to meet you."

"Are you eager for me to meet him?"

"I'd be lying if I said that I didn't want to keep you all to myself."

I wonder if I met his friend the night of the gala. "What is your mate's name?"

"Brady."

"I don't recall meeting a man by that name, but I met a lot of men that night."

I wonder if Rachel knows him. It's possible that she's been on a date with him.

"Brady stayed back while we were introduced, per Cora's request. She didn't want to overwhelm you."

She didn't want to overwhelm me? That's a hoot. "Umm, that entire event was the epitome of being overwhelmed."

Hutch reaches out, returning his hand to my thigh. "I hope that I didn't contribute to overwhelming you."

"No, it was the other men." They made me feel like a fresh piece of roadkill surrounded by starving vultures.

"Good news. You're done dealing with that shite."

"Thank God for that."

Hutch's fingers skim back and forth across the top of my leg. It's beguiling and yet somehow soothing. "Tell me about your week."

God, I can barely think with him touching my thigh like that. "I worked on my manuscript a couple of days, and then my roommate and I went shopping one day."

"What is your manuscript about?"

"It's a psychological thriller. Stalker becomes boyfriend kind of thing. Maybe." I shrug. "It's still very early."

"Can I read it?"

"There's not anything to read. I'm still working on the outline."

"Ah, I see. Did you buy anything when you went shopping?

I grin, thinking of the lingerie. "Girl stuff."

"Did you happen to bring any of this new girl stuff with you?"

"I brought all of it."

Hutch takes my wine from my hand and places it on the coffee table. "I'm not thirsty for wine and I don't think that you are either."

He slides closer and I twist so that I'm facing him. His eyes leave mine, moving lower, and he looks at my mouth. "You have great lips."

"I like yours too." They're so soft and full and framed perfectly by the scruff on his face.

"Do you always wear red lipstick?"

I lick my lips. "I never wear red lipstick."

He touches his thumb to my bottom lip. "You're wearing it tonight. And you wore it the other nights that I saw you." He noticed and remembers.

"Only because I thought that you might like it."

"I do like it. It's sexy and it looks beautiful on you."

"Thank you."

I lick my lips again and press them together, preparing for the kiss that could be coming.

Come on, Hutch. Kiss me. I want you to.

He leans closer and sucks my bottom lip into his mouth, gently tugging on it. It's not one of those gross I'm-going-to eat-your-face-off kind of sucks. It's a sexy kind of suck. The foreplay kind of suck.

His mouth opens, covering mine, and our tongues fall into a rhythmic wave. It's a seductive swirl of soft, wet velvet and wine. And damn, I think that the wine tastes even sweeter on his tongue.

I push my fingers into the back of his hair, and everything moves faster. Our kiss is no longer slow and sweet. It's carnal and demanding.

Pulling away, I pant for air, and his eyes connect with mine. "Do you want me to stop?"

This relationship isn't normal. It has its own set of rules and those don't include the norm. It's okay to have sex for fun and not for love. This has nothing to do with my stupid heart.

Placing my hands on each side of his face, I drag my fingertips through his facial scruff. "Don't stop."

An angel on one shoulder, a devil on the other. And even that dark bastard is asking me what the hell I'm doing.

"Are you sure?"

I'm about to cross a line, and when I do, I can't return. "I'm sure."

Hutch places his hands on top of mine and turns his face into my palm, kissing it through a wide smile. "Not here."

He gets up from the couch and takes my hands, pulling me to stand. With his hands holding mine, I follow him down the hallway to his bedroom.

"Do you need your bag?"

"Yes."

My heart is pounding against the interior side of my chest. Each beat is pulsating in my face and ears and hands. I feel hot and cold at the same time. Shit, I think that I'm light-headed. Am I going to pass out?

I cannot pass out. That would be humiliating.

We grab my bag and go into Hutch's bedroom. His room wasn't on my house tour, so this is my first time seeing it.

King-sized bed. White and gray bedding. Light-colored furniture. Clean lines. Simple and masculine. I don't want to kill the mood by thinking about Hutch's late wife, but I don't see a woman's touch anywhere in this room. Has he changed the bedding? Did she once sleep here?

"I moved out of our bedroom. I never shared this bed with her." I turn and look at him. "I could tell that you were thinking about it."

Am I that transparent? "I'm sorry. I couldn't help but wonder."

"It's fine, Lou. No pretenses, remember?"

"Right." That's something that I'm going to need to remind myself of on a regular basis.

"With me, you can say whatever's on your mind. Never be afraid. Got it?"

"Got it." I look at the door to my left. "Bathroom?"

"Aye."

"I won't be long."

He tries to suppress a smile. Total fail. "I'll be out here waiting for you."

I close the bathroom door behind me and breathe in deeply as I look at myself in the mirror. Slow breath in, slow breath out. I repeat the process a few more times, hoping that it will help me gather some courage.

Calm down, Cait. Tonight is going to be fun. No pressure.

Except that I do feel pressure. A ton of it, actually.

I'm twenty-two years old, and I've had one boyfriend my entire life. My list of sexual partners comes to a grand total of one. Uno. I'm a girl who has almost no sexual experience, and I'm supposed to somehow know how to give an experienced man like Hutch the full girlfriend experience.

I lean toward the mirror and stare into my own eyes. Windows to the soul, they're called. Behind the green, brown, and gold flecks of color, my windows are slammed closed. Not so much as a crack for anyone to get a glimpse into my core where I've become so numb. My heart is desensitized because it's been betrayed by every person in this world who should have cared about me. But didn't.

Everyone except Rachel. She's the one exception in this shit show called my life.

Fuck it.

Those two words have seen me through a lot of shit, and they're going to see me through this too.

"Time to do this, Cait."

I brush my teeth and change into the pink baby-doll set I bought earlier this week. The baby-pink color is misleading. It looks innocent at first glance, and then you notice my deeply exposed breasts and the barely there G-string in the crack of my ass.

Misleading. The same could be said for me—I may look like a skilled inamorata, but I'm really only an amateur in disguise. And this sexy lingerie is my masquerade.

I brush my hair, detangling the bottom layer that constantly moves against my back and shoulders, and twirl the ends back into loose curls. Lucky me. My hair is actually cooperating tonight.

I smooth the few unruly tresses and think about what tonight is going to be like with Hutch.

Will he be hot and kinky?

Will he be dominating?

Will he only care about his own pleasure?

So many unanswered questions.

My body tingles as I imagine his hands moving all over me. My nipples get hard when I imagine his thumb and index fingers rolling and pinching them. And his tongue licking them. I'm wet and he hasn't even touched me yet.

Another epiphany.

Tonight isn't about the money. It isn't about our arrangement.

I want this man.

You are about to make yourself a true inamorata, Cait. I hope you know what you're doing because there is no going back after this.

I come out of the bathroom, stopping in the doorway when Hutch's eyes move over my body. I place my hand on the doorframe and shift my weight to one foot, doing my best to look seductive instead of scared to death.

"Fuck." I don't hear the word come out of his mouth, but I read it on his lips.

I'm wearing sexy lingerie, and Hutch has stripped down to his boxer briefs. There are zero pretenses happening in this bedroom right now. It's after ten o'clock and both of us know that we won't still be unfucked at eleven.

He comes to me and cradles my face, placing a soft kiss against my mouth. "You're beautiful, Lou."

Lou. I hate hearing him call me that when we're about to be so intimate with one another.

He should be calling me Cait. And for a brief moment, I consider telling him so. But I don't. I can't. He's a client and this will come to an end. I can't ever allow myself to forget that.

Our mouths open at the same time and his tongue moves slowly in a wave against mine. I melt against him and the already-present tingles in my core spread throughout my body.

His lips leave mine, traveling along my jaw until they reach the side of my neck. I tilt my head to the side, and he pushes my hair away, kissing and sucking and nipping at my skin.

His mouth moves up and hovers over my ear. "One look is all it took. I saw you and I wanted you."

He grips my butt cheeks and pulls me against him, pressing his hard cock against my stomach. "I haven't been able to stop thinking about you since that night."

"I've thought about you too." A lot. More than I care to admit.

His hands migrate to my hips, and he uses his hold on them to pull me toward the bed, kissing me en route as though he can't get enough of me. I feel his desire for me and the sensation is intoxicating.

He stops kissing me and grins. And that smile… it's pure seduction. It could make a nun forget her profession of vows.

Hutch turns us around and the backs of my legs press against the mattress. He lowers himself to his knees in front of me and pushes my gown up, fisting it over each of my hips. Holding the fabric out of the way, he kisses my stomach and ignites a frenzy of amazing tingles between my legs.

Holy shit, I can't believe how turned on I am. I think I'd let this man do anything that he wants to me right now.

His fingers hook the waistband of my pink and black-lace G-string, dragging it down my legs. My head spins hard. I'm afraid of tumbling over, so I use his shoulders to balance myself as I lift one foot and then the other.

He tosses my G-string on the floor and pushes his nose into the part between my upper thighs, inhaling deeply. "Fuck, you smell good."

I want to be appalled. The good girl inside of me says that I should be, but I'm not. I'm something else entirely.

Turned on. Horny. Ready.

That's what I am.

His hands glide up my legs, starting at my ankles and

stopping at my butt cheeks. He squeezes and pulls me hard against his face, placing his mouth so close to that spot that is silently pleading for his kisses. I moan, I honest-to-fuck moan, proving how desperate I am for him to keep going.

He gazes up at me and smiles when his eyes connect with mine. The contact doesn't break, not even when he leans forward and licks me in one long, upward stroke.

The glide of his soft, wet, velvety tongue. The sight of him licking me. His eyes on mine, watching me watch him. It's so damn erotic.

"Sit, mo maise."

Mo maise. Mo translates into my, but dammit, I don't know what maise means. Homework for later, I guess.

I sit on the bed and he grabs behind my knees, pulling me quickly across the bed until my butt is almost hanging off the edge. Whoa, wasn't expecting that kind of sudden movement.

He places my feet on the bedrails and pushes my knees apart, rubbing my inner thighs in long, even strokes. "You're so tense. Relax. I want you to enjoy this."

I'm tense because I don't know what's coming next. I can only speculate about what he's going to do to me. And then it happens. My question is answered when his head dips between my thighs.

Oh. My. God.

I moan again when he licks me. I moan because I can't not moan.

His slick tongue glides up and down through my slit, occasionally hitting that sensitive nub at the top. I'm so tempted to reach down and spread myself apart because I want to feel more. I want to feel everything. I think I'll die if he doesn't give it to me, and at the same time I think I'll die if he does.

He inserts a finger, pumping it in and out of my

opening while his tongue performs some kind of magic. A new and unfamiliar sensation builds deep within my groin, and the sensation grows stronger and stronger. A rush of warm pleasure quivers deep inside of my pelvis.

Oh God, right there. It feels so good.

What is that? Am I having an orgasm?

I. Think. I. Am.

I fist the top of his hair and lift my hips up. "Ohh… uhh."

My response must excite Hutch because he licks and sucks harder. And I would almost swear that I hear him slurping.

My legs become nothing more than quivering, boneless appendages in the aftermath of my orgasm.

My orgasm.

I just had my first O.

And it was magnificent.

Hutch presses a final kiss against my slit. "You taste so fucking good after you come."

You taste so fucking good after you come. I'm not 100 percent sure what that means. More homework, I guess.

What's next? Does he want me to blow him?

Duh, Cait. Stupid question. Of course, he does. Guys always want their cocks sucked.

I hope that I don't disappoint him. Blowjobs are another area where I lack experience, but I'm eager to make him feel good. I hope that counts for something.

He stands and I slide off the edge of the bed, preparing to drop to my knees in front of him. "My turn to make you feel good."

His hands wrap around the sides of my waist. "I haven't been with a woman in a long time. I'm afraid that I'll come as soon as your mouth slides down my cock."

"You don't want me to?"

He places his fingers beneath my chin and lifts, planting a kiss against my lips. "Trust me. I want your mouth around my cock, but I need to be the one in control this time. I don't want this to be over before it begins."

"I understand."

I sit on the bed and scoot to the center, lying flat on my back. I watch as he pushes his boxer briefs down and crawls over me. When we're face-to-face, his hand comes up to my cheek, cradling it. "You're beautiful."

I smile. Of course, I smile. What woman doesn't love it when a handsome man tells her that she's beautiful? "Thank you."

Lowering himself against me, Hutch settles between my legs with his erection pressing against my slit. I love the feel of his warm, heavy body lying on top of me but the tip of his bare cock so close to my opening makes me nervous. "We need to revisit the condom conversation."

He lowers his mouth to mine and places a soft kiss there. "What have you decided?"

Hutch provided proof that he was disease-free. While that's important, it isn't the only driving factor in my decision. "I believe that sex without condoms should be shared between two people who care deeply for each other. I want to save that for the man that I hope to love one day."

He looks at me for a moment before finally replying. "Fair enough."

"I'm sorry. I know that's not what you were wanting to hear."

"It means something to you, Lou. Don't ever be sorry about that."

Hutch leans over and reaches into the nightstand drawer, taking out a foiled square. He kneels between my legs, tearing open the package with his teeth, and I watch him roll the condom down his erection. "Inspecting my competency?"

I laugh aloud. "I trust that you know what you're doing."

"Admiring my cock then?"

"Actually, I am."

He smiles and lowers his body on top of mine again. He uses his knees to push my legs apart and positions the crown of his blood-filled cock against the wet, throbbing split between my legs. He enters me with one hard, smooth motion and I grip his biceps, squeezing hard. I try to suppress my gasp, and the noise that I make comes out sounding like a whimper.

He pulls back with deliberate leisure. It feels like he's going to slide out completely, but then he thrusts into me again. His length, coated with my slick juices, slides out smoothly and then glides in balls deep over and over.

Hutch slows his pace and squeezes his eyes shut. His face looks pained, and I'd swear that he's trembling. "You feel so damn good. I'm not ready for this to end."

I reach out, wrapping my hands around each side of his face. He opens his eyes, and I can see that he's struggling to make this last for as long as possible. And he's losing the battle.

Why is he fighting so hard to prevent the inevitable? Is he thinking that he gets to come one time tonight and that's it until next time?

"It's okay to let go. You can have me as many times as you want."

Hutch's forearms are pressed into the mattress on each side of my head and they move down, wrapping around the top of my shoulders. His head lowers to mine, our foreheads pressed together, and he groans when he spasms inside me. "Oh fuck, Lou. Fuck."

Cait. Pretend that he's calling you Cait.

He stills and the only sound that I hear is his moving breath and the tick of the second hand on a clock somewhere in the bedroom.

My legs fall apart, relaxing with my feet flat against the mattress, and his weight anchors me to the bed. He remains inside of me, and it's nice to feel him like that instead of his body immediately pulling away.

He smiles and presses a kiss against my lips. "You… you…"

"What?"

He shakes his head. "Nothing."

"There are no pretenses between us, remember? Say what's on your mind, mister." I like this part of our relationship. It gives me the right to insist on hearing his thoughts.

"You are…" His smile widens. "Wee down there."

I laugh, thinking of how to respond to that. "Thank you. I think."

"It's a compliment. Trust me."

He pulls out of me and sits up on the side of the bed, peeling back the condom. "Be right back. Gotta take care of this."

He gets up and I shamelessly watch him walk to the bathroom. The man's ass is perfect and worthy of being admired.

He returns to bed and lies on his back beside me, hands tucked behind his head. No cuddling but that's okay; I didn't expect any.

He breathes in deeply and slowly exhales. "It's unbelievable what a good shag can do for you."

"You feel better?"

"Fuck, do I. I feel fab."

"I'm glad that I was able to help."

Hutch rolls toward me and lies on his side, his upper body propped up. His eyes roam my body for a second, and then he reaches out, cupping the underside of one of my breasts. "A perfect fit."

"It seems like we're having a lot of perfect fits tonight."

"Aye, we are."

His thumb and index finger roll my nipple, making it hard. "You're not staying in the bedroom across the hall. That part of the agreement became null and void the second that I was inside of you. Agreed?"

I guess that's not up for discussion. But it's okay with me—I don't want to stay across the hall anyway. "All right. How often do you want me to sleep over?"

"Depends on my work schedule but I'll try to give you as much prior notice as possible. I understand that you have your own life away from here."

Hutch paid a lot of money for every moment of my time. He doesn't have to be considerate of my personal life, and yet he chooses to be. "Thank you for that."

His hand moves to my opposite breast and he plays with my other nipple, making it hard too. "You haven't said anything about the sex being good for you? Was it?"

This man is asking for affirmation? Does he really not know that he's a sex god?

I grin, feeling the heat of embarrassment in my cheeks. "You just gave me my first orgasm. Does that answer your question?"

"Are you kidding me?"

"True story."

"You're twenty-two. How have you not had an orgasm?"

"No one has ever gone down on me."

"And you've never rubbed yourself to get off?"

"No."

"That is hard to believe."

"Well, believe it. That was my first one."

"Well, fuck." He pauses a moment. "What did you think of it?"

Don't hold back, Cait. Tell him how much you liked it. He's as good as asking to be praised. "I've never felt anything so good. I want you to do it again. All of the time would be great."

A booming chuckle resonates from deep within his chest. "You liked it that much, aye?"

"It was incredible. I had no idea that an orgasm would feel so good."

"It's only the first of many, Lou."

His hand abandons my breast and moves to my stomach, rubbing it in a circular motion around my belly button. Every rotation moves a little lower until the tips of his fingers are grazing the top of my slit. And all of those throbbing little tingles begin to buzz again.

God, I want more from him. And I want it harder, faster, deeper. I want his tongue inside of me. His fingers. His cock. I want it all.

He leans closer and his mouth presses against my ear. "We're going to have a lot of fun together this summer. I'm going to give you a lot of orgasms."

Maxwell Hutcheson is getting the girlfriend experience from me. What he doesn't yet realize is that he in turn is giving me the boyfriend experience.

Win.

10

MAXWELL HUTCHESON

Closed eyes. Writhing on the bed with the bed sheets fisted inside her hands. Mouth in the shape of a delicate O. Echoes of pleasure filling the room. Everything about last night was perfect.

I already knew that Lou was beautiful, but I discovered something new about her last night: she's even more beautiful when she comes.

Inside her. That is where I want to be. And it's where I intend on being a large part of the next three months. Preferably bare, but I no longer see that happening. Any hope that I had for being inside her without a condom is gone after last night's discussion. She sees skin on skin as something to be shared by people in love. I won't push her about it again.

The morning after sex. This is the part where things can get messy between a man and woman who aren't in a loving, committed relationship. But not with Lou and me. We both understand what our companionship is about and where it's going. Or not going.

This is exactly what I needed in my life. She's everything that I wanted.

My NOLA girl.

Lou is sleeping on her stomach and the sheets have worked their way down into a bunch just above the curve of her bum. I'm tempted to reach out and squeeze it, but I resist. She's probably tired after being woken up three different times during the night to fuck.

She stirs a wee bit when I get out of bed but doesn't wake. I leave her to sleep in for as long as she likes. I want her to be well rested for later.

I also want her to be nourished. I wonder what she would like to eat when she gets up. She seemed to really appreciate the basket of pastries and champagne that I sent her. I think I'll call and have another one of those delivered.

I wonder if she prefers coffee or tea? Sweet or savory breakfast? There are so many things that I don't know about her. But I'm going to know.

I'm a coffee drinker, always black and piping hot, and I'm on my second cup when Lou comes up behind me and snakes her arms around my waist. She plants a kiss on the side of my neck and my cock twitches. "Good morning, Hutch." I love hearing her call me that.

I turn my face toward her and kiss the corner of her mouth. "Good morning yourself. Want some coffee?"

"No, thank you."

"Tea?"

"Juice works for me."

I point to the basket on the counter. "I had champagne and fresh pastries delivered. Orange juice is in the refrigerator if you want mimosas."

She kisses the side of my face. "You're already spoiling me."

"I promised you that I would."

She goes to the basket and pulls back the wrapping. And that's when I see that she's wearing my shirt—the white button-down that I stripped off last night and tossed across the chair. And fuck, she looks better in it than I do.

"Exactly how hungry did you think I'd be this morning? This basket is even bigger than the one you sent to my flat."

Ah, she lives in a flat and not a house—it's a wee bit of personal information about her real life. And I'm adding it to my list of facts regarding this mysterious woman. It doesn't mean much now, but it could be useful information in the future.

"You're the one who said that you were a foodie."

"I need calories." She smiles and takes a croissant out of the basket. "Last night was a vigorous workout."

"Not more than you can handle, I hope?"

"No worries. I'm young. I can keep up."

My life has fallen into a stale, stagnant rut, but Lou is pulling me out of the funk. She makes me feel younger. I haven't felt this alive in years.

She walks around the bar and goes to the cabinets beside the dishwasher. "Glasses?"

"Cabinet to the right. Champagne flutes are on the top shelf but hold on." I get up and go around to fetch the glass for her—she'll never be able to reach it.

After I give her two glasses, I place my hand on top of her head and move it toward my chest. "You are a wee thing. I didn't notice that until now."

She looks up at me. "You, sir, are not a wee thing."

"I hope not. No man wants to be told that."

"No, I suspect not."

"I'm pretty sure that you shrank overnight."

"I shrink four inches every night when I take off my

shoes." She lowers her voice. "It's my superpower. What's yours?"

"I'm pretty sure that I showed it to you last night right before you had your first orgasm."

"That mouth of yours has superpowers all right." She winks at me and smiles. "Keep that shit up. I like it."

Lou goes to the fridge and reaches in for the orange juice. The bottom of her shirt rises, and I see her bum peek out below the hem.

Fuck, I love having a woman in my life again. And in my bed. Especially when she's as sexy as Lou is.

"Have you eaten breakfast yet?"

"No. I was waiting so we could eat together."

"That's sweet."

Lou pours two mimosas and prepares two breakfast plates. Frankly, it catches me a wee bit off guard. Mina would never have done anything like that for me. She would have expected me to get my own.

I don't know Lou well, but everything that I've seen from her so far is the opposite of Mina. And that's not a bad thing.

"What do you plan to do after graduation?"

She chews a few times and covers her mouth with her hand. "I'm thinking about moving back to the US."

I wasn't expecting to hear that. "You don't like Scotland?"

"I like Scotland very much, but I moved here to be raised by my father and his wife. That turned out to be a total shit show. There's nothing keeping me here."

That is such a shame. Everyone should feel loved and wanted by their family.

"Won't you miss your roommate?"

"Of course. She's my best friend. And literally the only

person on this earth who has never let me down. Everyone needs someone like Rachel in their life."

Her roommate and best friend's name is Rachel. Is that a slipup? Or is Rachel her Inamorata name? Another detail to add to Lou's fact sheet.

"Do you have friends and family in the US?"

"Nothing more than distant family that I don't really know, but New Orleans still feels like home to me."

She's been gone for six years. It may not feel as much like home as she thinks. "You should visit before moving back."

"That's not a bad idea."

My mobile rings and I'm instantly annoyed when I see who it is. I'd love nothing more than to never talk to Mina's sisters again, but I know Blair's MO. She's persistent. She'll keep calling until she gets me.

"I'm sorry. I have to take this."

"No worries. It's fine."

"Hello?"

"Good morning, Max. How are you?"

"I'm well, thank you."

"How is Ava Rose?"

"She's good."

"She's good? That's all you've got for me?"

No. I have something much different in mind for you, Blair.

"Wonderful. Perfect. Take your pick."

"I'd like to see that for myself."

What she'd really like is to drop by unannounced and annoy the fuck out of me. It's a habit that she needs to break.

"You know that you can come by anytime." The words nearly choke me, but I can't make her feel as though she isn't welcome.

"I might come by tomorrow."

Oh fuck no.

"Tomorrow's no good. We won't be here."

"Well, I don't know if you remember or not, but I'm calling because it's Mum's birthday. We're having a surprise party for her on Tuesday night."

Fuck, I don't want to spend one of my evenings celebrating my mother-in-law's birthday when I could be with Lou instead.

Come up with an excuse, Max. Lie if you have to.

"I'm meeting with a big client on Tuesday evening. I can't skip it."

"Reschedule."

"I would but this is a very important client. Thomas wouldn't want me to do that." That's no lie. My father-in-law is a real hard-arse when it comes to money and his company. Blair knows this.

"It's Mum's first birthday since we lost Mina. She needs to see Ava Rose. Dad will understand why you had to reschedule."

Ava Rose is Lundy's granddaughter. I can't keep Mina's daughter from Lundy on her birthday because I want to stay home and be with Lou. That's a dick move. No two ways about it. "I'll check my schedule and see if I can move some appointments around."

Lou holds up her empty glass and grins, silently mouthing "Another?"

I cover the microphone of my mobile and whisper, "One more."

"Who are you talking to?" Damn, Blair has sonars for ears.

"Ava Rose."

"Tell my sweet lassie that Auntie Blair loves her, and I'll see her in a few days."

"Will do."

Fuck, I was so close to no longer being part of the Lochridge family. But instead, I'm forced to endure them and without Mina as a buffer. It's brutal.

I end my call with Blair and wait for the questions to begin. But they don't. Lou doesn't ask who I was talking to or demand to know who Ava Rose is. That would never happen in a normal relationship.

"Sorry about that."

She shrugs and shakes her head. "Nothing to be sorry about."

"Mina's family is still a big part of my life. A bigger part than I like."

"I gathered that."

"I'm going to be tied up with them on Tuesday evening. That means that you'll have a free day, but I'd like to ask you to do something for me on your time off."

"What?"

"Go shopping for more girl stuff. Buy more of what you wore last night. A lot more."

Lou looked so fucking hot last night. I want her to wear lingerie like that every time we're together.

"I can do that. Any special requests?"

"I want to see you wear it all."

She smiles and clears her throat, poorly disguising a girlish giggle. "Even a pearl G-string?"

A pearl G-string? Fuck me. "I would pay good money to see you wearing a pearl G-string."

"All right. It's on my shopping list."

"One more request. Be here waiting for me when I come home Wednesday. Wear the pearl G-string and nothing else."

She smiles. "Yes, sir."

I'm not keen on her carrying an overnight bag every

time she comes and goes. "Buy clothes, personal items, whatever you need so you don't have to pack a bag anymore."

"How do you plan to explain that to the staff?"

My friends and family already dictate too much of what happens in my life. I'll be damned if my employees are going to as well. "My staff members aren't my friends or family. I don't explain any part of my life to them."

"They won't talk?"

"They won't if they want to continue working for me. What happens in this house, stays in this house. They know that."

"If you say so."

She doesn't sound so sure but I am. I've been very clear with all of them.

"I do say so. And I also say be here Wednesday night wearing that pearl G-string."

"Done."

11

CAITRIONA LOUDEN

I'M TRYING TO FIGURE OUT HUTCH'S FANCY-ASS SHOWER faucet when he comes into the bathroom. "I have to go out and tend to the horses. Do you want to go with me?"

Hutch has traded his plaid pajama bottoms and white T-shirt for a pair of khaki cargos and a plaid button-down shirt. I can see a few sparse hairs peeking out at the top of his shirt, but I know that there's more underneath—a lot more—and I recall the way that I ran my fingers through the coarse patches last night.

Hutch is a fine specimen of a man. Very fine indeed.

"I would love to visit the horses. Can you give me fifteen minutes to shower?"

"No need to shower before we go to the barn. Do it after we get back."

"I smell like sex." A lot of sex.

Hutch chuckles. "The horses won't care. I promise."

"I care." I scrunch my nose. "I'm funky."

He leans against the doorway, his arms crossed. "Listen, lass. My face was between your legs three hours ago, and you smelled good enough to eat." One of his brows lifts. "Literally."

Well, he has told me repeatedly how good I smell to him.

"Fine. I'll shower after we come back, but I need a minute to change. I can't go in your shirt."

I had no idea that my new companion was a horse lover so thank God that I threw jeans, a T-shirt, and Chucks into my overnight bag at the last minute.

Hutch doesn't make a move when I begin unbuttoning the shirt that I'm wearing. "Are you going to stand there and watch me change?"

"Planning to unless you ask me to leave."

I don't want him to go. I like that he wants to watch me. "No, it's fine. Stay."

After I'm dressed, he watches me braid my hair, and we both smile when our eyes meet in the mirror. "What is it?"

He shakes his head. "Nothing."

"You're smiling so it must be something."

He shrugs. "I like having you here."

"I like being here."

"Last night was everything that I hoped it would be."

"It was for me too."

"So far this relationship is proving to be the best idea that I've had in a long time."

"Well, I don't know what kind of ideas that you've had in the past, but I think that this one is a pretty damn good one."

I reach into my bag and take out an elastic band, wrapping it around the end of my braid.

"I'm already thinking about tonight."

I let go of my braid and let it fall down my back. "I am too."

"Well, Miss…" Hutch stops and chuckles. "I don't know your last name, real or otherwise."

I don't want to hear him call me by another fake name. But I also won't tell him my real name. "Miss Hutcheson."

"Miss *Hutcheson,* aye?"

"Yes. Lou Hutcheson."

"All right, Miss Hutcheson. If we don't get out of here, I'm going to strip you out of those jeans and throw you across the bed. So come on, lass, before I forget about the horses and have my way with you again."

I'm surprised when Hutch grabs an old, worn leather hat from a hook on our way out the door and places it on his head. I didn't think that he could get any hotter, but I see now that I was wrong.

I sit beside him on the ATV and look at him in that rugged getup. So damn different from the custom designer suits that he usually wears. "What?"

"You're a very sexy man."

Hutch leans over and presses a kiss to my mouth. "You're a very sexy woman."

"I'm mediocre. You're something… very not mediocre."

"You're wrong, Lou. Nothing about you is mediocre."

I help Hutch feed Sol, Prissy, and Nevan and tend to their stalls. I said that I wouldn't pick up dog shit for anyone, but here I am shoveling horse manure.

Damn.

When we finish caring for the horses, Hutch drives me around the property, showing me how far his land extends before we return to the house. It's a simple laid-back Saturday afternoon because we're the only two people on his estate. But that won't always be the case.

I'm curious to see what happens when the staff returns. Will they hate me? See me as a woman who is trying to replace the late Mrs. Hutcheson? I wonder if they liked her.

Hutch and I spent most of the day talking so we aren't incredibly chatty during dinner, but we share a lot of smiles and what I like to call knowing grins. Because we both know what's going to happen later tonight.

I'm bent over loading the dinner plates into the dishwasher when Hutch moves behind me and grabs my hips, pulling my body against his. I stand upright and he leans around to kiss the side of my neck while he grinds his erection against my ass. "I want you to go into the bedroom and get ready for me. I'll finish up here and meet you there in five minutes."

"Five minutes isn't very much time to get ready."

"Five minutes is all that you're getting. I've been thinking about this all day, and I don't want to wait another minute to have you."

He kisses my neck again and releases me. "You'll find a surprise on the bed. I want you to put it on."

"What is it?"

"You'll see." His hand comes down and swats my ass. "Clock is ticking. Go."

The awkward newness is already gone. I'm excited for this. Impatient to feel him inside of me again. And eager to see what he has left for me on the bed.

Black lace bra. Matching strappy G-string. Black lace garter belt and thigh-highs.

Damn. That's hot.

But where did this stuff come from? And when did he buy it?

I don't have time to ponder the question for long because I have to be ready. He'll be here soon.

I snatch the lingerie from the bed, along with my black heels, and go into the bathroom. I unbraid my hair and work to tame it. It's a little unruly, but I don't think that Hutch will mind. Long, wild tresses will go great with this risqué getup.

"Time's up," he calls out from the bedroom.

"Okay, but sit on the bed and close your eyes." I open the door and find him doing exactly as I've instructed. "No peeking."

"I wouldn't dare."

I move across the room and stand before him, my hand placed on my hip. "Open your eyes."

The bluest of blue meets hazel and the corners of his mouth turn upward, forming deep indentions in his cheeks. "Fuck. You look even better than I imagined."

We reach for each other at the same time and Hutch's mouth comes down hard against mine. My lips throb from the rough nature of his kiss, but I don't mind. I can't wait to see what this man has in store for me.

He stands, strips his shirt over his head, and moves to stand behind me. "Lie on the bed, facedown."

I climb onto the bed on all fours and lower my body to the bed. And wait for whatever comes next.

I hear the sound of a zipper, rustling of clothing, and then the sound of the opening drawer.

The bed dips when Hutch crawls over me from behind. All that I feel is the hot skin of his chest grazing my back as he moves up my body. And then his weight presses me deep into the mattress.

He pushes my hair out of the way and presses his lips against the side of my neck. He slowly moves his mouth to my shoulder and chills erupt over my body when his teeth nip at my skin.

His hands are all over me at once as though he can't touch me enough. And as though my body has a mind of its own, my back arches and his hard cock presses against my ass.

Is that what he wants from me tonight?

I hope not. I've never done that before, and it scares me.

His hand creeps around to my stomach and then down between my legs. His fingers push the fabric of my G-string to the side and he spreads the top of my slit, exposing the sensitive nub normally hooded by flesh.

"Ohhh, Hutch."

"Ah, there it is."

His fingertips circle my clit and I temporarily forget my fears regarding what Hutch may want to do to me. The only thing that I feel in the moment is pleasure.

His erection prods me from behind. I'm still not sure what his plan is, but I decide that I'm not afraid. He can do anything that he wants to me as long as his fingers continue doing what they're doing right now.

He pushes my legs apart with his and positions his cock at that familiar place, gliding it inside of me slowly, stretching my channel until he is fully sheathed. I must admit that I'm relieved when he doesn't attempt to explore uncharted territory, but I don't have time to think about it for long because he grasps my hip and pounds into me from behind.

Oh God. I've never done it like this before. It feels so deep and full. His cock feels so much bigger than it did last night.

The synchronization between the thrust of his cock and his finger stroking my clit is perfection. He's playing me as though he's an accomplished musician and I his exquisite instrument.

I'm hurling toward the edge of orgasm quickly. Too quickly. I don't want this to be over yet.

I want to tell him to slow down to prolong this feeling yet pound me harder and faster to increase the intensity of the climax. But I don't have time to ask for either because I tumble over the edge into an oblivion of pleasure. "Ohhh."

"Say my name when you come."

The quaking ecstasy begins to contract within my core. I become entangled in a flood of ecstasy, but I somehow manage to find my voice. "Hutch… Hutch… Huuutch."

"You're mine, Lou. No other man touches you." His voice—it sounds as though he's speaking through clenched teeth.

His final thrusts are slower but more powerful. And then everything stops and he remains inside of me.

I collapse against the bed with exhaustion, covered in a thin sheen of sweat, and he crumples on top of my back. His weight pushes me into the mattress, and his panting is loud against my ear. "I won't share you with another man. I'm the only one who touches you."

I think that Maxwell Hutcheson's world is secretly a very dark place, and I know nothing about it. I also think that it frightens me, but it's too late now. I'm already a part of it. I couldn't walk away from this even if I wanted to.

"Do you understand, Lou?"

"Yes."

"Say it."

"I understand."

"No. Say that you're mine and no other man will have you."

"I'm yours and no other man will have me."

"Good." He pushes my damp hair away from my neck and places a kiss below my ear. "Tell me your name."

"My name is Lou."

He kisses my neck again. "All right. Another time then."

Caitriona Brooke Louden.

I may tell him many things over the next three months, but I'll never say those three words to him.

12

MAXWELL HUTCHESON

Lou is trembling beneath me, and I'm afraid that it has nothing to do with her orgasm.

Was I too aggressive with her? I think so. And now I must show her that I can also be gentle.

I lift myself off of Lou's back and kneel between her parted legs. Beginning at her shoulders, I kiss her skin gently. I slowly work my way down her back, tasting the salty moisture created during our sexual frenzy.

Gliding my hands from her waist to her shoulders, I massage the tense muscles in her back. It takes several minutes, but I feel her eventually relax under my touch. "Feels good?"

"Very."

I work her muscles and contemplate how to justify my possessive outburst. Hard as I try, I can't figure out how to rationalize something that isn't rational.

I don't know. Maybe I let my past betrayal get into my head? The truth is that I'm not exactly sure what happened to me just now. I only know that I want her with me, only me, and no one else. And while I haven't earned her loyalty, I have paid for it.

I migrate upward, kissing her shoulder again, and I skim my nose across the nape of her neck. She smells so good—a fab concoction of fruit, sweat, and pheromones.

I rest my cheek against the center of her back, my own personal way of submitting to her even if she doesn't realize what I'm doing. I stay that way while I try to regain some of the footing that I may have lost with her after my irrational commands. "I'm sorry if I was too demanding."

"It was intense." She pauses for a moment. "But I'm not opposed to intense."

She isn't angry or upset with me?

Her upper body lifts off of the bed, and she looks back at me over her shoulder. "However, you've confused me."

I roll off of her and lie on my side facing her. She does the same and props her head in her hand with her elbow pressed into the bed. And her eyes… they're so full of questions.

It takes me a moment to gather my words. "We may only have an arrangement for a few months, but you're all mine during that time. Only mine. I won't share you with another man, Inamorata client or otherwise."

"There is no other man. But I have a question for you." She reaches out and circles her fingertip around one of my nipples. "Will you do the same for me?"

"Be yours?"

She nods. "Yeah. Be mine and only mine until our arrangement ends?"

I wasn't planning on being with another woman. I thought that was established, given the circumstances that brought us together. "Aye. Just you and me until it ends."

"Yeah, just you and me."

~

When I open my eyes, I see that Lou is asleep on her stomach. She isn't a morning person. Not even a wee bit.

We've only spent a couple of nights together, but I'm already learning things about her: she's a stomach sleeper, doesn't want to cuddle when it's time to go to sleep, and she likes her own space in the bed.

It's Sunday morning. My last day of this weekend with Lou. Sure, we have upcoming days together, but this could be the last one without the staff around. As much as I'd like to, I can't send them away every time Lou comes over, and I need to take advantage of their absence today.

Instead of getting up to have my usual cup of coffee, I stay in bed. I want to be next to her when she wakes. Because I'm ready to fuck her again.

I can't help myself. She enchants me. I can't even look at her without getting hard.

Lust has no mercy.

I lie next to her and study her sleeping form. I lie beside her for so long that I'm on the verge of going back to sleep when I feel movement on the mattress.

My eyes spring open and she's staring at me. Hmm. The watcher becomes the watched.

"Happy Sunday, Hutch."

"Happy Sunday to you, sleepyhead."

Her forehead wrinkles. "I can't be called the sleepyhead if I'm the one who wakes up first."

"I've been waiting for you to wake up for so long that I fell back asleep."

"Right, sure you did."

"I did."

"What kept you in bed instead of getting up to have your coveted hot black tar?"

"You kept me in bed." I reach out and grab the back of her thigh, pulling it toward me so it wraps around my waist. "And this."

I'm inside her twice before we leave the bed and then again in the shower. And for good measure, a fourth time before we leave my house to take her home. Well, not home exactly. I'm taking her back to Inamorata's office. She isn't ready to let me know where she lives. I understand—I've not proven myself to her yet. But I will in time.

As I drive, I berate myself for not being more daring with Lou this weekend. I should have fucked her all throughout the house since the staff was gone. The kitchen. The living room. On top of the dining room table. It would've been the perfect time to christen those places. They'll probably be impossibilities after the staff returns to the house.

All in all, we had a wonderful weekend. I'm not ready to let her go. "I want you to come over tomorrow night. I'll pick you up after I leave work."

"What time?"

"Around six but I'll text and give you an exact time."

"I'll need a one-hour notice to account for travel from my flat to the train station and then the walk to Inamorata's office."

That is ridiculous. "You should just let me pick you up at your flat."

"You're very aware that I don't allow clients to know where I live."

She says clients, plural, as though she has so many. I don't like that. "I'm not an ordinary client."

"No, you definitely aren't ordinary."

"I'm your first and only. And don't forget that I gave you your first orgasm. Doesn't that make me special?"

"One of a kind."

I turn off the car and walk with her to the entrance of Inamorata. "I don't like the idea of you walking to the train from here."

"It's fine. I do it all the time."

"I could have taken you to Waverley instead." It's at least a half-mile walk to the station from here. And she's wearing heels.

"I needed to come here first and check in with Cora."

"So she can see that you're alive and well after our first weekend together?"

"Something like that."

"At least let me pick you up at Waverley station tomorrow night and save you the walk to Inamorata's."

She nods. "All right, that I can do."

I reach for her hands and give them a gentle squeeze. "Can I call you later to say good night?"

"You can call me anytime you like for any reason."

I lean in and frame her face with my hands, kissing her hard. I want her to still taste me on her lips after I'm gone. "I'll see you tomorrow evening."

She smiles and presses a quick kiss to my mouth. "Until then."

The bodyguard, or whatever Inamorata calls the titan guarding the entrance, opens the door for Lou. He takes her bag from me and lifts his chin, a gesture that I assume is intended for me. "Evening to you, sir."

"Good evening."

I stand at the doorway and watch Lou disappear into the building.

"May I help you with something else, sir?" the mountain asks.

"Just watching her for as long as possible. I wasn't ready to let her go." I chuckle beneath my breath because I actually just admitted that to Goliath.

"I understand, sir."

Glad that you understand, Goliath, because I sure as fuck don't.

BRADY TAPS HIS KNUCKLES AGAINST MY OFFICE DOOR. "Want to go and grab a pint with me tonight?"

I gesture for Brady to come into my office. "Got plans already. Lou's coming over."

"Come on, mate. You can make time for one drink."

I look at my watch. "Can't. I'm leaving in fifteen minutes to pick her up."

"Will you at least tell me about your weekend with her? Does Cora need to get a pink rosebud for the lass to wear on her left shoulder?"

Brady's question doesn't sit well with me, not even a wee bit, but I have no intentions of letting him know that. He can be a dobber sometimes, and I don't want to hear any shite out of him.

"Lou doesn't need a single rosebud. She needs a whole fucking bouquet."

"Ah yeah? Tell me about it."

He'll have to hear the short version. "I sent the staff away, and we spent the entire weekend at the house."

"Where was Ava Rose?"

"She stayed with my parents."

"What did Lou have to say about her?"

"I haven't told her yet."

Brady chuckles. "I hate to break it to you, mate, but that isn't a secret that's going to keep for long."

My best mate knows all of my secrets, but he doesn't understand the daily shite that I go through dealing with the aftermath that Mina left behind. "I'm going to tell her, but I wanted one normal weekend together before she hears the rest of the story."

"Have you not told her because you're afraid of what she'll say about it?"

"I just told you why I haven't told her."

"Lou is an inamorata. Technically, your employee… if you think about it. She's with you to do a job. She doesn't get to have an opinion about anything in your personal life. Don't forget that."

"I'm telling her everything tonight." And I hope that she understands. I need her to understand.

Closing my laptop, I push away from my desk. "I hate to run but I really need to be on time." I want to be there when Lou arrives. I can't stand the thought of her waiting for me at Waverley. A lot of unsavory people frequent that station.

"All right, mate. Have a nice evening with your inamorata. And let's try to grab that pint together one night soon."

"Aye."

I'm standing by the car waiting for Lou when she comes out of the station. Her dress is casual and although she's wearing heels, they aren't the four-inch fuck-me pumps that she usually wears.

I want to take her in my arms and kiss the fuck out of her, but I don't dare take the chance of being seen.

"You look ravishing. But then again, you always do."

"Not too casual?"

"You're dressed perfectly for an evening at home."

"I came out of the station and saw you wearing this designer suit, and I thought that our plans might have changed."

"I came straight from work. We're still having a quiet night at the house."

"I happen to like our quiet nights at your house."

"Me too."

Lou seems content when it's only the two of us. Unlike Mina, socializing with the most influential people in Edinburgh isn't on her list of must-dos.

Once we're in the back seat, I reach for Lou's hand and bring it to my mouth, kissing the top. "Three things on the agenda for tonight. First, Sonny is cooking dinner for us."

"Perfect. I'm starving."

"Second, I have someone for you to meet."

Lou does that furrow thing with her eyebrows when she's confused or concentrating. "You told me that I wouldn't meet anyone in your life."

"True, but this someone is different, and I think that you'll understand the exception that I'm making after you meet her."

"Her," Lou mutters beneath her breath. "Oh gosh. Now I'm a bundle of nerves."

"There's really no reason for you to be nervous."

"But I am." She smooths her hand over her dress. "I shouldn't have worn this. It's too casual. Do I need to change?"

"No. You look perfect just as you are."

"Is she joining us for dinner?"

"No. You'll meet her afterward."

Lou is tense during the drive to the house and on edge while we eat dinner. She hardly says two words. Makes me wish that I hadn't brought up the meeting at all. I want to enjoy my time with her this evening, not spend it reassuring her that she has no reason to be nervous.

"You said that there were three things on the agenda, but you never told me what the third one was."

"How about I don't tell you and I show you instead?"

It's been a whole day since I've had Lou beneath me. I want her.

Now.

Lou takes my offered hand and stands. "You're making me even more nervous."

"Don't be, mo maise."

That furrow on Lou's brow is back. She mutters something under her breath, but I can't make out what.

"What's wrong?"

"I don't know what mo maise means. I meant to ask Rachel about it, but I forgot."

"It means my beauty."

She smiles. "My beauty. That's sweet."

I hold Lou's hand, leading her to my bedroom. She stops outside of the doorway and pulls her hand away. "Wait."

"Why? What's wrong?"

Lou wraps her arms around her upper body. "Is this your way of trying to get me to do a threesome?"

A threesome? Where in the hell did that idea come from?

"No. God, no. Why would you think that?" I step closer and hold her face. "It's just you and I, Lou. That's what we said last night. Remember?"

"You told me that I was going to meet someone after dinner, and now you've brought me to your bedroom."

Okay. I get it now.

"I didn't bring you here to meet anyone. We have a wee bit of time on our hands. I just wanted to make good use of it." I brush my thumb over her cheek. "I missed you today."

She smiles and I know that all is well again. "I missed you too."

"Come with me?"

She follows me into the bedroom, and I sit on the bed, pulling her to stand between my legs. “Get up here, lass.”

She climbs up on the bed and places a knee on each side of my hips, straddling me. Her dress rides up to her waist, and I can see that she’s wearing black knickers.

“I thought about you all day. I could hardly concentrate on work.”

“I thought about you too.”

Her eyes are on mine when she licks her lips and leans forward. It’s just the surface of lips on lips for the briefest moment and then our tongues find one another. Our kiss is soft and sweet, but it isn’t enough. I need more.

Grabbing the back of her head, I pull her closer and deepen our kiss. My fingertips dig into the flesh of her bum, and I pull her body against mine. Hard. “I need to be inside of you.”

She places her palms on each side of my face and presses her forehead to mine, nodding. “I need that too.”

I push her dress up her body and pull it over her head. Unfastening the back of her bra, I free her perfect round tits and palm them. “So damn beautiful.”

Her spine arches as her head drops back when I suck one of her rosy tips into my mouth. I lick her nipple and after it hardens, I hold it between my teeth and suck in air around it.

“Tell me what you want me to do to you first.” Dirty talk from Lou’s mouth—that’s what I’m after tonight. “All you have to do is ask.”

Her lips are parted, harsh breath moving in and out. “You know what I want.”

Lou loves for me to go down on her. I know this. She doesn’t have to tell me, but tonight is about giving her a voice in the bedroom. “Say it.”

Her cheeks are bright pink, and her eyes are downcast.

"Look at me, mo maise." She hesitates a moment and then does as I tell her. "Look into my eyes and tell me what you like."

She touches her fingertips to her chest. "I like it when you start here."

"Start here doing what?"

"All of it."

I palm one of her breasts. "Rub? Kiss? Suck? What do you want me to do?"

She swallows and her throat bobs. "I want you to rub them and suck my nipples."

Okay. Now we're starting to get somewhere.

I cup her breasts and simultaneously knead them, taking one into my mouth. I suck her nipple for a moment and then roll my tongue around its spiky tip before moving to the other.

I stand and flip us over so that she's lying on the bed beneath me. "What do you want me to do to you next?"

"Take off my panties." My NOLA girl is warming up. She didn't hesitate that time.

Grinning at her, I tug downward on the waistband of her lacy black knickers. I drag them all the way down her shapely legs and toss them on the floor next to her dress and bra.

"I await your next instruction, mo maise."

She tugs on my shirt. "Take off your clothes while I watch."

Her eyes roam my body as I unbutton my shirt and drop it into the growing pile of clothes on the floor. A button yanked open and a lowered zipper later, I'm in the buff same as Lou.

I lift my brows. "Next?"

She bites her bottom lip and it slowly slips out from

beneath the clench of her upper teeth. "I want your mouth on me."

I hope that she doesn't believe that she's going to get off that easily. "Too vague. You'll have to be more specific."

She touches the center of her abdomen below her belly button. "Start here and work your way down until your face is buried between my legs."

Ahhh fuuuck. That was hot.

This is starting to become a lot of fun.

I crawl over her and kiss the center of her abdomen, inching toward my final destination. Her legs part as I move lower and I bury my nose against her slit, inhaling deeply. Her incomparable aroma fills my nostrils and my mouth instantly waters. I already know how good her quim is going to taste.

"Say it, Lou. Tell me to do it and I will."

She pushes her fingers into the top of my hair and tilts her hips upward. "Lick it and then tongue fuck me."

Kiss me down there—that's what I expected to hear out of Lou. Not lick it and then tongue fuck me.

She just took this game of dirty talk to a new level.

I drag my tongue up her center and flick the tip back and forth over the stiff wee bean sitting at the top of her slit. And then I hear a sharp intake of breath when I push my tongue inside her.

"Oh God… that feels so good."

Her words are breathless and barely audible. But I don't need words, dirty or clean, right now. Her panting and moaning tell me everything that I need to know.

Lou's back arches off of the bed and her body quakes. I feel those barely there quivers against my tongue and then the sweet and salty taste of her orgasm hits my tongue. Lou's sex nectar. I've never tasted anything like it.

Her body relaxes and her breathing slows. I place a final kiss against her slit and crawl up her body. Lying on top of her, I cradle her face with my palms and shower her mouth with kisses. "What do you want now?"

She bites my bottom lip and tugs on it. "Fuck me."

Don't have to ask me twice.

I pull away and reach into the drawer of my nightstand for a condom. I bite the corner of the foil square and rip it open. "Talk dirty. Tell me all of the filthy things you want while I put this on."

"I want to get on my hands and knees and scream into the pillow while you fuck me hard and fast from behind."

It's like she's reading my damn mind.

I grip Lou's hips and flip her over facedown on the bed. I wrap my arm around her waist and lift, raising her bum into the air. She gasps when I drive into her in one quick motion, burying myself bollocks deep inside of her. I pull back and thrust into her again, harder each time, over and over. I don't stop even when she screams my name into the pillow.

Groaning. Trembling. Ecstasy. My body is overtaken by all three when I find my release.

Lou is good at this. Very good. And I don't just mean the sex. She makes this—the girlfriend experience—feel real.

13

CAITRIONA LOUDEN

HUTCH COLLAPSES BESIDE ME ON THE BED. HE PUSHES HIS thick, muscular leg beneath mine and forces my thigh to hitch across his legs. He always touches me in one way or another after sex. I'm surprised by how much I like the physical contact. I'm not a touchy-feely kind of person, but it feels different with him. I like it when he touches me.

"What time is it?" he whispers and lifts his head, looking over at the bedside clock. "Almost ten."

Hutch kisses the side of my face and strains to sit up. "As much as I'd love to lie here naked with you for the rest of the night, we need to get up and get dressed. You have someone to meet."

This late? And right after he's just fucked my face into the bed?

My heart takes off in a gallop and I reach up to smooth my hair. "I need to freshen up, so I don't look so… freshly fucked."

"You look beautiful."

He doesn't understand. I would sooner die than meet a woman from his life and have her know that we just fucked. "I'm sure that I look like I've been ridden hard. Give me a minute."

I redress and mentally scold myself for allowing Hutch to toss my dress on the floor. I knew that I was meeting someone. I should have taken more care to not wrinkle it.

I smooth my hair and apply a fresh coat of red lipstick. "Do I look all right?"

"You look much better than all right, Lou."

"I don't want to embarrass you by looking a mess."

"You could never embarrass me. And you're going to see that all of this fuss is unnecessary."

I run my hands down my dress. "All right. I'm as ready as I'm going to be."

I follow Hutch out of his bedroom, and he leads me up a staircase. We haven't visited the floor above, not even when he gave me the house tour. His house is enormous, and in all honesty, I didn't realize that we had skipped it.

We stop at a closed door and Hutch turns the knob, opening the door slowly. I'm taken aback when I see a middle-aged woman sitting in a glider chair, reading a book.

"Mr. Hutcheson?" If I couldn't make out the surprise on her face, I would hear it in her voice.

"Good evening, Mrs. McVey."

"I would have kept the lassie awake if I had known that you were coming to see her."

The lassie?

It's in this moment that I take notice of my surroundings: pale pink walls, rose gold and metallic gold froufrou decor, white furniture.

Baby crib.

"It's fine. We won't be long."

"I'll step out and give you some time alone with her. I'll

just be in my room next door. Let me know if you need anything."

I walk over to the crib after the woman is gone and see a sleeping baby girl, her thumb in her mouth. And I don't know what to make of it.

Hutch approaches, standing beside me at the crib. "This is Ava Rose." He pauses a second. "Hutcheson."

"You told me that you didn't have children." And I believed you. What else have you lied about?

"Ava Rose isn't mine. She's my deceased wife's daughter."

She's an infant. Not an older child from a previous marriage. This doesn't make sense to me.

"When we met, you told me that you wanted to be transparent with me. This doesn't feel like transparency to me."

"That's a fair point, but please give me a moment before you jump to conclusions. I'll explain everything."

Rachel has told me that I'm judgy and she's right. That's what I'm doing right now, but I can't help it. Trusting people has made me the cynic that I am today.

I'm judgmental because I've been betrayed. I'm suspicious because I've been played. I'm emotionally unavailable because I'm afraid. And I'm unapologetic about it. Why shouldn't I be? No one ever apologized for making me this way.

"No one knows what I'm about to tell you with the exception of my best mate, Brady. This is a secret that must remain undisclosed."

"All right."

"Swear to me. Swear that you'll keep my secret."

"I swear."

Hutch looks at the sleeping baby. "I've never wanted children. I'm missing the gene that drives a man to want to father a child. Mina knew this before we married, and she told me that it was fine. She said that she didn't need children to be happy with me."

I've always known that I wanted children. The decision to not have children is something that I don't understand, but I don't have to understand it to be able to respect his decision.

"We were married for a few years when she told me that she wanted to have a baby. For me, nothing had changed. I still didn't want to be a father, but sometime during the early years of our marriage, she changed her mind. And with Mina being Mina, she thought that her feelings were the only ones that mattered."

Mina sounds like so many people in my life who couldn't care less about who they hurt in the process of getting what they want.

"A year passed, and she didn't bring it up again. I thought that it was behind us, and she was over it." Hutch chuckles but it's not an amused kind of laughter. "She wasn't even close to being over it."

Hutch pauses and grips the railing of the crib.

"I don't know when she stopped taking her birth control pills. I only know that she tried to trick me into getting her pregnant. When it didn't happen, she went to a doctor who started her on fertility medication."

Hutch makes that same bitter chuckle again.

"I was picking up a prescription at the pharmacy. The man behind the counter told me that Mina had a prescription ready for pickup if I wanted to get it and save my wife a trip. I paid for both but didn't look at Mina's until I got into the car. It was a fertility drug."

Mina was trying to get pregnant, even taking fertility drugs, and didn't get pregnant by Hutch. But she did get pregnant by someone else. Does that mean Hutch is sterile? It sounds as though that could be the case. Maybe that's part of why it's so ingrained within him to not want children.

"I was trying my damnedest to get over her deception, but our marriage was crumbling right before my eyes. The trust was gone. I couldn't even think about having sex with her for fear of being tricked into a baby. That's when I knew that it was over. I was planning to ask Mina for a divorce, but she got into the car accident before I was able to do it."

Mina was killed in that car accident. There are some big missing pieces to this story.

"Mina was declared brain-dead, but her family couldn't accept the prognosis. They had it in their heads that she was going to miraculously wake up and be fine. No one could fault them for having hope, and I knew that with time, they would see the reality of the situation. And while I was waiting for them to accept what had to be done, the doctors discovered that Mina was pregnant."

Oh my God.

"Our friends and family didn't know that Mina and I were on the verge of divorce. They assumed that Ava Rose was my daughter."

There's one twist after another to this story. I can see why Hutch didn't go into this the night that we met. It's too much to take in one sitting.

"What was I to do, Lou? At what point should I have told our grieving friends and family that Mina had betrayed me and the bairn inside of her wasn't mine?"

What a winless situation.

"Everyone was thrilled about the baby, even my own parents and siblings. They all kept calling it a miracle, a piece of Mina that I would always carry with me. I couldn't bring myself to tell them the truth. It would have broken their hearts."

Hutch stayed silent, allowing the people within their lives to have this last bit of happiness, instead of speaking the truth. "That must have been brutal for you."

"I've never endured a more difficult situation in my entire life."

And so here he is. The woman that he was going to divorce is dead, and he's left to care for a baby that he never wanted. A baby who was fathered by another man.

"Who is her father?"

"That may be the worst part of the story. I don't know."

"You don't have a suspicion?"

He shakes his head. "She was clever in covering her tracks."

All of this must be a kick in the balls for him. "It's okay to be angry about this. It doesn't make you a bad person."

"Mina's recklessness has changed my life forever. Angry doesn't begin to cover it." Hutch looks at the baby. "I don't know how to be a father to her."

"I think that all new parents need time to adjust."

"Time isn't going to fix what's wrong with me. I'm not cut out to be a father." He sinks his hands into the top of his hair and fists it. "Fuck, you must think that I'm horrible."

"I don't think you're horrible, Hutch. You're just a man who was thrown into a situation that he wasn't prepared for and doesn't know how to deal with it."

"I make sure that she's taken care of. She has four well-trained nannies who give her the best of care."

"I'm sure that her nannies are wonderful, but children shouldn't be raised by staff members."

"Maybe I'd feel differently if she were mine."

My mother and father made me and look at where that got me. "Biology means nothing. Love means everything. The rest will fall into place."

"And what if it doesn't? She's already three months old."

"She is going to know you as her father, and trust me, she is going to want your love. The way that you treat this little girl will affect her for the rest of her life. It will mold her into the woman she becomes. It's a very serious responsibility. If you can't love her, then you should tell everyone the truth and give her to someone who can love her."

"I'm going to do better. I have to do better—for her."

"Yes, you do."

"You don't know how much I needed this talk. I have no one that I can say these things to."

"I hope that I've been helpful."

"You're making me think about so many things that I've not considered. I need you to keep encouraging me, Lou. I need it so badly."

I reach down and stroke Ava Rose's cheek when she stirs. "I'd like to spend time with her if it's all right."

"Aye, spend as much time with her as you like."

Maxwell Hutcheson. I don't know what to make of him.

This man has many layers. And I look forward to peeling back each one and seeing what's beneath.

14

MAXWELL HUTCHESON

IF GIVEN THE CHOICE, I WOULD CHOOSE AN ARSE BEATING over enduring the company of my in-laws. But I must push through until it's over. And until the next time.

I've tolerated these people for years on account of Mina. And now I must tolerate them further because Lundy and Thomas are Ava Rose's grandparents. Elsie, Beth, and Blair are her aunts. They are her real family. Her blood. Her clan.

Not me.

"Has the pediatrician told you when to introduce solids?"

Solids? There's a slight delay in my brain as I consider what Elsie is talking about. And then it clicks.

"He said that we'd talk about that at the next visit." Lie.

"The pediatrician is a she. You said he," Elsie says.

"Right."

I don't take Ava Rose to her checkups. I don't make decisions about her diet. I get a weekly report from Mrs. McVey concerning her health and well-being. As long as her nanny tells me that she's healthy, I don't ask questions.

"Mina was allergic to eggs, so you should be careful when giving those to her." Elsie rubs her fingers over Ava Rose's inner wrists. "This looks like a patch of eczema. Have you shown it to the doctor?"

Eczema. Seems like I remember Mrs. McVey saying that the doctor had diagnosed Ava Rose with a mild case and would be treating her with a cream.

"Aye, we're applying a cream on it."

"What kind of cream?"

"I don't recall the name."

"Something over the counter?"

"Aye." I have no idea.

"It doesn't look as though it's helping."

"We're going to reevaluate the eczema at her next visit and switch to another cream if the rash hasn't improved."

"You should tell the doctor that you want a prescription steroid. It's best for eczema."

Aye, Elsie. I'm sure that you would tell the doctor how to do her job. You tell everyone what they should be doing. It's what you do best. You have an opinion on everything.

"I'll do that."

"You and this wee lassie are lucky to have us." Elsie adjusts Ava Rose, so they're face-to-face. "What would you do without us?"

Oh, I don't know. Live in peace? Experience tranquility?

I told myself that I was going to stick it out and stay until nine o'clock, but two hours of judgment and criticism are all that I can tolerate from these bollock busters. I may explode if I have to listen to them for another minute.

"I'm afraid that Ava Rose and I must be going. I have an early meeting in the morning." Another lie.

Blair gets up and takes Ava Rose from Elsie. "You can't leave yet. We haven't even cut the cake."

I need Thomas's help on this one. "I'm meeting with Nichols in the morning. I have some things that I need to prepare."

"Dad, tell Max that family is more important than business," Blair says.

Come on, Thomas. Don't fail me now. Choose business over family. You always do.

"Well, I think you can stay long enough for cake. Your preparations will hold a wee bit longer."

Fuck. I have worked for this man for ten years, and he has ridden my arse every single one of those days. Always demanding more out of me at the firm. Always forcing me to choose my work over my personal life. He's never chosen family over business a day in his life and he picks now to be a family man?

Un-fucking-believable.

"Blair called you about the party on Saturday. You should have prepared for the meeting before now," Beth says. And they're the first words that she's said to me in months. She has been especially bitter toward me since Mina's death.

"Max works hard at the firm. Don't use that as a weapon against him." Blair says.

The fuck? Blair is defending me?

"Right. He has plenty of time to work but never time for family. No time to bring Ava Rose to see us."

It's just like Beth to not see that the door swings both ways. "I don't keep Ava Rose from you. You're welcome to come and see her anytime you like. You know that." But you don't because you are too busy. And the effort to do something for someone other than yourself would kill you.

"Mina would have brought her to see us."

I'm not so sure about that. Mina was always tied up doing Mina things.

"It's a terrible tragedy that she isn't here to bring Ava Rose to visit."

"And whose fault is that?" Beth says, her words forced through clenched teeth.

And here we go again. I killed Mina because I pulled the plug. "Mina wasn't going to come out of the coma. You know that."

"That's not what I'm talking about."

"Then what are you talking about?"

"She wouldn't have gone away that weekend if you hadn't been obsessed with work and your own personal success. She'd have been home instead." Beth glares at me. "You should have been a better husband to her."

And Mina should have been a better wife to me. A wife who didn't try to trick me into a child. A wife who didn't cheat on me. A wife who didn't get pregnant by another man.

There are so many ways that I could respond to Beth's claim. And I want to. Believe me, I want to. I'd love for these people to know everything that Mina did and finally understand that I'm not the bad guy here.

Beth's husband wraps his arm around her shoulder. "This isn't the time or place."

She wipes the tears away from her eyes and cheeks. "You're right. This is Mum's birthday party. It should be a happy occasion for her. Shall we sing happy birthday and cut the cake?"

Blair lowers her voice, "Please stay, Max. Don't leave on account of Beth's outburst."

"We'll stay long enough for cake."

What should only take fifteen minutes or so turns into another hour. And while I sit there, an idea occurs to me.

They want to spend more time with Ava Rose? I'm going to give that to them in a way that doesn't include me.

"I'm going to be out of town on business next week. Would you like to keep Ava Rose while I'm away?"

Beth turns and looks at me, her eyes meeting mine. "We would love to keep her."

"All right. I'll have one of the nannies deliver her to you on Monday morning and return for her on Friday."

"Thank you, Max," Blair says. "It's very kind of you to offer."

~

"WHAT?" LOU SAYS.

"Nothing."

"You aren't thinking about nothing with a wicked grin like that on your face."

She isn't wrong. "I'm thinking about this pearl G-string and how you look in it." And how I just pulled it aside and fucked you while you wore it.

Lou did exactly as I asked. She was at my house when I came home tonight, wearing nothing but the naughty G-string when I came into the bedroom.

And damn, she looks like pure perfection in it. But then everything about Lou is turning out to be perfect. The way we communicate, the way we interact, the way we fuck. It's as though she was made for me.

"I'm happy that you like it."

Unable to resist, I reach for my phone on the nightstand and turn on the camera, focusing on her. "You look too damn good to not have your picture taken."

"I'm available for you to see in person anytime you like. You don't need a picture of me."

"I won't see you while I'm away on business next week."

"I didn't know that you were going away. When are you leaving?"

"Monday."

She bites her bottom lip, trying to suppress a smile. "What exactly will you be doing while you look at a picture of me wearing a pearl G-string?"

"You know exactly what I'll be doing."

She places her hand over her face. "I have bed head."

"Aye, you do, and you still look like a real stunner." Her messy hair will be a good reminder of the shag that we just had.

I grab both of her wrists in one of my hands and hold them hostage over her head. "You look perfect."

She turns her head to the side. "Do you have any idea how vulnerable it feels to have your photo taken while you're naked?"

I lower my face to hers and kiss the corner of her mouth. "Relax, Lou. No one's going to see these pictures except me."

"Hutch! I'm not going to let you take pictures of me like this."

I'm still holding her wrists above her head when I kiss her neck and whisper against her ear. "Come on, Lou. Please let me."

She doesn't say no, so I nuzzle my nose down her neck and plant a kiss below her earlobe to convince her. "Please, Lou."

"How long will you be away?"

"Five days."

"Five days," she mutters under her breath. "And you need a picture of me to get you by, huh?"

"Aye. Being away from you is going to be torture." Lou

feels like a hit off of the best drug that I've ever had. Being apart is going to be brutal.

"You can take a few pictures but no nudes."

Fuck me. I didn't think that she'd go along with it.

She places her hand over the camera lens. "Not yet. I get to brush my hair first."

She goes to the bathroom and returns a few minutes later with freshly brushed hair cascading over her shoulders. She climbs onto the bed, kneeling before me. "How do you want me?"

How do you want me? That question coming from a woman like her is every man's fantasy.

"Lie down."

She falls to her back and pulls the sheet under her arms, covering her naked breasts. "Like this?"

"Aye but spread your hair across the pillow."

She rises and holds her hair away from her neck as she lowers herself against the pillow. When she releases her thick, wavy locks of chestnut, they fall in all of the right places.

"Better?"

"Perfect." You have no idea how perfect.

Plump pink lips. Her fingers touching her mouth. Smiles and grins. Solemn and sexy. I get a lot of shots of Lou lying on her back, but there's one that I really want.

I put my hands on her knees, spreading them apart.

"No crotch shots."

"I'm not finished positioning the sheet."

Gathering the bedsheet between her legs, I twist it so that only a thin strip of material conceals her. I bunch the end between her breasts and take one of her arms, laying it over both breasts. She's covered to some degree so it's not really a nude. And she lets me take the photos.

Damn… she looks sexy.

I lie down beside her when I'm finished photographing her and twist to kiss her lips. "Thank you for letting me do that."

She picks up my phone and holds it above us. "My turn now."

"I can assure you that I don't care anything about seeing pictures of myself."

"Very funny." She turns it on selfie mode and adjusts the angle. "Say cheese, Hutch."

Photos of Lou and me in bed together aren't wise. It would be disastrous if anyone ever saw them. But I'm confident that no one will ever see them. They're on my phone. In my control.

Lou thumbs through the photos. "We look like a real couple in these pictures."

I don't reply. Instead, I kiss her on the neck and then the mouth. I move lower and suck her breast into my mouth. And our photo shoot is forgotten.

15

CAITRIONA LOUDEN

I'm settling into my role as Hutch's companion. Tonight marks two weeks since our agreement and so far, I don't regret it.

He and I are beginning to establish a routine. I do as I like while he's at work, and I'm always at his beck and call when he comes home. I don't mind. This arrangement works for both of us. Probably better than it should.

"I thought that we might go into the village for lunch today. I could show you around Kirkliston."

Hold on. Wait a minute. "I thought that we couldn't be seen together."

"We can't be seen in Edinburgh, but the village is a different story. My family, friends, and business associates have no reason to visit Kirkliston."

Lunch with Hutch in a public setting? "I'd love to."

The boyfriend experience. I might not have paid for it but it's what I want from him.

"Don't get too excited. There are only three places to eat and they're all casual. Maybe even a step below."

I don't need formal or fancy. "I don't mind casual."

"Your choices are Chinese, a fish and chips and burger joint, or hearty food. I believe that Americans call it comfort food."

I'm a southern girl. I'll choose comfort food every time. "Hearty."

"I've eaten there a few times and I enjoyed it."

"What time should I be ready to go?"

"I have some things to take care of this morning, but I should be finished by noon."

"All right. I'll be ready."

"Sleep a wee bit longer, mo maise." A wicked grin spreads across his face. "You'll need your strength tonight."

I look at the clock and see that it's only fifteen minutes after five. That is early by anyone's standards. "Maybe another hour. Or two."

Hutch kisses my forehead. "Sleep as long as you like."

I hear the shower turn on and I consider leaving the bed to get inside with him. But then I remember what he said. *You'll need your strength tonight.*

He's not kidding. Sex with Hutch isn't for the weak-hearted. Or weak-legged. The man fucks like a tempest. But he can also make love like the ocean rushing over a sandy beach. Both are beautiful and powerful at the same time.

We make eye contact when he leaves the bathroom, and he comes over to sit next to me on the bed. He strokes his fingers across my forehead, pushing my hair away from my face. "I love having you in my bed at night, but I think that I may love seeing you in it in the morning just as much."

"I love it too."

He leans down and places a sweet kiss against my lips. "Sleep well, Lou."

Lou. Oh, what I wouldn't give to hear him call me Cait instead.

I reach for my cell and scroll through the pictures that Hutch sent to my phone after our photo shoot. Of course, I only requested that he send the ones of us. I don't care anything about seeing myself nearly naked.

Thumbing through the photos, I have a thought that keeps repeating in my head—he makes it so damn easy to forget that this isn't a real relationship.

I put my phone away and close my eyes. When I open them again, Hutch is sitting on the bed next to me. "Time to wake up, sleepyhead."

I lift my head and look over at the clock. Shit, it's almost ten o'clock.

I strain to sit up. "I didn't mean to sleep so long. I'll get in the shower now."

"Hold on. We've had a bump in the road since we made plans this morning. The nanny isn't feeling well."

"Mrs. McVey?"

"Aye."

"I hope it's nothing serious."

"I don't think so. Sounds like some kind of stomach bug. Whatever it is, the baby can't be exposed."

"No, definitely not."

"I'm trying to reach the other nannies about coming in to take over Mrs. McVey's shift, but no one is answering my calls." I hear the annoyance in his voice.

"Don't be irritated with them. They value their time away from work just as you value yours."

"I understand that, but I pay those women a lot of money to care for Ava Rose."

Why is he so upset? "This isn't a big deal. We can still go to lunch and take her with us."

"It is a big deal, Lou. I don't know how to take care of her."

"You may not, but I do. I'll take care of her." Heidi used me as her own personal nanny when my younger sister Lola was born.

"Are you sure?"

"It'll be fine. Taking her with us changes nothing."

16

MAXWELL HUTCHESON

Ava Rose is strapped across the front of Lou's body inside one of those baby-carrying sling things. I've seen mums in public using them but never the nannies. Not that I've spent that much time observing them with her, but I'm surprised that Lou found that kind of baby gear in the nursery.

I watch the way Lou carries Ava Rose against her chest, and her tender nature baffles me. Protective. Caring. Nurturing. Those are the words that come to mind when I try to think of how to describe the way she looks. No one ever looked more like a mother than Lou does right now. And oddly, it's not a turnoff.

Ava Rose whimpers, and Lou rocks back and forth, patting her back through the sling. "Shh… it's okay, baby girl."

A wee bit of rocking, patting, and Lou's soft voice—that's all it takes to soothe Ava Rose back into a peaceful slumber. Unbelievable. The baby would probably be screaming her head off if I was the one holding her.

"What are you having to eat?" Lou says.

"Steak and Scottish ale pie. What about you?"

"I can't resist the macaroni and cheese."

Americans love their macaroni and cheese. "I thought that you might go with that."

Our server comes to take our order and leans forward, peeking into the carrier at Ava Rose. Lou adjusts the baby and her sling, giving the woman a better view.

"What a beautiful bairn. How old is she?"

"Three months," Lou says.

"That was my guess. Let's see. Who does she look like?" The waitress studies Lou for a second and then looks over at me. "I think she looks like her mum. Am I right?"

Lou lifts a brow. "I don't know. What do you think, Hutch?"

"Aye, she looks very much like her mum." Which isn't a lie. Ava Rose is similar to Mina in many ways.

"Then she's a lucky lassie because she has a beautiful mum."

"Thank you."

"Are you ready to order?"

We place our orders, and Lou leans across the table, lowering her voice when the waitress leaves. "It seemed rude to not thank her."

"Aye."

I don't tell Lou, but the truth is that I don't dislike the woman's assumption that we are a happy husband and wife. Makes this feel even more like the real thing. I miss being a husband and I still long for a loving, faithful wife. A devoted partner in life. I may not want to be a father, but I do want to be a husband again one day.

Ava Rose fusses again and this time the rocking, patting, and soft voice don't soothe her. "She's wet. I'm going to change her."

Lou and Ava Rose haven't returned when our food

arrives. "Steak and Scottish ale pie for you and macaroni and cheese for your wife. Can I get you anything else?"

Your wife.

"I don't need anything, but will you come back and check after… my wife returns?"

"Aye."

Lou and a more content Ava Rose return from the toilet. "Perfect timing."

"The server is going to come back and see if you need anything else."

"Looks good to me."

She picks up her fork and digs into the macaroni and cheese, her eyes widening while she releases a sexy moan. "Mmm… that is delicious. I haven't had mac and cheese that good since I was back home."

Home. A reminder that she still considers the US to be her home.

I watch Lou cradle Ava Rose with her right arm while she eats with her left. And then it strikes me. "You're left-handed?"

Lou smiles and swallows. "All day long."

"My dad and brother are left-handed."

"My dad is too. My mother despised that I inherited that trait from him. She tried to force me into being right-handed." Lou holds up her left hand. "As you can see, that nonsense didn't work."

That sounds like a cruel thing to do to a child.

"Your parents didn't get along?"

"It wasn't a matter of them getting along. He left her and went back to Scotland when he found out that she was pregnant with me. He said that he didn't want a baby."

My news about not wanting children must have rekindled some painful memories for Lou.

"His leaving devastated my mother; she was so in love.

But things got really bad when he married Heidi and started having babies with her. She went off the deep end and started using alcohol and drugs to numb the pain. And I became a little kid who paid for the hurt he had caused her." Lou looks down at Ava Rose. "You can't ever do that to this child."

"I would never mistreat Ava Rose on account of her mother's actions."

"You're bitter about your wife's betrayal. You're going to be for a while yet, and that's completely understandable. I would be too, but you can't let the pain fester and harden your heart. And you can't ever take it out on Ava Rose."

"I won't."

Lou looks up at me. "Always remember this conversation, Hutch. Months from now. Years from now. When I'm gone from your life and only a distant memory in the back of your mind, remember this conversation."

Despite our short time together, I'm already certain that Lou will never become a distant memory in the back of my mind. "I'll remember."

"And never forget how important you're going to be in her life."

I nod. "I won't."

I wanted a woman in my life again. A woman to warm my bed. A woman to lie beneath me. But with Lou, I feel like I got so much more, as though she was introduced into my life for a purpose greater than my own selfish needs and desires. But these are thoughts that can never find a voice. They must be kept to myself.

~

SITTING ON THE EDGE OF THE BED, I TAKE A MOMENT TO watch Lou sleeping. Deep, even breaths with a steady rise and fall of her chest. A quiet whistle from her nostrils each time she breathes. The sheets yanked away from me during the night, covering her and the floor on her side. These are the things that I've become accustomed to with Lou, all in such a short time. And I relish it all.

Five days without her. How will I manage? I don't want to go a single day without seeing her.

Crazy.

I lean over and kiss her upper back, inducing a slight stir but not enough to wake her. I do it again and this time she makes a seductive moaning sound. It makes my dick come to life, but I don't have time to satisfy his needs again this morning. I'm already running later than planned.

I kiss the bare skin on her shoulder. "I'm leaving."

She rolls over and smiles. "Don't go. Stay with me."

She has no idea how badly I wish I could stay. "I would if I had a choice."

"Hold on. Give me one minute in the bathroom."

She dashes into the bathroom and returns a moment later, still naked from our early morning goodbye sex.

"Kiss me one more time before you go."

She climbs on top of me and presses her mouth to mine. I know that letting her do this isn't good for my dick. How will I ever leave without burying myself inside of her?

"I'm running late because we've already had several one-more kisses. I really have to go."

"I know. My fault. Sorry."

"I'm not sorry." Schedule be damned.

"Call me when you can?"

"I will. Promise."

17

CAITRIONA LOUDEN

One foot in, and then the other. I pull the black Versace dress up my body, wiggling as it glides over my hips. Reaching behind my back, I tug the zipper upward until it hits a point where it won't rise any farther. I lower it and try again without luck.

Shit, shit, shit. The zipper can't be broken on this dress; I've never even gotten to wear it. And the thing cost a fortune.

Three times I repeat the same process. Still, no luck.

I open my bedroom door and call out to Rachel, "Can you please come in here and help me?"

She whistles when she comes through the door. "That is one dynamite dress."

"Thanks." This dress looks killer on me. It hugs and accentuates every curve I have. Butt. Boobs. Hips. I love this dress. And I hate that I'm not wearing it for Hutch tonight.

He's been gone for three days and I miss him far more than I should. Because I shouldn't be missing him at all. He isn't mine to miss.

"I can't get the zipper up." I spin around and pull my hair off my back and shoulders. "The dress doesn't feel too tight. Does it look like there's a thread caught in it or something?"

She comes to me and examines my dress. "Not that I can see."

I stand taller, suck in my stomach, and poke out my butt and boobs. "Try it now."

She pulls upward and the zipper smoothly glides to the top. "Got it."

I step away and smooth my dress. "Looks okay?"

"Stunning."

"I love your dress too."

"Ah, thanks. It was a gift from Claud."

Rachel and I haven't gotten to talk about him in a while since I've been spending so much time at Hutch's house. "How's your relationship with him?"

"He's still booking all of my appointments, even when he can't see me." It's one thing to book her time for dates, but it's something entirely different to book her time so that no other client can see her.

"And you're still happy about that?"

"Ecstatic."

"Then I'm happy for you."

"Everything is still going well with Mr. Hutcheson?"

"Wonderful. Or at least it was until last night when I told him about the Inamorata cocktail party tonight."

I understand why Cora would want all inamoratas to attend the party. She wants the clients to see her wide variety of choices in women, but I'm not a choice.

"What happened when you told him that you were attending the party?"

You're not available for the taking by other clients.

Stop acting as though you're still an inamorata. You're not.

Those men at that party are going to want you.

"He was very verbal about his dissatisfaction. He acted possessive of me and came off jealous that I was going to be around other clients." Can't lie. I loved every dominating word.

"Of course, he doesn't want you to go. In his mind, you are his."

"Would it be crazy if I felt the same? Like I am his?" Surely it is. The man bought my time. Not me.

"It's not crazy if you're falling in love with him."

"I'm not." I can't. Falling in love with Hutch would be the stupidest thing I've ever done. Even stupider than trusting a bartender to be faithful to me.

"Is something more than sex happening between the two of you?"

"No."

"Do you want something more?"

I can't have those kinds of thoughts. "Doesn't matter if I do. It can never happen."

"And why not?"

"His circumstances are complicated. There isn't room for a romantic relationship in his life now or anytime soon." And if there were, it wouldn't be with an escort. I'm certain of that.

"Love has a way of not caring about complicated circumstances."

Maybe love doesn't care but Hutch does. In fact, he cares very much about his complicated circumstances. And I don't see that changing anytime soon.

"CHAMPAGNE?"

"Yes, thank you."

I sip from the glass of bubbly and watch the twirling couples on the dance floor. Old, balding, big-bellied men. Young, beautiful, physically fit women. Not all, but the contrast between most of the dance partners couldn't be more dramatic. And I could be in the arms of one of these men right now. That thought elicits a shudder throughout my body.

Thank God for Hutch.

"Lots of new clients tonight," Cora says.

I turn at the sound of her voice. "I thought it would be a light turnout since it's a Wednesday night."

"A man doesn't care what day of the week it is when there's a chance of getting his knob polished."

"Yes, I suppose that all of them would clear their calendars for that."

"I assume all is well with Mr. Hutcheson? You're getting along?"

"We get along perfectly."

"You've overcome your aversion to sex?" Cora says.

I never had an aversion to sex. I simply wasn't inclined to sleep with a man I didn't know and take money in exchange for it. It's a reasonable line to have. And it's a line I've crossed. "My reluctance was short-lived."

"As one would expect with a man like Mr. Hutcheson. He is quite handsome."

I admit that it wasn't difficult to change my mind about him. "He is good-looking but he's also a good man."

"I'm happy that you're pleased with your arrangement. Perhaps we'll be able to find another like it after you fulfill your obligation to him."

"Thank you for the offer, but I won't have a need for more money." Not with the current balance in my bank account.

"Every girl of mine has her own personal reason for

being an inamorata. Ask around and you'll quickly find out that those reasons aren't always about money."

I can't imagine doing this for any other reason.

"I appreciate your interest in me, and I'm thankful for your taking me on when I needed the money, but I don't plan on making this a career. I'm going back to uni in September."

"All right. We'll leave it at that for now, but please know that you have a place at Inamorata if you ever change your mind."

"You're very kind. Thank you."

Even if I wanted to continue at Inamorata, I couldn't. Being with Hutch has ruined me. I can never be an inamorata to anyone else.

The first glass of champagne goes down so easily that I have a second. And then a third. I'm toying with having a fourth even though it's against Cora's rules. But why not? Hutch isn't here and I can't be booked by Inamorata clients. Sure, I must behave and represent Inamorata in a positive light, but that doesn't mean that I can't enjoy a fine champagne. And who's keeping up with my drink tally anyway?

Warm. Relaxed. Buzzed.

Check. Check. Check.

"Looks as though someone has exceeded her drink allowance. Mum won't be pleased about that."

Chambers, Cora's son. My body shudders at the sound of his voice.

When I met him, he instantly gave me the creeps. I don't have an explanation as to why, but I've never been able to shake the feeling. I only know that something below his seemingly professional surface makes me cringe.

I hold up my glass, bringing it to my lips and downing the final drink while he watches. "Guilty as charged."

"Don't worry. I won't tell Mother."

"Oh, I'm not worried." I'm spoken for by Hutch. Paid in advance. There's not a lot that Cora can say to me.

"I've noticed that you aren't making connections with clients tonight."

"Because I'm not available for booking."

"What does that mean?" he says.

If Chambers is the important partner that he claims to be, Cora would have told him about my arrangement.

"My time has been bought and paid for in full through August 31."

"By whom?"

"Mr. Maxwell Hutcheson."

"Never heard of him. I want to meet this man."

"He isn't here. He's away on business."

A man steps between us and wraps his arm around Chambers's shoulder. "Listen up. Mr. Hutcheson is a possessive bastard. He's quite fond of Miss Lou, and he won't be pleased to hear that you're harassing her."

"I am not harassing her. I'm merely doing the job that Mother asked me to do."

"What job is that?"

"I'm to check in on all of the inamoratas and see if they need anything."

"Errand boy. Figures. Well, this inamorata is fine so you should fuck off."

Chambers shoves the man's arm away. "Mother will hear of this, Mr. Young."

"Aye, she will."

I don't know who this man is, but I'm grateful for the interruption. "Thank you for that."

"I hate that wanker. I haven't met an inamorata yet who likes him and that includes his mother."

So it isn't just me? The bad vibes that I get off of the guy aren't just in my imagination?

The man offers his hand. "I'm Brady."

"You're Hutch's Brady? His best mate?" The one who brought him to the Inamorata gala?

"Guilty."

Brady introduced Hutch to Inamorata. He was Hutch's foot in the door at the gala. We'd have never met if it weren't for this man.

"It's so nice to meet you."

"It's my pleasure, Lou."

"Hutch is out of town on business." What a stupid thing to tell him. Not only are they best mates, they're colleagues. "But I'm sure that you already know that."

"Aye, I do."

"Hutch tells me that you've been an Inamorata client for a while?"

"Aye, since my divorce two years ago."

"My best friend is an inamorata. I'm wondering if you've ever booked her. Ra—" I've already let Rachel's real name slip in front of Hutch. I can't let that happen again. "Her name is Meg."

"I've never booked an inamorata by that name. In fact, I can't recall ever meeting a Meg. How long has she worked for Cora?"

"Several months."

"Is she here tonight?"

"Yes, somewhere." I look around and spot her with her steady Inamorata client. "There she is on the dance floor. Long blond hair. Green dress."

"It's too bad that I've never booked her. She's beautiful."

"She is." Inside and out. I've never had a more loyal friend in my life.

"I'd be interested in booking her. That is, if she wears a rosebud."

I'm not sure what her official rosebud status is these days. "She has a steady client who books her out in advance so that no other client can see her."

"Oh? Sounds similar to your arrangement with Max."

It feels odd to hear that name. I only think of him as Hutch now. "I suppose that our arrangements are a little bit similar."

"Your arrangement with Max… it's good for him. It's been a long time since I've seen him this happy."

He's happy? I am too.

"He's a wonderful man and I enjoy our time together."

Talking about Hutch makes me miss him so much. I'm wishing for the millionth time tonight that I was with him when my phone vibrates in my hand.

HUTCH: You look beautiful in that dress.
LOU: How would you know?
HUTCH: Because I'm looking at you right now.

Oh my God. Hutch is here?

My heart speeds and my head springs upward. I search the sea of faces, but I don't see him anywhere.

He's messing with me.

LOU: Very funny.

I'm awaiting his reply when I feel large hands grasp my hips from behind. Warm breath hits my ear and my breath catches in my throat. "I'm right here, mo maise."

I turn in his arms and look at him. "Hutch?"

"Surprised to see me?"

"Yes. I thought you wouldn't be back until Friday."

"That was the plan, but I worked overtime so I could come back sooner."

So he could be with me?

He takes my face in his hands and kisses me hard. When he lets me go, he pulls back and looks in my eyes. "Come home with me."

I nod. "Let's go."

18

MAXWELL HUTCHESON

"Thanks for keeping an eye on Lou until I could get here."

"I have to tell you, Max, that I find all of this odd. I understand your arrangement, but I don't understand your agenda."

"I have only one agenda, Brady. I paid a lot of money for Lou's time and loyalty. Both belong to me. She shouldn't even be at this cocktail party." These men don't have the right to so much as look at her while she is in a companionship with me. If I'd had my say, she wouldn't have attended this party at all.

"I get it. You don't want to share your shiny new toy."

"And I won't."

"Can't say that I blame you for feeling that way, not after the amount of money you paid her."

"Exactly." But that isn't all of it. This is about something more than the money.

I glance at my mobile. "How long does it take to let Cora know she's leaving?" Feels like I've been waiting a long time.

Another five minutes passes and she still hasn't returned. Something feels off. And I know that I'm right when I see Lou rushing toward me.

I glance at the hallway leading to Cora's office and then back to her. "What happened?"

Her eyes won't meet mine. "Nothing. Let's just go."

"You've been crying, Lou."

"Can we just go? Please? Now?"

I don't feel like going. Someone has done something to her, and I want to know what that is.

"Did you have an argument with Cora?"

"No. Nothing like that."

So something did happen. "Did one of the Inamorata clients do something to you?"

"No."

I grasp her chin and force her to look at me. "Tell me what happened."

A fresh collection of tears begins to pool in her lower lids. "Let's talk about it in the car."

She's baiting me to get us out the door, away from whoever hurt her. I hope she isn't under the impression that I'm too dumb to sort that out. "All right."

We leave Inamorata, saying nothing on the walk to the car, but I can't stand it another second once we're in the back seat. "Tell me, Lou."

Her head lowers and she stares at her hands in her lap. "It was Cora's son."

"What did he do to you?"

"Please tell Calvin to drive. I want to leave this place."

I nod at Calvin but she's wrong if she believes that distance will save Cora's son if he has somehow hurt her. I won't hesitate to tell Calvin to turn this car around.

I reach for her hand and bring it to my lips after the

car is moving. "All right. I've done everything that you've asked."

The spill from the streetlights flashes on her face as we drive, and I see the tears flowing down her cheeks.

"I went to Cora's office. She wasn't there but her son Chambers was. He got between me and the door and shut it. He wouldn't let me out."

I already know how this story is going to go. How far, I don't know, and that will be the deciding factor for my next move.

"He told me that I wasn't leaving until I gave him what he wanted." Lou sniffles and reaches up, wiping her lower lids. "He was so fast and so strong. I tried to push him away and he didn't budge."

Anger. Fury. Rage.

Tightening fists. Grinding teeth. Shaking body.

"He told me that I was nothing more than a whore and I should stop fighting him. I was so scared that I couldn't think straight, but then my mind cleared, and my self-defense lessons kicked in. I put my hands around his head and pushed on his eyeballs until he let go of me. And then I kicked him in the nuts and ran."

I want to kill him.

I think that I will kill him.

"Calvin, turn the car around and go back to Inamorata."

"No, no, no."

That man has taken advantage of Lou's vulnerability. I'm not having it. "I won't let that bastard get away with doing that to you."

"He didn't get away with it. Ask his balls."

Lou doesn't get it. She got lucky this time. He could have done so much worse to her and he probably has with some of the other inamoratas. "He deserves more than a kick in the bollocks."

"Please don't, Hutch. He's an asshole, no doubt about it, but he's Cora's son. I don't want this to become a problem between her and me."

Lou was an inamorata when we met, and she'll be an inamorata after our arrangement ends. She doesn't want problems because she could need Cora to broker future arrangements with Inamorata clients.

There could be clients to have her after me. I don't like the way that makes me feel.

"I know his kind. You've hurt his ego and now he's going to be driven even more to have you."

Her eyes widen. "Meaning what?"

I don't want to frighten her, but she needs to be smart about this. "Does he know where you live?"

She brings her hand to her forehead and mutters a profanity under her breath. "Cora would have my name and address on file. Do you think he'd be crazy enough to come after me at home?"

"Who knows what's in his head? But I'm afraid it might not be safe for you to stay there right now. I think you should move into my house for the remainder of our arrangement. At least we know he can't get to you there."

"How can I live with you without exposing our relationship?"

Concerned Lou. Thinking of me instead of her safety. "Don't worry about that."

"How can I not worry about it?"

I pull her close, so close that our foreheads are touching. "Your safety is what matters most, and I won't leave you vulnerable to him. Understand?" She nods and our heads move together. "Going back and forth from your place to mine is getting old anyway, right?"

"I could do without it."

"Ava Rose will like having you around more. She enjoys your visits."

"She said that, huh?"

"Aye, she did."

Lou becomes quiet. Not the immediate acceptance that I was hoping to hear. "Come on, Lou. Say that you'll move in with me."

She hesitates before answering. "You're sure that you want me to be in your home full time?"

"Aye."

"I'll move in but only if you'll promise to tell me if I need to leave before August 31. I don't want my presence to be a problem for you."

I bring her hand to my lips and kiss the top. "I promise."

Okay. It's a done deal; Lou is moving in with me for the next two and a half months. And I'm more excited about that than she could possibly imagine.

Lou's silent during the remainder of our ride home, and I'm worried about the thoughts going through her head. I hope she isn't putting any merit into being called a whore by Cora's son.

I give her hand a squeeze where it rests on my thigh and she turns to look at me. "He's wrong. You're not a whore."

She lowers her head. "I took your money. Isn't that what a whore does?"

"We are two consenting adults who have a great time together because we're friends. We enjoy spending time together, and it has absolutely nothing to do with the money. Do you understand that?"

She nods and whispers, "Yeah." But her voice isn't very convincing.

"Come here, mo maise." I pull her into my arms and hold her tightly, saying nothing. Words aren't what she needs right now.

She is relaxed against me when we arrive at my house. That's when I realize that she has fallen asleep.

I brush her hair from her face, and she reminds me of a sleeping angel. A beautiful sleeping angel, one that I hate to wake.

I brush my fingers against her cheek. "Lou, we're home."

She stirs a wee bit but doesn't wake. I scoop her in my arms and slide across the seat when Calvin opens the door.

"What are you doing?" Her voice is barely more than a whisper.

"I'm carrying you to bed."

"It's okay. I can walk."

"I want to carry you." I want to take care of you, Lou. I want to make you feel safe.

She wraps her arms around me and rests her head against my shoulder. "I'll allow it but only because I've had a lot of champagne and I'm really tired."

"Is there a particular reason that you had a lot of champagne?"

"Because I missed you."

I lower her on to what I have come to think of as her side of the bed. "I missed you too. That's why I worked so hard and came back early."

I slip off one of her heels and then remove the second one, dropping both on the floor next to the footboard.

"Thank you."

"I'm happy to do it."

Her eyes remain closed as she says, "I don't mean carrying me to bed or taking off my shoes. I'm talking about treating me like I'm somebody instead of nobody."

My NOLA girl is showing me who she is deep down inside: a woman who is damaged, a woman who is carrying a scar that is as old as she is, a woman who longs to be loved. She's filled with heartache and it penetrates her bone deep. I know because it deeply resembles my own pain.

I brush my fingers down her cheek. "You're a special person, Lou. You should always be treated like someone special."

She reaches for my hand and holds it against her face but doesn't say anything.

I want to tell her how her heart belongs to someone she's yet to meet, and she'll be loved and adored by one bloody lucky man someday. She'll have his babies and he'll love her in a way like she's never known before.

But I can't tell her these things. I can't bring myself to say the words. And I don't know why.

19

CAITRIONA LOUDEN

I OPEN MY EYES AND I'M ALONE. WAKING IN HUTCH'S BED without him isn't surprising. The man is an early bird.

I love waking in his bed, but I wish he were here with me. The thought barely enters my mind and then it hits me. I remember what happened with Chambers last night and why I won't be waking in my bed at home for a while.

Oh my God. Chambers. What a dick.

I hope Rachel isn't upset that I'm going to be living with Hutch. But how can she be when she's been spending more nights at Claud's than at home?

I pick up my phone from the nightstand to call her and see her texts.

RACHEL: You disappeared. Are you ok?
RACHEL: Can you text me back and let me know you're all right?
RACHEL: Just met Brady. He told me you left with Hutch. Glad you're ok but I'm pissed off b/c you left without a goodbye.

Rachel's missed texts came in after I was asleep. Shit. She's going to kill me. Might as well take my ass-chewing and get it over with.

She answers on the first ring. "Well, thanks a lot for saying goodbye last night."

"I'm sorry. I didn't mean to worry you."

"It's okay. Brady assured me that all was well. He also told me that Hutch came back early from his business trip to be with you."

"He did."

Rachel sighs. "That man is falling in love with you, Cait."

Rachel loves to make something out of nothing. "Maxwell Hutcheson is possessive of what's his and my time belongs to him. He's paid through the nose for it. He doesn't want other men having a single minute of it."

"He may be possessive of your time, but he's also possessive of you in general. I'm on the outside looking in and I see it clear as glass. He's falling, you silly lass."

"Hutch is lonely. And horny. I fulfill both of those needs for him. That's not love."

"All right. I'm not going to argue with you about it. But in time you're going to see that I'm right. And then I'm going to say I told you so."

No one loves saying I told you so more than Rachel. I wish I wouldn't have to disappoint her this time.

"It's the other way around. When our arrangement ends and I never see him again, I'll be the one to say I told you so."

"And what would you say if I told you that I'm falling in love with Claud?"

Falling in love. Those are three very frightening words. "Are you, Rachel?"

"I think I am."

I'm not surprised. She glows every time she talks about the man. "Has Claud told you how he feels about you?"

"No, and I haven't asked. I'm afraid that he only sees me as a good time that he paid for."

Rachel didn't see what I saw last night at the party. Claud only had eyes for her. "Your relationship with him is more than that. He doesn't allow other men to book you. That means something and I think that you should ask him what."

"And what if it means nothing?"

"It'll be painful but at least you'll know where you stand with Claud."

"I guess a painful truth is better than a false hope," she says.

"Agreed. But I don't think you have anything to worry about."

"I don't want to think about it right now. Makes my stomach nervous. Tell me about Hutch showing up at the cocktail party."

"I was shocked. I thought he was still in Italy on business."

"You were at the party one minute and gone the next. He wasted no time in stealing you away."

I have to tell her about Chambers. Warn her. "Listen, Rach. You have to be careful around Chambers. I went to tell Cora goodbye last night, and he cornered me in her office. That bastard tried to rape me."

"The fuck? Are you all right?"

I feel nauseated just thinking about his hands on me. "The only reason I got away from him was because I remembered what I had learned at the self-defense classes."

"I was warned by one of the other inamoratas to not be alone with him. It was right after I started working for

Cora and I forgot about it. She wouldn't go into details when I asked why but I guess I know now."

I don't know our chatelaine as well as Rachel does. "Do you think that Cora would do anything about it if she knew what her son was up to?"

"I think so. Assaulting her inamoratas is bad for business and above all, Cora is a professional. She takes care of her girls."

Cora definitely cares about her inamoratas. She wouldn't want any of us to be harmed.

It may cause a problem between us, but I don't have a choice. He could be hurting other inamoratas. "I have to tell her what happened."

"I agree."

"Hutch was furious. He believes that Chambers will come after me at home, so he wants me to live at his house for the remainder of our relationship."

"Ladies and gentlemen, I present exhibit B," Rachel says.

"Oh, stop reading into something that isn't there. He's just looking out for my safety." I'm going to change the subject instead of engaging her ridiculous theory. "Call me next week and we'll go see a movie or do some shopping."

"Sounds like a plan."

I end the call and reflect upon how different our lives are today than even two months ago. Rachel and I have partied, worked, and lived together. During the last year, we've hardly been apart for more than a day, and now our time together is barely existent. I miss that nerd.

I leave the bedroom to go in search of food and find the refrigerator door open when I enter the kitchen. I tiptoe over to Hutch with the agility of a lioness and wait for him to close it so I can take him by surprise with a morning kiss. But it's me who's caught off guard when the door swings shut.

Shit, shit, shit.

I'm standing face-to-face with Sonny. And I'm wearing a T-shirt that barely covers my panties.

He smiles at me. "Good morning, Miss Lou."

"Just Lou."

He turns around, busying himself with taking the eggs to the counter and I reach for the bottom of the T-shirt, pulling it lower on my legs as if it's somehow going to magically stretch into a dress.

"May I cook you something for breakfast? Omelet? Waffle?"

How could I forget about the staff being back in the house? "A waffle would be lovely. Thank you."

"Tea or coffee?"

"Neither. I prefer juice." I hold up my index finger. "Please excuse me. I'll be back in just a moment."

I pull the shirt over my panties and streak toward the bedroom, praying that I don't encounter any of the other staff while on my way.

You are so stupid, Cait. This is your first official day of living in Hutch's house, and you're already screwing it up. He isn't going to let you stay if you can't do better than this.

I'm rummaging through the new clothes that Hutch had delivered for me when I'm startled by warm breath on the back of my neck. "You're up."

A panicked screech leaves my throat and I spin around, landing a slap across Hutch's chest. "Don't sneak up on me like that." He smiles and any irritation that I might feel disappears. "You scared the shit out of me."

A deep chuckle rumbles from his chest. "I'm sorry. Scaring you wasn't my intention."

He kisses the side of my neck and his hands creep around my waist, slipping into the back of my panties, gripping my bare butt cheeks in his hands. "I had something very different in mind besides scaring you."

I don't know if he will after I tell him what happened in the kitchen. "I just ran into Sonny in the kitchen… while I was wearing this."

"I bet he didn't mind that one bit."

Ew. Sonny is old enough to be my grandfather. "You aren't mad at me?"

"It's going to be impossible to keep our relationship a secret from the staff with your living here and sharing my bed. And as I told you before, I don't owe any explanations about my personal life to them."

"So we aren't going to make any kind of effort to hide the truth from them?"

"It's probably not the best idea for you to walk around the house in your knickers, but I see no reason to go to the trouble of trying to fool them. They're intelligent people. They'll figure it out. And they'll either keep their gobs shut about us or they'll find other employment."

His hands leave my butt, and he moves them lower, grasping the back of my thighs and lifting me up. As though my legs have a mind of their own, they instantly wrap around him.

"I haven't had you since Sunday night. It feels like a lifetime ago."

That's right. Hutch rushed home from his business trip to be with me last night. And after the Chambers incident, he put me to bed without making any kind of advance toward sex. He handled me with kindness and patience last night. Because that's the kind of man that Hutch is.

He's so damn lovable. And the woman I was three

weeks ago would throat punch the woman I am today for having that kind of thought about Maxwell Hutcheson.

He carries me from the closet to the bed, lowering me to the mattress. He stands upright and I watch as he unfastens his belt and trousers. My heart pounds against the interior of my chest, as does my clit between my legs, aching for his touch.

Hutch lowers his body and his mouth devours mine, swallowing all of my moans with his kiss.

"Fuck, you have no idea how much I missed you." His voice is so low that I question if I heard him correctly.

Hutch slides his hand beneath my T-shirt and cups the underside of my breast, rubbing his thumb back and forth over my nipple, making it harden. "I'm going to wreck you."

I'm going to wreck you. I don't have a lot of time to decipher what that means because his hands are already on my hips, pulling down my panties.

A breathy whimper slips from my mouth before I'm able to contain it, and I don't even have it in me to be embarrassed. I'm turned on and I want this. No reason to pretend that I don't. "I want your cock inside of me."

"My tongue insists on having you first."

He kisses me from mouth to groin, his lips exploring my body on its downward path to between my legs. But not before his tongue takes a brief detour, prodding my navel, and then resuming its southern route.

He stops moving when his face is between my legs and looks at me. Well, not actually sure that I can say me. It's my lady bits that he's looking at.

His eyes dart to mine and he grins before looking down again. He buries his nose in the top of my slit, taking a deep whiff. Breathing it in. Sucking my aroma into his lungs. "Tell me that your pussy is mine."

The tingles in my body are throbbing, attempting to match every beat of his heart, synchronizing us as one. "My pussy is yours. I'm yours."

"That's my good lass." He kisses my slit, flicking his tongue over the top, teasing my clit. "Spread your legs. I want to taste what belongs to me."

My legs fall apart, and Hutch stiffens his tongue, moving it up and down my slit and plunging deep into my opening. My eyes are closed but they're in danger of rolling backward in my sockets when his tongue rubs that spot, the glorious one inside the roof of my vagina.

Hutch's finger brushes through the leaking body fluids below my opening and spreads it between my butt cheeks, wetting the area. Rubbing and lubricating me back there.

Revolted. Appalled. Outraged. I am none of these things. And although I've never allowed anyone in through the back door, I would let Hutch come in if he knocked.

He teases my tight, puckered ring with the tip of his finger while he eats me out, and the two set off the first of many rhythmic uterine contractions deep inside my pelvis. "Hutch… I'm… coming."

My breathing slows but my thighs continue quivering while I ride out the aftermath of the climax that just shook me to my core. I relish the warm sensation glossing over my entire body as it washes through me.

Hutch reaches into the nightstand drawer, and then I hear the familiar sounds of a ripping foil packet and the stretching of lubricated latex over his cock. He grabs my ankles and pulls me to the edge of the bed where he's standing. "Put your legs around me, mo maise."

I position my legs around his waist, and he slides inside of me in one fluid motion. "Fuck, Lou. How are you always so tight?"

He grasps my waist tightly and holds me in place,

pounding into me without a bit of mercy. And still I want more. In one quick motion, I move my legs from his waist to his shoulders and within a minute, it does him in. He thrusts deeply one last time and groans a few profanities, followed by my name.

My ankles are hooked over his shoulders and he's smiling down at me. "That was so damn good."

"Yes, it was."

Hutch kisses the inside of my inner thigh and allows my legs to fall onto the bed. He reaches for my hands and pulls, helping me to stand.

Grabbing my panties from the floor, he holds them out for me and kisses the inside of my thigh as I step into them. My hands grip his shoulders for balance as he pulls them up my legs. "Men usually take panties off. Not put them back on."

"I do both." He pats my butt when my panties are in place. "Get dressed and go enjoy the breakfast that Sonny is cooking for you. In that order this time, please."

"You won't eat with me?"

"And I've already eaten. Twice, as a matter of fact." He grins and winks.

"Such a clever lad you are."

"As much as I hate it, I have to go to work." He puts his arms around me and kisses my forehead. "See you this evening."

Forehead kisses. Those are the things that romantic relationships are made of. There's no place for them in sex-for-money relationships.

This is going to end badly for me.

20

MAXWELL HUTCHESON

Lou doesn't know that it's my birthday or that my only birthday wish is to stay home with her. But I can't; I have to go to my parents' house for my annual birthday dinner with the family.

Dammit. It's my birthday. Shouldn't I get to do what I want to do?

Lou's only been in my life for a month, but it feels like much longer. Our situation has expedited the process of getting to know each other. I can't remember ever feeling so well acquainted with a woman this early in a relationship.

I'm surprised by the way that I feel as I drive away, leaving her behind at the house. I want to go back for her. I even consider saying to hell with all of it and turning my car around. I'm not sure what the hell I'd do once I did, and it's a reminder of why that isn't a possibility.

I walk through the front door of my parents' house and Mum comes into the foyer, kissing the side of my face. "Happy birthday, my boy."

"Thanks, Mum."

Her eyes lower and lock on Ava Rose. "Oh, there's my sweet granddaughter."

Lying by omission to my parents about Ava Rose's paternity makes me feel like shite. They truly believe that I had finally changed my mind about wanting a child. They believe that Ava Rose is my biological daughter. Their granddaughter.

I've considered being honest with them. Of course, their hearts would initially be broken, but I know that they'd continue to love Ava Rose. They'd make no difference between her and their other grandchildren. That's the kind of people that they are.

So how did I end up like this? What happened to make me so damn opposed to parenthood? I can't put my finger on it.

Mum takes the car seat from my hand and carries Ava Rose into the living room where the rest of the family is. "Look who's here."

Everyone leaves their seat, and the whole family gathers around Ava Rose, studying her, talking to her, playing with her. They are all so in love with that wee baby lass. I wish that I could feel what they feel. If I could will it and make it so, I would in a heartbeat.

I feel broken. Like my instinct telling me to not have children was there for a reason.

"Oh, Max. I can't believe how much she's grown since we saw her."

"She has a healthy appetite." At least that's what the nannies tell me.

Mum rubs her hand over the top of Ava Rose's head. "She has new hair coming in. Looks even brighter to me."

"You think?"

"She's definitely going to have Mina's red hair and brown eyes."

"Then she'll be a lucky girl." Mina was a beauty. There's no arguing that.

"True, but I had hoped that Ava Rose would have your blue eyes."

Impossible for that to happen when she doesn't have any of my DNA. "Maybe she'll inherit something else from me."

"Let's all hope that she doesn't inherit your smart-ass mouth," Ian says.

"*My* smart-ass mouth?"

I punch my brother in the upper arm. And maybe I give him a nice whack with my knuckles so he'll really feel it.

"Ow. Fuck, Max"

"Puss."

"Boys," Mum says. Her tone. Her narrowed eyes. The combination has always had the power to make Ian and me settle down.

My sister Sara nods in the direction of her sons. "Leo is a sponge waiting to absorb new and interesting words so he can regurgitate them. Mind your language please."

Nothing would please me more than to teach Leo—and later Mason too—some naughty words to repeat. If she's wise, my sister won't allow me to be alone with those wee rascals.

Dinner is delicious as always, and catching up with my family is nice. I enjoy seeing them dote on Ava Rose even if I'm unable to do the same.

"Family picture while we're all together," Mum says.

"Max, you have that new fancy mobile. You take the picture and then text it to all of us."

There are nine of us here tonight. "Exactly how will that work? My arm isn't long enough to fit everyone into the frame in selfie mode."

"We can prop it up on something and use the timer," Sara says.

I'm not a photographer. "I don't know how to set up the timer."

"I can do it," Ian says. Figures. His generation knows everything about mobiles.

"Max, hold Ava Rose. Sara, hold Mason. Leo, stand in front of your mum and dad. And everyone be still and smile for Nana's family photo."

One photo. Two. Ten. We finally give up and decide to settle for whatever we happen to have already gotten when Ava Rose and Mason both start crying.

Ian thumbs through the family photos on my phone. "Damn, I don't think it's possible for Leo to ever be still. He looks like a blur in all of these."

"The laddie is on the move all of the time."

"Damn, Max. What have you been up to lately?" Ian asks.

"Not much. Just busy at work." I feel like his question is implying something else, but I don't know what. Until it clicks.

Fuck. Ian is looking at the pictures of Lou on my mobile.

I dash across the room and reach for it. "Give me my fucking mobile. Now."

"Not so fast." He holds me at arm's length with a hand on my chest and continues thumbing through the pictures as I shove him out of the living room into the adjoining hallway.

"Give it to me, Ian."

"It's a good thing I didn't call Mum over to pick which one of the family photos she wants you to send."

"Give me my mobile. Now!" I hiss through gritted teeth.

"She looks familiar."

Shite. He's probably seen Lou at uni. "She's no one."

"She doesn't look like no one to me."

He twists the mobile to examine a picture from a different angle. "Damn, Max. Just damn."

Fuck. Fuck. Fuck.

This is bad.

I yank my mobile out of his hand, and he has this look in his eyes. I think it's respect? Admiration? Maybe envy? "You have a girlfriend. A hot-as-fuck girlfriend."

"Shut up. You can't say anything to anyone. And she's not my girlfriend."

Ian chuckles. "You are such a fucking liar."

"She's not my girlfriend. We're just having a wee bit of fun together."

"Those pictures look like you're having a lot of fun."

I don't want to have this conversation with my brother. He's still a kid on so many levels.

"A guy does what a guy has to do. I get it. This is a judgment-free zone. But I feel like I know her from somewhere."

He's going to figure it out. I might as well tell him the truth. Or part of it. "She's a student at uni."

"Fuck, Max. You're dating a college girl?"

Oh hell. I didn't even think about the age difference.

"She took some time off from school so she's not that young." Not a complete lie. Lou did take off a year. "And again, we're not dating."

I don't want to talk about Lou this way with him. She's my secret—one I don't want to share—and he's showing way too much interest in her.

"Are you serious about this lass?"

"No way."

Ian laughs. "I think that you don't like it worth a damn that I saw nudie pics of the girl you're shagging."

That part I can't deny. It makes me sick that he saw parts of Lou that were supposed to be for my eyes only. "She's not naked in these pictures." Well, she is, but she's mostly covered by the sheet.

"I have eyes and they work, you dobber."

Sara comes into the hallway and sees the scowls passing between us. "What are you two fighting about now?"

I glare at Ian, a warning to keep his mouth shut about Lou. "We aren't fighting."

Sara comes over and stands beside me. "Let me have a look at the pictures."

"No need. I'll just send all of them to you."

"No, Max. The pictures are really good. Let Sara see them."

I give Ian a look that says I'm going to beat the fuck out of you later. "Sure."

I hold my mobile, controlling Sara's preview of our family photos, beginning at the end. Fuck, I can't go too far back. How many did we take?

"Mum, you need to come see the pictures," Ian calls out.

Fucker. I'm going to beat his arse into the ground.

"Hold on a second. I need my glasses."

Fuck me.

Mum comes to me and takes the mobile from my hand, wearing her reading glasses. Grand. She'll be able to clearly see Lou's barely covered tits when she flips beyond our family pictures.

"Here, Mum. Let me help you."

She slaps at my hand. "I know how to work a mobile, Max. I'm not that damn old."

She holds my mobile at a distance, studying the first photo. "Ugh, my eyes are closed in that one."

She thumbs through the second, third, fourth, and fifth pictures. And my stomach is in a huge knot. I'm about to be fucked. I feel it coming.

She has to be looking at the last family photo. "I think that's it. I'll send them all to you."

Here it comes. One more flick of her thumb and it's over. She's going to see the proof of what I've been doing.

Her smile fades, as does the color from her face. And I know that she's looking at it—the picture of Lou and me in bed together. The one where I'm kissing the side of her face.

She passes my mobile to me and smiles. "Your screen is too small. Email them to me so I can have a better look on my laptop."

I look down at my mobile and confirm it. It's Lou and me in bed. Fuck.

The image isn't graphic so thank God for that. Her eyes are looking right at the camera and her hand is cupped around my jaw while I'm kissing the side of her face. It's actually a very romantic-looking picture. We look like two people in love. There's nothing shameful about it except for the fact that my wife has only been dead for three months. And that alone makes me feel ashamed.

My mum must think that I'm a pure bastard. And that kills me.

I wait until I find Mum alone in the kitchen. Of course, everyone goes missing when it's time to clean. That's always the case.

"Need help, Mum?"

"No, darling. It's your birthday. You shouldn't have to clean up."

I ignore her decline for help and stand beside her, holding a dry towel. "You wash. I'll dry."

"All right."

She passes one, two, three plates to me, and I dry each. It takes that long for me to grow the bollocks to bring up what she just saw. "I know that you saw the picture."

I don't have to say which one. We both know which picture that I'm referring to.

She hesitates a moment before replying. "I saw it."

"I need to know what you're thinking."

Mum doesn't answer immediately. "She's a bonnie lass. No doubt about it."

"You're also thinking she's a bonnie lass who is not my wife?"

Mum breathes in deeply and exhales slowly. "Mina is gone. No one expects you to be a grieving widower forever."

"Mina's family doesn't feel that way."

"They can't expect you to not move forward with your life."

Has she met the Lochridges? "Trust me. They can and they do."

"They can think whatever they like but that doesn't make it so, Max."

"And what is your opinion? Do you think it's too soon for me to have another woman in my life?"

"I think that only you can know when it's time to move on. If you feel ready, then it's time."

I wasn't expecting to hear this out of my mum.

Have I made this situation into something it's not? I'm not sure.

21

CAITRIONA LOUDEN

I'm alone in Hutch's house. But I'm not scared. I'm bored. And lonely. I want Hutch to be here with me. And Ava Rose. I've gotten used to my playtime with her. I miss her too.

I call Rachel but don't get an answer. Only voicemail. "Hey, Rachel. I guess you're out with Claud, but I'm alone tonight. Hutch has gone to his parents' house, and I thought you might want to come over and watch a movie or something. Call me if you get this message in time. If I don't hear from you tonight, I'll still see you tomorrow."

I turn on the television but can't find anything to watch. I decide that Hutch and Ava Rose's absence might be the perfect time for me to take advantage of the huge tub. A bubble bath and soothing music. That's what I need.

When the bathroom is nice and steamy, I twist my hair into a topknot and slip into the hot tub of bubbles and water. The fragrance is delicious—vanilla and black cherry. One of my favorites.

I close my eyes and relax against the back of the tub,

listening to "Someone Like You" by Southern Ophelia. I love that song so much. Damn. Charlie William's voice has that perfect country rasp. My kind of music.

I'm singing the slow-tempo lyrics when I see motion in the mirror through my peripheral vision. I turn around to see if my eyes are playing tricks on me, which is a real possibility considering how easily I get spooked, but there's nothing wrong with my eyes or my mind.

Holy shit. I jolt when I see the woman standing in the doorway of the bathroom staring at me, my heart galloping like a racehorse out of the gates. How long has she been standing there watching me? For some reason, I suspect a while.

I gather bubbles in my hands, covering my body. "Who are you?"

"Who am I?" She laughs. "I think the question is who are you?"

"I'm Lou."

"Where is Max?"

"He's gone to visit his family in Glasgow."

"Looks as though you've made yourself quite at home while your employer is away."

She assumes that I'm part of the staff. That's good. Very good. "It was hard to resist this tub while Mr. Hutcheson is away."

"I don't think that my brother-in-law would approve of you taking such a liberty."

Shit, shit, shit. This woman is one of Mina's sisters. "I'm certain that you're right. I've overstepped my boundaries."

"You don't have luxuries like these where you come from." I can't tell if that's a statement or a question.

"No, ma'am."

"You're American?"

"I am." I see no reason to discuss my circumstances with her.

"What do you do for Mr. Hutcheson?"

I fuck him. "I help with the housekeeping."

She laughs, but it's easy to see that she isn't amused. Her eye-roll tells me that she's irritated by the thought. "You're much too pretty to be a housekeeper."

Being told that you're pretty is typically a compliment, but it doesn't sound like one coming from her.

"You never told me who you are."

She's tall and slender, wearing an elegant taupe dress with matching heels. Her natural red hair is cut in a medium-length bob with bangs that are too blunt, reminding me of the blunt manner in which she walked into this house uninvited and began interrogating me.

"Blair. I'm Mina's sister. In case you didn't know, Mina is Max's late wife."

"Yes, he told me about her. I'm sorry for your loss."

"I'm sure that you are." Her voice is low, low enough that I'm not sure if she intended on my hearing her catty remark. The only thing I know for sure is that my gut is telling me there's something more to Blair's unannounced visit.

Is she checking up on Max? Trying to catch him with a woman? From what Hutch has said, that's a stunt Mina's sister would try to pull.

"I'll tell Mr. Hutcheson you came by." Bye-bye.

"I left a birthday gift for Max in the living room. Make sure he gets it."

"Birthday?" I whisper.

"Yes, today is his birthday."

"Oh. I didn't know."

"I wouldn't expect you to know. There's no reason for the hired help to be told anything about his personal life."

Wow. She really enjoys putting me in my place.

It's Hutch's birthday and he didn't say a word. And why should he? I'm only his paid fuck buddy. Nothing but an employee, just like all of the other staff members. She's right. There's no reason for him to tell me things about his personal life.

If there was ever any question about where he and I stand, it's now clear.

22

MAXWELL HUTCHESON

Lou. I'm missing her. I'm missing her far more than I ever thought possible.

I wanted to leave my parents' house after dinner and go home to her, but I couldn't. My family was enjoying their time with Ava Rose too much. They don't get to see her as often as they'd like, and it would have been cruel to take that time away from them.

A compromise struck me: leave Ava Rose with my parents and go back to Lou. The house staff is gone for the weekend because I'm away. It would be just the two of us in the house again. Another weekend alone. Exactly what I want for my birthday.

I enter the house and go to my bedroom, turning on the bedside lamp. I smile when I see Lou sleeping on my side of the bed… and wearing one of my T-shirts. Isn't that a sign that she's missing me too?

It's one in the morning and I only want to get naked and climb into bed with her, but I don't. She's easily spooked, and I don't want to frighten her. Instead, I sit on the bed next to her and brush her soft cheek with the back of my fingers. "Lou."

She stirs a wee bit but doesn't wake. Such a deep sleeper. "Lou, baby."

Baby? Where did that come from?

She opens her eyes and smiles when she sees me. "You came back." She looks over at the clock. "At one in the morning?"

"I wanted to be with you." I cup the side of her face. "It's sort of a habit I've developed."

She places her hand on top of mine and turns her face, kissing my palm. "I sort of have the same habit."

A wrinkle forms over her brow. "You had a visitor this evening. Your sister-in-law Blair."

Oh fuck. It's never good when one of Mina's sisters drops by. "How did that go?"

"How do you think it went?"

"Not fab."

"I was taking a bubble bath in the tub… your tub… in your bathroom… in your bedroom."

"Shite," I mutter under my breath.

"I'm sorry."

"Don't be sorry. You did nothing wrong." Blair is the one who's wrong for showing up like that.

"I didn't know she was in the house. The doors were locked. I'm sure of it. I checked twice before I got into the tub."

How did Blair get into the house? Would Mina have given her a key?

"It startled me when I looked up and saw her standing there, staring at me. What's even creepier is that I feel like she had been watching me for a while before I noticed her."

"What did she say?"

"She asked who I was. I told her that I was a housekeeper, and I played it off like I was overstepping my boundaries while my employer was away. She didn't stick around for long after that."

It's just like Blair to come around and stick her nose in my business. She always has. I don't know why she can't be content with managing her own husband and marriage.

"You did as much damage control as you could, considering the situation. There's nothing to be done about it at this point."

"Are you angry?"

"Not at you." But with Blair? Aye. I'm furious with her.

I remove my jeans and T-shirt and crawl into bed with Lou, wrapping my arms around her from behind. There are times when I need to fuck her, but now isn't one of them. I'm content to hold her in my arms.

"She left a birthday gift for you. It's in the living room."

The secret is out. "I'll open it tomorrow."

Lou is quiet and so am I. All I can hear is the thump of my heartbeat.

"Our birthdays are only a week apart."

"Yours is next Friday?"

She makes a sound, but I'm not sure it can be considered a confirmation.

Thump. Thump. Thump. More heartbeats, but now they're a wee bit faster.

"Why didn't you tell me that it was your birthday?"

Is that sadness that I hear in her voice?

"Because leaving you behind while I went to celebrate my birthday somewhere else made me feel like a dobber."

"You went to celebrate with your family. I would have understood."

She would have understood. I know that. "I should have told you. I'm sorry."

"I would have liked to have gotten you a gift."

I'm in a place in my life where I don't need material gifts. "You give me your time. That's all I need."

She turns over and we're lying face-to-face. "I disagree. You are deserving of so much more." Her words ooze with seduction and blood rushes to my cock.

Who am I kidding? I didn't drive all the way from Glasgow to hold her.

I lower my hand, cupping it over her knicker-covered pussy. "Am I deserving of this? Because it's what the birthday boy really wants."

"Perhaps but I have something else to go with it."

Together, we push her knickers down her legs, and she kicks them away beneath the covers. Same order with my Y-fronts and then the T-shirt that she's wearing.

Hot skin on skin. There's nothing like it.

My palm presses against her mound, my fingers grazing her entrance while my free hand wraps around her bent thigh and pulls her against my hard cock. She quivers against me as the tips of my fingers drag along her slick slit.

"Already soaking wet," I whisper against her mouth.

"For you, always."

My index and middle finger slide through her slick, feminine juices until they're deep inside of her. Curling them around to hit her G-spot, I stroke her and it's so fucking satisfying when she moans my name.

Her hips thrust against my hand, slow at first and then faster, until she implodes on the inside.

Her breathing slows and she opens her eyes. "It's not my birthday. This is supposed to be about you and the gift I want to give you."

"Getting you off makes me happy."

"It makes me happy too. But now it's your turn."

Lou moves on top of me, her knees pressed together between my thighs, and crawls down my body.

Fuck. She's going to suck me off.

I melt into the bed when her lips wrap around my thick cock, the back of her teeth lightly scraping down my length. I try but I can't stop the few drops of pre-cum that spill into her mouth.

Ooh, happy fucking birthday to me.

I haven't had a blowjob in a very long time. I don't even know how long it's been. Mina never sucked my dick; she thought that it was beneath her.

Lou has tried to go down on me a few times, but the timing has always been off. I was already close to coming, and I was afraid the feel of her mouth would send me over the edge. And it probably would have. Just like it's threatening to do now.

"Mmm," she moans, her mouth stuffed with my erection, sounding as though she's enjoying this blowjob as much as I am. And that in itself is a huge turn-on.

Her mouth bobs up and down my cock, and the beginning of the end starts. But I'm not ready to let it happen. "Slow down, Lou. I don't want to come yet." I want to make this last for as long as possible.

I grasp the back of her head, and she whimpers when I guide her off of my dick. Grinning at me with her mouth red and shiny with saliva, her body quivers. The air between us is permeated with the smell of sex, the scent thick and heady. And I can't resist pulling her mouth to mine for a dirty kiss.

She's still on her knees between my thighs, her legs pressed together, and I reach around to play with her from behind.

I slide my fingers into her pussy and find that it's dripping wet. I steal some of the wetness dripping along her slit and she tenses and gasps when I rub it over her puckered hole.

Her eyes flutter when I slowly slip a single finger into her tight ring. She tenses around it, proving to me just how good my cock would feel buried deep in her tight bum.

I've never tried anal sex. But I want to. I want to with Lou.

She moans, rocking her bum up and down my finger. "You can do it if that's what you want. I'll let you."

"If it's what I want?" I chuckle. "Baby, you don't know how many times I've fantasized about anal with you."

"I'll need you to be slow and easy. I've never done it before."

"No worries, mo maise. I'll be gentle with you."

She moves away and gets on her hands and knees. I grab a condom from the nightstand and my hands shake as I roll it on. Fuck, I feel like a lad about to have his first shag.

Kneeling behind her, I glide the top of my condom-clad cock through her slick juices to be safe. I don't want this to be ruined because I haven't done everything to make it pleasurable for her.

I lean over and press my front to her back. She looks back at me over her shoulder and I kiss the corner of her mouth.

"This is my first time too. Our first times will be together," I whisper.

I push my cock between her cheeks and her already-quivering body shakes violently. "Don't be afraid. If you don't like it, I'll stop."

"I know."

Despite the urge to thrust into her deep and hard, I rock into her slowly, a wee bit at a time. A game of advance and retreat.

"Are you all right?"

"Yes."

"Do you want me to stop?"

"No. Keep going."

A mixture of relief and pleasure floods me, and I think I'll die of ecstasy when I'm inside her all the way to the hilt. "Fuck, Lou. You feel so damn good."

I hold that position for a moment before pulling back slowly and advancing again. "You're okay?"

"Yes." She rocks with me on her hands and knees. "Fuck me, Hutch."

The fuck? "Are you sure?"

"Yes. I want it."

Still afraid of hurting her, I gradually pick up speed until I'm pounding my cock inside of her. And I swear to God that the woman is meeting me thrust for thrust. Maybe even harder.

No shame. No mercy.

We're fucking each other like two savages, neither of us more of a beast than the other.

I grip the back of her hair and pull her head back until my mouth covers her ear. "You are mine."

I'm not asking. There's no edge of romance to my voice. I'm honest-to-fuck demanding her to be mine.

Lou is mine.

MINE.

M. I. N. E.

"I am yours, Maxwell Hutcheson."

Her words are affirmative, her body submissive. She's mine to do with as I please—I know by the way her body is yielding to mine. I could hurt her if I wanted to and she'd let me. But I don't want to hurt her. I never want to hurt Lou.

My hand slips around her waist and my fingers find her engorged clit, rubbing it in a circular motion.

"Make me come. I want to know what it feels like this way."

Anything. That's what I'd give to her in this moment.

"There?"

A few loud pants leave her mouth. "Yes, that's it."

A few moments later her body shudders, as does mine. We fall off the edge together, free-falling through oblivion. With my arm wrapped around her torso, just below her breasts, I pull her against my chest so that we're kneeling together on the bed, my cock still buried deep inside of her.

And that's the way we orgasm.

When we spiral down from the high, we fall to the bed. Both of us covered in a thin sheen of sweat. Both of us exhausted. Both of us thoroughly fucked.

But me even more so.

Because I can't fall in love with this woman.

Lou isn't going to be here beyond the end of the summer. Some fucker who isn't playing the part of a grieving widower/single dad is going to come along and sweep her off of her feet. Or at the very least pay her to be his companion. And I won't be able to say shite about it.

I may be fucking her, but I'm the one who is getting fucked. And I'm doing it to myself.

23

CAITRIONA LOUDEN

THE BLAIR WITCH PROJECT. THAT'S WHAT I'M CALLING IT. And I'm glad it happened. Hutch was forced to tell me about his birthday and well… I was able to give him a gift that neither of us will forget anytime soon.

It's seven o'clock and Hutch is still in bed with me. That's not like him at all, but it was late when he came home. And even later when we finally did go to sleep.

Hutch reaches out and flattens his hand over my bare stomach. "How do you feel this morning?"

I inhale deeply and stretch the muscles in my body from head to toe. "I feel…" I can't help but laugh. "Thoroughly filled, spread, and stretched."

"Last night's activity is deserving of all those descriptors?"

"Definitely." And many more.

"Not sore?"

"No." And I'm surprised by that. I expected to be. "I feel quite well."

"I'm glad. I wouldn't want you to have discomfort on our day out. I want to take you riding."

"On the horses?"

Hutch's naughty grin appears. "Aye, unless you have something else you'd like to ride."

"No one told me that you were so funny. Oh, wait. You're not."

"I can be funny."

"You can be mildly humorous at times." Hutch may have been funny at one time, but I think it's been a long time since he's felt like joking and laughing. I'm happy I bring out that side of him.

"I already know you're going to love riding Prissy."

Ah, shit. My plans for today pop into my head. "I thought you were going to be gone until Sunday evening. Rachel and I are supposed to go shopping today."

"That's fine. I have to go out of town again next week, and I have some things I need to take care of before I leave. We can ride another day."

I poke out my bottom lip. "You're going out of town again so soon? You just got back."

"I know. I don't want to leave you again but it's a big client. I have to go."

"Where to this time?"

"Alicante."

"Are you kidding me? Italy last week. Spain this week. I'd hate to have your job."

"It's not as fun as it sounds. I actually have to work while I'm there. And I don't enjoy free time because I'm alone."

I've never been anywhere. New Orleans and Edinburgh. That's about the extent of it. "I wouldn't care if I was there alone. I'd go out and do everything I could."

"How about you go to Alicante with me?"

"Really?"

"Aye. Why not?"

I want to. I want to sooo badly. "Could we pull it off without anyone knowing?"

"I'm the only person from the firm going on this trip. I don't know how anyone would find out anything."

"You're really willing to take that kind of gamble?"

"For the chance to take you to a place where we can be free to do as we like? Aye. I would take the risk, no hesitation."

He believes it will be fine so why should I question it? "I'd love to go."

Ah, man. I'm going to Alicante, Spain. I don't know anything about the place, but I'm not telling him that. I'll do a search on it later.

Hutch reaches over and grabs his wallet from the nightstand. "You'll need some new things for the trip."

I look at the credit card he's offering me. "I can't let you pay."

"Why would I not pay?" he says.

"You've already given me so much."

"Have you forgotten that I'm supposed to have the full girlfriend experience?" He leans down and kisses my mouth. "And part of the full experience means that I get to buy nice things for my girlfriend."

I could almost forget for two, maybe three, seconds that all of this is pretend. And during those two to three seconds, I'm so damn happy.

"I'll let you pay if you agree to do the real relationship thing while we're in Alicante. Neither of us mentions our arrangement or our agreement or references the girlfriend experience in any way. Let's just do life together the way a real couple would."

Hutch can never really be mine, and I just want to know what having a man like him to love me feels like.

Even if it's only for a couple of days and even if it's not real.

"The real thing, huh? I'm game if you are."

"It'll be fun."

"This is a business trip for me, but we'll have plenty of time to play too. While you're out shopping today, buy a few dresses and swimsuits. I'd like to request skimpy bikinis. And also buy some new lingerie. You know the kind that I love to see you wear."

I reach out and grab the back of his neck, pulling him in for a kiss. "No one has ever been so good to me."

He cups his hand around my face. "You deserve good things in your life, Lou."

Maxwell Hutcheson came into my life at a moment when I felt like an insignificant waste of everything that makes up a person. I thought that I might shrivel up and disappear. I wanted to shrivel up and disappear. And just when I thought that I might, he saw me.

Dammit.

This man is finding his way into my heart. And I'm allowing it because he's the first one ever strong enough to penetrate the protective wall around it.

I CALL RACHEL WHEN I'M ALMOST AT OUR FLAT. "HEY, I'M three blocks away. Are you ready?"

"I need five or ten more minutes."

Of course, she does. She's never ready on time. Won't I ever learn to tell her to be ready thirty minutes earlier?

"I'll wait in the car."

"No way. Come up."

Ugh. Asking me to come up means that she actually

needs more than fifteen minutes. "All right. Buzz me in. I don't have my key."

Calvin stops in front of our building. "She isn't ready so I'm going up."

I reach for the door handle, but it doesn't work. It's just like Calvin to force me into allowing him to open my door. "Thank you."

"You're welcome, Miss Lou."

"Just Lou."

"Mr. Hutcheson wouldn't like that."

I wink at Calvin. "Then Mr. Hutcheson doesn't have to know. It'll be our little secret."

Calvin grins. "All right, Lou."

"I could say that I won't be long but that's probably a lie." Rachel probably still has a wet head.

"There's no hurry."

I walk into our flat and see that Rachel's housekeeping skills haven't improved while I've been gone. Cereal bowl on the coffee table. Coffee cup on the end table. Shoes on the floor where she kicked out of them. "Rachel… come on. Really?"

"Sorry. I haven't had you here to do the cleaning."

The dynamics of our friendship are odd. Rachel has a wonderful mom. She grew up being parented by a woman who took excellent care of her. I didn't have that. My role model sucked, yet I'm the one who takes care of Rachel.

"You're grounded until this mess is cleaned up."

"Haha, very funny."

"The driver is waiting. Do try to not be too long."

"Yes, Mummy."

Rachel and I haven't seen each other since the night of the cocktail party. We have a lot of catching up to do and we decide that it's best to do it over burgers and beer.

Rachel bites into her burger and a mayonnaise-mustard combination squeezes out of the bun, landing on her shirt. "Well, I'll be damned."

"I don't know why you didn't see that coming." The food at this pub is messy. Delicious, but messy.

She uses her napkin to wipe away the condiment from her shirt. "So... how's the long-term companion thing?"

"Things are really good with Hutch." Better than they should be. I don't think I'm supposed to be this happy about being someone's whore.

Being a whore is one thing. Being his whore is something entirely different.

"What about living together? How's that going so far?"

"I like living with him. But we sort of got busted by his sister-in-law."

"Busted how?"

"His late wife's sister came to the house while Hutch was away. She let herself into the house and came to his bedroom. I was in the tub taking a bubble bath."

"Oh shite. How did you explain that?"

"I pretended to be taking advantage of the boss being away."

"So the sister-in-law just walked into Hutch's bedroom? She didn't call out for him?"

I've been so flustered over the whole thing that I haven't considered that. "Fuck, you're right."

"Don't you find that odd?" Rachel says.

"I do and now that I think about it, she showed up looking like she'd spent hours getting ready." Her hair, her makeup, her outfit—all of it was pristine. And sexy.

"She could be one of those women who always looks well put together."

"She comes from money so that's a possibility. Or she

could have gotten all fixed up for her dead sister's widower."

"Is she married?"

"I have no idea." But I plan on finding out.

"You live in his house. You're the woman in his bed every night. He went to a lot of trouble to have you. He wants you. Not her."

Rachel is right. He wants me. He tells me often and I believe him.

"Our relationship is supposed to be uncomplicated, an arrangement with clear expectations, but nothing about it feels clear anymore. The lines are blurring."

"Because you're falling in love with him. I think I've told you this already."

"I don't want to, but he's so good to me. He's making it very hard to not fall in love with him."

I can't believe I just admitted to that.

Rachel's mouth is a straight line. She's trying so hard to hold in that "I told you so."

"He's taking me to Spain next week."

She kicks her legs beneath the table, nails me in the shin. Damn, that hurt.

"Shut the hell up," she says.

I reach into my purse and hold up the credit card he gave me. "We're staying at a luxurious beachfront house, and he wants me to buy new clothes and bikinis for the trip."

"He wasn't lying when he said he would show you the time of your life," Rachel says.

"I felt guilty when he gave me his credit card. He's already given me so much money."

"He's delivering on his promise. And you have two more months with him. Live it up. Let him spoil you and don't feel guilty about it for a second."

Rachel's right. Hutch and I discussed what he wanted out of this relationship. He told me that he wanted to pamper me and make us feel genuine. This is him following through with his part of the bargain. If he wants us to feel real, I can give him real.

24

MAXWELL HUTCHESON

FUCK MY LIFE. MINA'S FATHER IS RUINING EVERYTHING I wanted to do for Lou's birthday.

I can't believe that Thomas decided to send one of the new guys to Alicante with me next week. I've always made that trip alone. It's as though he can sense that I was making special plans for the new woman in my life.

Lou is turning twenty-three this Friday. Or at least I think that's when, based upon her statement that our birthdays are a week apart.

She hasn't mentioned hers again. I believe she would tell me the date if I asked her, but I prefer to surprise her with a special gift. And I think she's going to love what I've gotten her.

I tip the bellhop, and Lou and I tour our honeymoon suite at Glenskirlie. Aye, I booked the honeymoon suite in hopes that it might somehow make up for missing Alicante.

Lou walks over and runs her fingers down the sheer fabric draped over the canopy. "I can't think of a word to describe this room. Romantic isn't enough to do it justice."

She sits on the bed and bounces a wee bit. "It's pretty and comfy."

"Then we should be able to fall asleep as soon as our heads hit the pillows."

She grins and shakes her head side to side. "I certainly hope not. This bed was made for things other than sleeping."

"I'm open to any suggestions you may have."

"That's a discussion to be had tonight."

"As keen as I am to have that discussion, it will have to wait until much later tonight. We have plans. Big ones."

God, I love when she smiles like that. Genuine happiness. It can't be faked. "What kind of big plans?"

"I'm taking you to a concert."

"What kind of concert?"

I've considered keeping it a secret and letting her figure it out when we get there, but I can't hold it in any longer. "Southern Ophelia is playing at the Hydro tonight."

Her eyes widen. "Southern Ophelia? You mean with lead singer Charlie Williams? The *country* music band from the US is here? In Glasgow? Tonight? And we're going?"

"Yes to all of those questions."

Lou squeals and jumps in place. "Oh my God. Do you know how much I love Southern Ophelia?"

"I sort of gathered it by how much you listen to their music."

"Charlie Williams is the hottest guy in country music. I would drink his bathwater."

"I get the picture, Lou. You like Charlie Williams."

"I don't like Charlie Williams. I looooove Charlie Williams. And I don't know how to thank you enough."

"No worries, mo maise. I have some ideas about how you can thank me later tonight."

She presses a sweet kiss to my mouth and rests her forehead against mine. "Is that so?"

"Aye. I have very naughty ideas."

"You always do. And I'm happy to oblige."

The tickets cost a small fortune but our seats are bloody good. Center stage, second row. Lou is ecstatic about her nearness to the stage. I'm not sure I am since I didn't consider how mesmerized she was going to be by the close proximity to her country music star crush.

Fuck, I think I may be a little jealous of the way she's looking at him.

Lou sings along, never missing a word. It's easy to see that she knows every lyric by heart.

Grabbing my hands, she places them on her hips. She takes a step back and her whole body rubs against mine while she sways to the rhythm of the music. Damn. My NOLA girl is entranced by the music, and I'm not sure that she realizes exactly what she's doing to me.

It's dark and all eyes are on the stage. No one is paying attention to us. I see no reason to not have a wee bit of fun with this, so I slide my hand from her hip to between her legs. She leans her head against my chest and looks up at me over her shoulder. "You just can't keep your hands off of it, can you?"

"How am I supposed to keep my hands off of it when your arse is rubbing against my cock?"

"I'm sorry. I shouldn't do that to you in public. Will you punish me later?"

Is that an invitation for kink? "Do you want me to punish you?"

"Maybe."

Lou places her arms on top of mine, tightening my grip around her, and sings, "I'm waiting for your heart to wake… so you will ask me to stay… my heart is impatiently waiting around… to hear the words it's begging you to say… but if I remain and the words never come… it's a pain I don't think I can take."

Fuck. Those lyrics are poignant.

Lou turns when the song ends, wrapping her arms around my neck. "I love that song. The lead female singer who once sang with Southern Ophelia wrote and performed it when she was them. She left the band and married the man she wrote the song about, so I guess his heart must have awakened."

"I remember the female lead who used to sing with them. She's hot as fuck."

Lou's palm comes down hard against my chest. "Shut up."

"What the hell was that for?"

"Don't talk to me like that about other women. I don't like it."

"Jealous?"

"Maybe."

"Well maybe I don't like the way you're swooning over the lead singer up there." Damn, I sound like a talking pussy.

Lou tightens her hold on me. "Any swooning that I do is completely for you. Got it?"

"Got it."

Lou stops at the entrance to the bar inside of our hotel. "I'm in the mood for a beer. What do you say about having a drink before we go up to the room?"

"Trying to postpone your punishment?"

Her face becomes a mask of confusion. "Punishment?"

She's forgotten so soon? "Aye. For rubbing your bum

against my cock at the concert."

She laughs. "Oh yeah. Forgot about that."

"I haven't forgotten."

"If I have a punishment coming to me then I should definitely have a drink. Maybe two."

The bartender places two beers in front of us, and we reach for the mugs at the same time, both of us taking a long drink.

"Mmm… that tastes good. And the cold feels good on my raw throat."

"You were quite the singer tonight."

"I had so much fun. Thank you for bringing me to Glasgow and surprising me with tickets to Southern Ophelia. It was amazing."

We only get tonight and part of tomorrow in Glasgow, and then we're back to Edinburgh. "It doesn't make up for missing Alicante with me next week."

"It's fine, Hutch. I understand why I can't go."

"I know, but I feel horrible for inviting you and then telling you that you can't go."

Lou has never traveled. I love seeing her eyes widen with wonder when she sees new things. Makes me want to show her the world.

"I don't want you to feel bad about it. Not for a second."

"I'll make it up to you another time."

"You already have, Hutch." Lou twists on the barstool. "I need to go to the bathroom. Did you see it when we came in?"

"Aye, to the left after we entered."

Lou leans closer and presses a sweet kiss against my mouth. "I may be a minute. You know that there's always a line in the ladies' bathroom."

"Want me to grab a table if one becomes available."

"Yeah, that would be great."

A table in the corner opens up and I dash over to claim it, placing my beer on the table right before another man making a move for the same table. I lift my chin, giving him the better-luck-next-time nod.

"You're bloody quick, mate."

"My wife prefers to sit at a table rather than the bar." My wife. I like the way that sounds coming off of my tongue.

"Your wife?" A chuckle follows his question.

What the fuck is that chuckle about?

"Aye, my wife."

"What the *wife* wants, the *wife* gets?"

"If you'd ever been married, you'd know the answer to that question."

"How long have you been married?"

"A month." That's how long it's been since our arrangement began. I can't believe that a third of our time together is already gone.

"Your missus looks more like a whore than a wife."

Did I hear that correctly? Surely not. No man would say that to a stranger about his wife. "Excuse me?"

"I don't think she's your wife at all. I think she's a cheap whore you picked up outside a Soho walk-up."

I stand, and what happens next, some might call a sucker punch. I call it a well-deserved lesson in how to not talk to a man about the woman he's with.

The rude fucker is lying facedown on the floor and I hope he gets up. I want him to come back at me. "Go ahead. Say something else like that and see what happens."

I hear a soft gasp behind me. "Chambers? How–"

Chambers. I remember that name and where I've heard it before.

I turn and look at Lou. "This is the man who tried to

rape you at the Inamorata cocktail party?"

The man chuckles. "As if it's possible to rape a whore. That's amusing."

Lou's attacker is in Glasgow ? In this bar inside of Glenskirlie? That isn't a coincidence. It can't be. "You followed us here?"

He stands and straightens his shirt and jacket. "I have eyes and ears everywhere… Mr. Maxwell Hutcheson."

I feel Lou's hand on my upper arm. "Let's get out of here. Please. I want to leave."

I see the bartender eyeing us while he's on the phone, and I'm certain that he's calling for security to come throw us out.

"Aye, let's get out of here."

I take Lou by the hand and we leave the bar. I open and close my fist after we get on the lift and realize how damn bad my hand hurts. I feel certain that I broke something in it, but I don't regret hitting that fucker. I'd do it again in a heartbeat.

"He's Cora's son? The one who attacked you at the cocktail party?"

"Yes."

"It's no coincidence that he's here. You know that, right?"

"Yes. And I'm afraid that you were right to think that he wasn't finished with me."

"I don't know what his being here means, but you're safe with me. I won't let him near you."

"I know."

Lou has ice sent to the room for my swollen hand, and I ice it down while she prepares for bed. I find it easy to forget the pain because I'm thinking of what's about to happen. And I don't want to wait any longer.

She watches me in the mirror as I move to stand

behind her and place my hands on her upper arms. I kiss one of her shoulders, and she reaches up to touch my injured hand. "You're bleeding."

She turns in my arms and takes my hand. "You need to wash this so it doesn't get infected. We'll get some ointment and bandages for it tomorrow."

She turns on the water and soaps a lather onto her fingers, washing my knuckles until the dried blood is gone. Still holding my hand, she looks up at me. "You punched Chambers before you knew who he was."

"Because he pissed me off."

"What did he say to you?"

Your missus looks more like a whore than a wife.

How in the world do I explain that to Lou?

Reaching out to hold her face, I lean forward and kiss her, and her lips on mine bring calmness.

When our kiss ends, I take her hand and pull her into the bedroom toward the bed. Sitting on the edge, I pull her hips toward me, and she stands between my legs. Her fingers play in my tousled hair. I love when she does that.

"Tell me what he said."

"He said 'Your missus looks more like a whore than a wife.'"

"Chambers knows that I'm not your wife. Why would he have called me that?"

"Because I told him you were." Fuck, I feel stupid telling her this. "I thought he was a stranger and wouldn't know the difference."

"You told him that I'm your wife?"

Fuck. It sounds even worse coming out of her mouth.

"I know. It's ridiculous and I'm a dobber for pretending to be your husband."

"Hutch…" That's all she gets out before her mouth slams against mine. At the same time, her hands are at my chest working to unfasten the buttons of my shirt. Unsatisfied with the slow progress, she reaches for the bottom and pulls it over my head while it's still buttoned.

Fuck. That was hot.

She undoes my belt buckle and yanks open the button on my trousers, this time more successful with the unfastening process. She slides my zipper down and puts her hand inside my Y-fronts, her hand enclosed around my cock as she glides it up and down. Damn, this lass knows how to give a hand job.

She kisses me hard while her hand pumps me. I'm so fucking close to coming, but she doesn't let me. "Where are the condoms?"

"Outer pocket, big suitcase."

She kisses my mouth. "Don't go anywhere."

Hell, there's no chance of that.

I get up and remove all of my clothes while she's digging for the condoms. She comes to me twirling a foil square between two fingers. "I'm putting it on you this time."

She'll get no argument from me.

Using her palms, she pushes me down on the bed and kneels between my thighs. She opens the packet and I lift my head, watching her put it on me. When she finishes, she gets off of me and stands at the bedside, shimmying her panties down her legs. Fuck, that wiggle thing that she does with her hips and arse wrecks me every time.

She climbs one knee at a time onto the bed and straddles me. My hands are splayed over her hips, waiting for her pussy to slide down the length of my cock. But it doesn't.

My tip is at her wet entrance. She's rocking her hips back and forth, teasing me. "You're my husband, huh? Show me."

25

CAITRIONA LOUDEN

HUTCH FLIPS US OVER AND A LITTLE BIT OF BREATH IS knocked from my lungs when I land on my back. He's kneeling between my legs and he hooks them around the bend of his arms, pushing them back and apart. He's not gentle about it. Not even a little. But his aggressive handling of my body is nothing compared to the merciless drive of his cock inside me.

"Ohh!" I scream.

Barbaric. Brutish. Blunt. That's how this is going to be.

Hutch's mouth sucks my earlobe, and his words sound as though they're squeezing through the spaces between gritted teeth and barely parted lips. "You're mine. Understand?"

There's an angry edge to his voice. And maybe that should frighten me, but instead, it turns me on.

I curl my body around his, pulling him even closer. "Yes."

"I want to hear you say it."

We're positioned sideways on the bed and each thrust

shoves me farther across the mattress until my head is hanging off the edge.

"I'm." Thrust.

"Yours." Thrust.

"No." Thrust.

"One." Thrust.

"Else's." Thrust.

He releases one of my legs and slides his hand down between them. "No one else touches you like this."

I'm panting as I rock against his fingers. "You're the only one who touches me like this."

These aren't romantic words exchanged between two people making love. These are possessive demands made by a jealous, greedy lover. A man dominating a woman.

There are times when Hutch is sweet and gentle, but this ain't one of them. I gladly take everything he has to give me.

Master me. Command me. Fuck me.

Love me.

He hits my sensitive sweet spot perfectly, and my body contracts around his cock, detonating his orgasm. "Ah… ah. Lou, I…"

I reach for his face and stretch upward, pressing our foreheads together.

What is it, Hutch? Do you want to say something else to me?

When our orgasms end, he relaxes against me. He stays that way for a while, our foreheads still pressed together, before pulling out and collapsing on the bed beside me.

I toy with the back of his hair while staring up at the beautiful sheer panels draped over the canopy above us, with one thought—this bed was meant for making love, but that isn't what we just did. This bed was meant to be shared by two people in love, but that isn't what we are.

But I can pretend.

And what a beautiful illusion it is.

~

I SMELL BREAKFAST. DEFINITELY BACON. MAYBE PANCAKES? I'm hungry, and it's difficult to pass up, but I'm exhausted. It was a late night. Very late.

I turn over on my stomach and pull the sheet up over my head, getting a few more minutes of sleep before I feel Hutch reach under the sheet to rub my bare butt cheeks.

"Good morning, birthday girl."

I lift the covers and look at him. He's grinning, so damn proud of himself. "How did you know today's my birthday?"

"You told me last week and I remembered, so get up for your birthday breakfast."

I remember mentioning that our birthdays were a week apart, but I thought it went in one ear and out the other. I never expected him to remember. No one does. Except Rachel.

"Give me a minute in the bathroom."

After slipping into the plush hotel robe and slippers, I go into the living/dining area. There I find a huge breakfast buffet spread across the table. It's a ton of food. We'll never be able to eat all of it.

"I had them send up one of everything for my wee foodie."

His wee foodie. That may be one of the sweetest things that a guy has ever called me.

He lifts a plate and hands it to me. "Birthday girl gets to go first."

While I'm plating my food, he pours coffee for himself and a glass of orange juice for me. He doesn't even have to ask anymore. We've been together long enough that he knows.

My drink preference. He knows that plus a whole lot of other things. Like how to touch me in all of the right places. How to say words that have a direct path to my heart. How to make me want to hold on to him forever and never let go.

He joins me at the table with a tall stack of pancakes. "Hungry much?"

"I had a famishing night, but I always eat this much in the morning. You'd know that if you were ever awake to join me for breakfast." His words are followed by a wink and a grin.

"Breakfast is important to you. Sleep is important to me. We all have our priorities."

He chuckles. "I'm aware."

"How's your hand today?"

He holds it up, making a fist and then releasing it. "It hurts, but I can move it. Maybe nothing's broken."

"I would feel terrible if you were injured on my account."

"You're worth a broken hand."

"No one has ever defended me like that." I'd be lying if I said that I didn't like it.

"No one gets to call you a whore."

"You can."

He stops eating and looks at me. "I'd never degrade you by calling you a whore."

"Not *a* whore. *Your* whore. There's a difference."

I can almost see the wheels turning in Hutch's head. "You're *my* whore?"

"Yes. Only yours."

"*My* whore." He grins. "I don't think that I'm supposed to like that, but I do."

"And I don't think I'm supposed to like being your whore, but I do. Very much."

He reaches out for my hand and brings it to his mouth, kissing it. "You never cease to amaze me."

"Dirty talk. Never underestimate the power of it."

When I finish eating, I push my plate away. "That was wonderful. And such a nice gift to wake up to. Thank you."

"I hope you don't believe that breakfast is your birthday gift."

"The concert last night and breakfast this morning. No one has ever given me better gifts."

He reaches into his pocket and pulls out a black velvet jewelry box, sliding it across the table to me. "Another gift."

Jewelry.

Why is my heart speeding? It's not as though this box contains an engagement ring. It also doesn't contain a piece of jewelry that will imply any sort of commitment. We may be pretending that he and I have something real, but that doesn't extend to this gift.

I reach for the box and crack it open. Inside is an ornate heart pendant hanging on a chain. "It's beautiful."

Is the heart symbolic of something? Or just the first pretty necklace that you saw? I need you to tell me.

"It isn't just a necklace."

My heart speeds. Is he going to say something that could change our relationship forever? "It's not?"

"See the split? Pull it apart."

I do as he instructs and the heart breaks into two pieces. "A USB?"

"You told me that you lost months of work when your computer crashed. You don't have to ever worry about that again. You can back it up to this USB and you'll always have it with you."

What a thoughtful and wonderful birthday gift. So why am I so sad?

"You don't like it?"

I force a smile. "I love it. It's perfect and proves how well you know me. Thank you."

I take it out of the box and pass it to him. "Will you put it on me?"

Turning around, I lift my hair. After he closes the clasp, he kisses the back of my neck.

I spin around and touch the heart at the dip of my neck. "Such a thoughtful gift. And beautiful."

He smiles, admiring his gift around my neck. "Looks good on you."

"Thank you."

"Go get ready. Let's go out."

We never get to go out in Edinburgh. There's always the risk of being seen together. "And do what?"

"Any damn thing we want to do."

He kisses the top of my head. Is it not the kind of kiss a man gives to a woman when he cares for her? The answer is yes. But is it pretend, a part of this game that we're playing? That, I don't know.

He smacks my ass. "Go, mo maise."

"Yes, sir."

I'M ABOUT TO GET INTO THE SHOWER WHEN I HEAR Rachel's ringtone. "Happy birthday to you…" And on it goes.

I went years without hearing anyone sing that song to me, but not since meeting Rachel. She is going to sing that song to me every year on the morning of my birthday or burst.

"Thank you."

"You should have told Hutch that it was your birthday."

"I sort of told him last week. Not the exact date but he figured it out. He took me to see Southern Ophelia last night and I woke to a huge birthday breakfast. And he gave me a gift."

"Do tell."

"A necklace. Heart-shaped with a USB inside so I can upload my manuscript and not lose it again when my shitty laptop crashes."

"Wow. That's really thoughtful. Is it yellow gold?"

"White. Coming from him, it's probably platinum. And there are stones on it. I'm pretty sure they're diamonds." A man like Hutch wouldn't give cubic zirconia to a woman.

"That's a great gift. Why do you sound disappointed?"

"I'm not disappointed." Lie. I am. And I should be ashamed.

"You are. I hear the disappointment in your voice."

No one knows me like Rachel. Sometimes it's great. Other times, not so much.

"I guess the practicality of it throws me off. I was hoping for something romantic."

"The romance is his knowing you and your needs on a deeply intimate level. He put a lot of thought into it."

"You're right. I don't know why I didn't see that." And I don't know what I was expecting.

"You long for more with him just like I want more with Claud. I get it, Cait."

"What's the latest on you two?"

"Claud asked me to leave Inamorata."

"Shut the fuck up." That's huge. "He wants you to leave Inamorata and do what exactly?"

"Take care of him. Let him take care of me."

"He wants you to live with him on a full-time basis?"

"Aye."

"Is that what you want?"

"Let's call it a stepping-stone toward what I really want."

"Marriage? Kids?" That fucking beautiful ever after we're all chasing?

"Yes."

"You love Claud enough to marry him? Have his babies?"

"I do." She didn't hesitate with that reply.

"Do you think he loves you?"

"Yes. Maybe not enough to marry me just yet, but he will. I'm going to make it happen."

"I'm happy for you, Rachel."

"I'm wondering what to do with our flat."

I have plenty of money and zero intentions of ever living in that shithole again. "Let it go."

"I thought that's what you might say."

"I'll come by soon and sort out what I want to keep and donate."

"You're next, you know?"

"I don't think so. Claud's circumstances are very different from Hutch's."

"It's going to happen for you. I believe that."

Hutch is unobtainable, same as every other thing in my life. I don't understand. Why is life so easy for some and so miserable for others?

Fairy tales are fairy tales because they're fictional. Made-up stories about a love that doesn't exist. A prince charming who doesn't breathe or walk or love outside of the black ink on white paper. I've surrounded myself with those stories for as long as I can remember. I blanketed myself inside of them, blocking out the cold of the world and everyone in it.

The princess always gets her prince charming. She always gets her happy ending. It's a cruel story to hear time and time again. Heartless actually. Because as a child these tales made me believe that I too would one day get my happily ever after.

Fairy tales. False hope. Lies printed in black and white.

Fuck that. Those were my words. I decided to give up on believing in fairy tales a long time ago. I buried the stories beneath the pain and hurt and disappointment in life but as hard as I tried, I could never make them go away completely. They're part of me, deep as bone. And that tiny spark of hope remains lit waiting to be doused again.

I'M GETTING OUT OF THE SHOWER WHEN MY PHONE RINGS. I see that it's my dad and it happens all over again. I'm a ten-year-old little girl who is thrilled because her daddy is calling to tell her happy birthday.

It's pathetic, this innate love that I feel for him when he has spent most of my life pretending that I didn't exist. Why are little girls that way with their fathers?

"Hello?"

"Hello, Caitriona. How are you?" Despite telling him time and time again to call me Cait, he continues to call me by my first name. But I can see why he would choose that—it's more impersonal.

"I'm good, Dad. And you?"

"Everyone's well."

I'm happy about that. My brother Owen tends to be sick a lot. "Oh, that's good to hear."

"I was calling to see if you could come by the house this evening."

Wow. My dad has a birthday gift for me? It wouldn't be a first, but I could probably count on one hand the number of times he's remembered my birthday and given me a gift.

"Sorry, I can't. I'm in Glasgow right now."

"What are you doing there?"

I'm having a romantic weekend with a beautiful man that I can't get enough of. "I came up for the weekend with a friend to see a concert."

"When will you be back in Edinburgh?"

"Tonight. Late tonight."

"Well, Heidi and I were hoping to speak to you in person, but I guess it can be handled over the phone."

"What's up?"

"Heidi and I have been trying to have another baby. It took a while this time but she's finally pregnant."

I feel like I've been punched in the gut. Again.

Really? He can't afford to support me while I finish my final two semesters of school, but he can afford to have another child?

My dad has always been a great father to his other kids. But never me. Not even when I was his only child. He has always made his love for my brother and sisters well known, but I had to plead for so much as a kind word. I did everything within my power to make him love me, aside from begging on my knees.

There are a lot of things I could say to him. But I choose one word. "Congratulations."

"Thank you. We feel blessed but taking care of four children is going to be a lot of work for Heidi. We want to talk to you about moving back in and helping her."

Is that what this call is about? He kicked me out and now he's asking me to come back and take care of his kids so Heidi can have it easy?

The asshole doesn't even realize that it's my birthday? "It's July 8th, Dad. Don't you know what today is?"

He's quiet for a moment. "I don't know, Caitriona. Is it a special day?"

"No, Dad." It's never been special to you or anyone else and it won't start being special today. "Forget that I brought it up."

"You won't be able to move back into your old room; we need it for the nursery."

I'm not considering this shit, but I have to ask because I'm so damn curious. "Then where would I sleep?"

"We haven't figured out where we'll put you just yet but don't worry. We'll come up with something for you."

"The futon in your office probably sleeps okay."

"Aye, Heidi mentioned that."

Oh my God, Dad. I wasn't serious.

"What about uni? I'm planning to go back in September." I'm dying to know if they expect me to quit school and take care of their kids.

"We've talked about this, Caitriona. We aren't going to pay for your tuition, especially now that another baby is on the way."

"I wasn't asking for money. I have plenty. I don't need any of yours. And you know what else I don't need? You."

"Caitriona—" That's the only word that I hear before I press END on my phone screen.

I don't know the exact moment that the tears started. Maybe it was when he told me that he was having another baby. Perhaps it was when I realized that he'd forgotten my birthday. Again. Doesn't matter. I only know that I can't stop the tears once they begin, and the more I try to hold them in, the more I feel like I might explode.

I jolt when I feel warm arms wrap around me from behind. “I’m here, Lou. I’ve got you.”

I melt against Hutch when he strokes my hair. Such a simple gesture yet so soothing. And so needed in this moment.

He doesn’t ask what has upset me. I imagine he doesn’t have to ask if he heard any part of the conversation with my dad.

He holds me and his embrace speaks volumes without saying a word. And I have hope for the first time in a while that maybe fairy tales aren’t full of lies and broken promises.

26

MAXWELL HUTCHESON

Lou's pain. It's old and deep and I feel it in the center of my core.

And I grasp it full circle now. I understand why Lou has been so adamant about protecting Ava Rose, striving so hard to make me comprehend why I can never do anything to make that wee girl feel the way Lou feels right now.

I'm angry, fucking angry, that Lou's father would treat her so poorly. I can't see how a father could hurt his daughter this way. Even if he doesn't feel a father-daughter relationship with her, he has a responsibility to cause her no harm.

Oh, the things that I would say to her father if he were in front of me right now. He'd know how to treat her when I was finished with him.

I sit on the couch and pat the cushion between my legs. "You. Right here."

She sits, leaning against my chest, and I kiss the top of her head. She's never said so, but I think she likes when I do that. She always seems to cozy up to me a wee bit tighter afterward.

Lou can be difficult to read at times, but now isn't one of those occasions. She's hurting and I want to be the champion that she deserves. God knows she doesn't get support from anyone else in her life, save her friend, Rachel.

This woman, so childlike in the moment, needs comfort. I simply hold her in my arms and that's all. I think it's what she needs, and I'm content to sit here doing it for as long as she needs me.

Let me take away your pain, Lou.

I don't know how long we stay that way, me holding her in my hands like a wounded animal, before her tears stop. But it's a while.

"I'm sorry for acting like this."

"He hurt you. Don't apologize because you feel pain."

She takes my hand and laces our fingers together. "I don't think you know how good you are at making me feel better."

She lifts her head from my shoulder and her eyes meet mine. Her lips part, and she inhales, but no words come.

"You make me feel better too so we're even."

She blinks rapidly and looks away, lifting my right hand and inspecting it. "The swelling has gone down, but I can see some discoloration beneath the skin."

"It's fine. Barely hurts anymore."

"It still looks painful." She brings it to her lips and kisses it.

"Your kiss will make it better in no time."

She smiles. "I'd still like to go out, that is if I've not ruined your mood with my tears and snot."

"You've not ruined anything."

"Good. Give me twenty minutes to finish getting ready, and I'll be ready to walk out the door."

I'm sitting on the couch waiting for Lou to get ready and I hear the buzzing vibration of her phone. I follow the sound, but it stops before I find it.

Missed call from Cameron Stewart. Who the hell is he?

Maybe her dad calling back? A relative or friend calling to wish her a happy birthday?

A boyfriend?

I want to know but I don't dare ask. Now isn't the time to initiate that kind of conversation.

Lou comes into the living room and I slide her phone between the cushions of the couch. I don't want her to know that I saw the call from this man. Or woman. Cameron isn't always a man's name.

Long chestnut hair hanging in loose curls. Hazel eyes. White casual dress. She looks like an angel.

I reach out to touch the heart pendant hanging around her neck. I'm pleased to see her wearing it. "It looks good on you."

She smiles. "You listen to me and this necklace proves that."

I reach out and tuck a stray lock of hair behind her ear. "I listen because I like what you have to say."

"Thank you again."

"You're welcome."

Lou and I spend the day exploring Glasgow, and I take her to a new but highly recommended restaurant for her birthday dinner. The food doesn't disappoint and neither does the atmosphere. Very romantic.

"How's the lamb?"

"Very good. Want to try it?"

"I do. I've never eaten lamb before."

"How have you never had lamb?"

"I grew up in New Orleans. Lamb isn't really a thing there."

"Right. You eat alligator."

"Sometimes."

She opens her mouth and wraps her lips around my fork. She pulls the bite of lamb off of it, and her nose immediately wrinkles. "Nope. Not for me."

"Seriously? You don't like it?"

"No. It tastes like… bad breath."

"I've never heard it described like that."

She picks up her drink and takes a big drink. "Does it always taste like that or did this restaurant do something to make it taste that way?"

"Tastes like normal lamb to me."

"Ugh, no. Just no. And in case you're wondering, I feel the same about haggis and black pudding. I won't eat that either."

"I'll keep that in mind."

Cameron Stewart. I can't get that name out of my head. The mystery of his or her identity is driving me mad. "Do you date much?"

She smiles and the candlelight illuminates her high cheekbones. "I have as of late. I've had a date almost every night for the past five weeks."

Not the answer that I'm looking for. "What about before me?"

"I dated a little."

"Any serious relationships?" I ask.

"Not especially."

I know that Lou is young, but I find it hard to believe that a beautiful woman like her has never been in a committed relationship. She wasn't a virgin. "You've never had a boyfriend?"

"I thought I was in love once. Turns out I was wrong."

That's all she has to say about it, and I get the feeling that I'm not the only one who has secrets. And I plan on finding out what hers are.

27

CAITRIONA LOUDEN

HUTCH AND I HAVE FALLEN INTO ROUTINES. WHILE HE'S AT work, I brainstorm on my new story and put down as many words as possible. At the end of the day, I back up my manuscript to the USB hanging around my neck. My story goes everywhere with me. I'll never lose it again.

Between brainstorming and typing on my laptop, I always find time each day to spend with Ava Rose. I believe that she enjoys our time together. Maybe I'm kidding myself, but she seems like a happier baby when she's with me.

I often take her for a walk around the grounds in her stroller—or her pram, as the nannies call it. A baby needs fresh air, needs to feel the sunlight on her face and the wind blowing on her skin, and the nannies never take her outside. They always keep her cooped up in the nursery. Seems highly unstimulating for a developing child if you ask me. But of course, no one has.

Sometimes Ava Rose and I venture into the village. I'm always amazed by how many people assume that she is mine. *Your daughter is beautiful.* I can't tell you how many times that I've been told that by the people of Kirkliston. I don't correct them. I'd be lying if I said that I didn't like the feelings I get when we're out and people mistake me for her mother.

I've fallen in love with this little ginger baby girl. I admit it.

Hutch and I are two months into our arrangement. Only one month remains. Actually, not even that long. Three and a half weeks. I have a life to return to in twenty-five days. I can't imagine what that is going to feel like. And I don't want to imagine it. Because I love the woman I become when I'm with him.

In a short amount of time, I've come to think of his house as my home. I've come to think of Hutch as more than a paying client.

I love him.

I. Love. Him.

How did I let that happen?

Our precious time together feels like a candle with wicks burning at both ends. Once the flame meets in the middle, all of this is over. I'll never see him again, never hear his laugh, never touch his skin. I'll never share his bed again.

Am I prepared to leave Hutch and Ava Rose? No, but it doesn't matter. The day is coming, and I'd better figure out how I'll say goodbye.

Hutch's long hours at work have given me a lot of free time for writing. Being here inspires me. Hell, I should at least be honest about it—Hutch inspires me. I know the stuff I'm writing is good, but the inspiration behind the words is bittersweet. I'm afraid that I've come to a place that I never wanted to be—writing grown-up fairy tales because I'm in love.

It's one of those days. I'm deeply entwined within the

fictional world that I am creating when I hear Hutch's voice. "I'm home."

I look up from my laptop. "Hey, you."

I abandon my work and go to him. "I'm glad you're home. I missed you."

"I missed you too."

He wraps his arms around me and kisses my mouth, pulling me close by using the grip he has on my butt.

"Dinner's ready. Can you break away to eat with me?"

My workday ends the second that Hutch enters the house. I won't waste a single moment working when I can be with him, but I love how he always asks. "I'm finished for the day now that you're here."

It's Monday. Cajun night. Another routine that Hutch and I have developed, thanks to Sonny.

"Oooh, looks good."

"Sonny said that it's Creole shrimp and Gouda grits."

"Shrimp and grits is one of my favorite dishes."

Hutch tries his first bite. "Mmm… I must admit that I enjoy our Monday night Cajun dinners."

"The food in New Orleans is amazing. I wish that I could take you to all of my favorite restaurants. You'd fall in love."

"I think I already have."

My heart speeds and my head tells it to slow down. He's talking about the food, you fool.

Stupid heart.

Hutch uses his fork to point at the food on his plate. "If I hadn't already been won over, this dish would do it for me. It's my favorite so far."

"Sonny does a great job, but you should let me cook for you sometime."

"You cook?"

"I do." I see the surprise on his face. "I spent a lot of

time at my best friend's house when I was growing up. Her mom was a great cook and she taught me a lot."

"I would love for you to cook dinner for me."

"All right. I'll be in charge of our next Cajun Monday."

"It's a plan. And speaking of plans… I have tickets for the Scottish Ballet in Glasgow."

"You like ballet?"

"I don't, but one of my clients has a granddaughter in the production. She's the star of the show and he gifted me with two tickets. He's insistent upon my attendance at opening night on Friday. I normally wouldn't consider attending but he is one of my biggest clients. I'm afraid he'll be offended if I skip out."

I've never seen a real ballet. "I'd love to go. What's the adaptation?" Adaptation? Is that the right word? I'm not really sure.

"Cinderella."

A fairy tale. It's impossible to get away from them.

"Sounds like fun."

"I was thinking that we could go on Friday night and stay until Sunday evening. We saw only a small portion of what I want to show you."

"I loved what I saw of Glasgow the last time we were there. I'd love to see more."

"Then it's a plan."

~

"Good afternoon. Are you checking in?"

"Aye, we have a reservation for Maxwell Hutcheson."

I smile to myself because I'll never be able to see Hutch as Maxwell. It's so damn formal and stiff.

"Ah, yes. Welcome, Mr. and Mrs. Hutcheson."

My internal smile broadens.

Mrs. Hutcheson. I don't hate being mistaken for her just as I don't hate being mistaken for Ava Rose's mother.

He doesn't correct the woman checking us into the hotel. And that means I get to pretend, even if only for a minute, that we are so much more than companions approaching our expiration date.

"Looks like we have you booked for a honeymoon suite for two nights. Checking in on the seventh and departing on the ninth."

"Correct."

Aww. He booked the same room again? That is so sweet. And romantic.

"Here are your keycards. You'll be on the fifth floor. Elevators are around the corner to the right. Bell services will bring up your bags."

Neither of us say anything as we rise in the elevator, and I can't resist stealing a glance at Hutch in the mirror. His eyes meet mine, and we both smile.

"We're in the same room as before, *Mrs. Hutcheson.*"

"I heard, *Mr. Hutcheson.* I think you could be trying to woo your wife."

"Perhaps."

After we're inside the suite, I go to the window and overlook the city. "Why did you leave Glasgow?"

"My job took me to Edinburgh."

"Do you ever consider coming back?"

"Aye."

"Then why don't you?"

"It doesn't feel right to bring Ava Rose to Glasgow when her family is in Edinburgh."

When is he going to get this through his head? "You are Ava Rose's father. Your parents are her grandparents. Your brother is her uncle. Your sister is her aunt. Her family is in Glasgow too. You should come back if it'll make you happy."

"I don't know."

"The Lochridges could still see Ava Rose whenever they like. You wouldn't be taking her far away."

Hutch shrugs. "It's something to think about."

HUTCH IS WAITING FOR ME ON THE SOFA. "SORRY. DIDN'T mean to take so long getting ready."

He looks at me and I don't mistake the long breath he inhales before slowly exhaling. "Worth. Every. Minute. You look beautiful."

I never tire of hearing Hutch tell me that I'm beautiful. "Thank you."

I'm wearing a fitted black cocktail dress and tall heels. My feet are going to hurt later, but the shoes make my legs look sexy. And that's what I want—to be beautiful for Hutch, even if it's painful.

I hold out a diamond pendant necklace, a gift from Hutch. "Will you fasten this for me?"

"Of course."

He fastens the clasp and steps away to look at me. "So damn bonny. But you're missing something."

"You can tell that I'm not wearing panties?"

"No knickers? Really?"

"That's for me to know and for you to find out."

"And I plan to." He takes my hand and kisses the inside of my wrist. "Your wrist looks like it needs something."

He goes to the dining table and fetches a long, slim jewelry box, cracking open the box and showing me the diamond bracelet inside.

"You spoil me."

"I told you that I would."

I wonder how many carats it is. A lot. That much, I know.

I hold out my hand, and he fastens the bracelet around my wrist. "It's beautiful, Hutch."

He takes my hand and kisses the top. "You're beautiful."

"Thank you. For the compliment and the bracelet."

We arrive at the Theatre Royal Glasgow and find that we have some of the best seats in the theatre. "Wow. We're in the box."

"It appears so."

Red velvet. Gold trim. Ornate ceiling. The theatre is incredible. "Have you been here before?"

"Many times."

Swirling ball gowns. Bursts of color. A magical world filled with scores performed by an orchestra. It's everything that I've always loved about this classic story but in a much different light. And as always, I'm sucked into the fairy tale. And I'm sucked into the possibilities of what could be with Hutch and me.

28

MAXWELL HUTCHESON

A FAIRY TALE. BALLET. ORCHESTRA MUSIC. I THOUGHT that sitting through the performance would be a miserable couple of hours, but I was wrong. I've never enjoyed a show at Theatre Royal Glasgow so much in my life. And there's only one reason.

"Where are we off to now?" Lou asks.

Dancing with Lou would be fun. "I know of some good dance clubs if you're in the mood."

My mobile vibrates and I choose to let it go to voicemail when I see that it's Ian. My brother will have to wait. Lou has my full attention right now.

"Let's do it."

I scan the club for faces I recognize, and I'm relieved when I don't see anyone I know. Hell, they all look like kids to me.

Kids? Shite, I think they're the same age as Lou. That's a kick in the bollocks.

"Oh, I love this song."

The song is slow but harsh with a lot of bass. Good for

dancing but not in a romantic way. The melody feels seductive. Erotic.

"What is this song?"

"'Love is Madness' by Thirty Seconds to Mars and Halsey. One of my favorites. I can't believe they're playing it."

I feel my mobile vibrate in my pocket and I continue to ignore it. How can I not when Lou is moving against me to the beat of this song and grinding her arse against my cock?

Vibration.

Vibration.

Vibration.

Fuck, can Ian not take a hint? I'm not interested in talking to him right now.

I take out my mobile intending to turn it off when I see the series of missed calls and texts from Ian and Mum.

IAN: Family emergency. Answer your phone.
MUM: Call me now.
IAN: There's been an accident.

Family emergency. Answer your phone. Call me now. There's been an accident. I see those series of words and my stomach flips, making me feel ill. The last time I heard those words was when Mina got into the car accident. And it eventually killed her.

"I'm sorry. I have a family emergency. I need to make a call."

Lou stops dancing and places her hand on my upper arm. "Let's go outside. You won't be able to hear anything in here."

Calvin pulls up and we get into the back seat. My mobile is pressed to my ear when Mum answers, forgoing her usual hello and pleasantries. "Max..." That's the only word she gets out before her voice breaks.

"What is it, Mum?"

"It's Sara. She's been in a car accident."

It's Sara. She's been in a car accident. I hear my mother say those words and it feels like history repeating itself in a new, cruel kind of way.

"How bad is it?"

Mum, you have to tell me that Sara survived. I can't go through this again. And not with my sister. Not with sweet Sara. She has a husband who adores her. He can't lose his wife. She loves her two boys with all of her heart. They can't lose their mum.

"All of us are at Queen Elizabeth University Hospital. They haven't told us anything yet."

So everyone is there. Everyone but me. Because I chose to ignore them.

"I'm on my way."

"I know you're anxious to get here, but please drive carefully from Edinburgh."

"I'm in Glasgow."

There's a distinct pause before Mum says, "That's good. We'll see you soon."

I end my call with my mother and I'm numb. This is my sister. And she could possibly be fighting for her life right now.

"My sister's been in a car accident."

Lou reaches for my hand. "I'm sorry, Hutch. Is it serious?"

"We don't know anything about her condition yet, but I have to go."

"Of course, you do." Lou leans over and places a kiss against my lips. "Go now. I'll catch a taxi to the hotel. But please call or text me when you have news."

She pulls the handle, opening the door, and I realize that I don't want to be without her tonight. I want her by my side. "Go to the hospital with me."

She stops, her hand still on the handle of the open door. "You're upset, Hutch. That's completely understandable, but you aren't thinking straight right now."

"I am thinking straight, Lou. I'm thinking straighter than I have in months, and I want you to be there with me."

"I hate to state the obvious, but your family is there. How will you explain me?"

I consider the words dancing on the tip of my tongue. If I say them, they will change our relationship. And I don't care. "I need you to be with me."

"Are you sure? I don't want you to make a decision you'll regret later because you're afraid for your sister right now."

My family is my family but not a one of them knows me the way Lou knows me. She's the only person on earth who's heard my darkest confession.

"I know exactly what it'll mean, and I'll have to answer some tough questions, but I'm prepared to do that."

"Okay. I'll come." She closes the door and slides closer, cradling my face with her hands. "All you ever have to do is ask. I'll do anything for you."

I know.

Introducing Lou to my family is going to change everything. I might regret this decision later, but right now, I can't imagine not having her by my side. I need her.

We find my parents, Ian, Adam, and the boys in the family waiting room. My brother-in-law is standing by a pair of doors, I presume the entrance to the area where Sara is being examined and treated. He looks helpless and lost. It's a feeling I remember well.

My mum looks up as Lou and I approach. She passes my younger nephew to my father and gets up, wrapping her arms around me and squeezing tightly. "I thought we'd never get you to answer your mobile, you wee jobby."

Wee jobby, also known as little shite. My mum's favorite nickname for me.

"I'm sorry. I had to turn off my mobile because we were at the theatre. Has there been any news since we spoke?"

My mum releases me. "Someone came out a few minutes ago and told us that Sara is in stable condition. She's having X-rays done now and when those are finished, she'll go for a CT. That's all we know at this point."

"Stable. That's reassuring." Or at least I think it is. No one ever used the word stable to describe Mina's condition. "Do you have any idea what happened?"

"Adam said that she'd gone out to dinner with some friends and was on her way home. We haven't heard anything about what caused the accident, but I'd suspect that the heavy rain we got earlier tonight is to blame."

That's right. There were puddles of water on the side-walk when Lou and I came out of the theatre.

Mum looks at Lou and then back at me and I know that the time has arrived. I have to introduce her to my family.

"This is Lou." Fuck. I hope Mum doesn't ask for a last name; she's never given me one. Hell, she's never told me anything but her Inamorata name. Her alias. That's a conversation that we need to revisit again. "This is my mother, Clarissa Hutcheson."

Lou's eyes widen when my mother pulls her into an embrace. "It's lovely to meet you, Lou."

"It's very nice to meet you too, Mrs. Hutcheson, although I wish it were under different circumstances."

"I wish it were different circumstances as well."

"I pray that all is well with your daughter and that she makes a speedy recovery."

"Thank you, dear."

My mum grasps Lou's hands. "You're even more beautiful than the picture I saw of you on Max's mobile."

Oh fuck. I think I can see the color leaving Lou's face right before my eyes.

"That's a very sweet thing to say. Thank you."

Mum bends down and picks up Mason, placing him on her hip. "I wish they'd hurry up. Sara needs to see her family. She needs to know that we're here for her."

"Son, are you going to introduce your friend to the rest of the family or is your mother the only one who gets that honor?" my dad asks.

The biggest hurdle is behind me. Meeting the rest of my family will be a piece of cake.

"This is my dad, Angus Hutcheson."

"Everyone calls me Gus," my dad adds.

I gesture toward my brother. "This is Ian."

Ian studies Lou and his eyes widen. "We had a class together at uni. Illuminated Manuscripts. Dr. Fraser."

Lou looks at Ian for a moment. "That was a while ago."

"Aye."

I can't tell if Lou remembers Ian or not.

"This is my sister's husband, Adam. And these wee laddies are my nephews, Leo and Mason."

"It's lovely to meet all of you."

"You're American?" my mum asks.

"Yes. I'm from New Orleans."

Lou recounts the story of how she came to live in Scotland, but it's a much shorter version than the tale she told me two months ago. This one lacks the details about her pain, her sorrow. She almost manages to make it sound like a happy event in her life.

An hour passes. And then another. With each tick of the second hand, my family and I become a wee bit more restless, and then a staff member finally comes through the doors we've been watching like hawks. "Sara Hillhouse's family?"

Adam leaves his seat the moment he hears Sara's name. "Aye, I'm her husband and these are her parents and brothers."

"Your wife is doing well. X-Ray and CT scans are negative with the exception of two fractured ribs. Because she lost consciousness after the accident, we'll observe her overnight and she should be able to go home tomorrow afternoon if no additional problems arise."

My mum releases the breath that she's been holding. "Oh, thank you so much. When can we see her?"

The man raises his arm and looks at his watch. "Mrs. Hillhouse will be transferred to a room within the hour, but you can visit her now. I'm sure you're anxious to see her."

"That would be wonderful. Thank you so much," Adam says.

"I think I should see Sara before the boys do." Adam's voice is low when he looks at Leo and Mason. "I need to know how to prepare them for what they'll see so they aren't frightened."

"I completely agree," my mum says.

"You all go in to see Sara first. Lou and I will stay with the boys," I say.

"She's your sister. You should go too. I can sit with the boys."

I know that I can trust Lou with the boys, but Sara and Adam are particular about who they will allow to watch them. "Lou takes care of Ava Rose. You can trust her with your children."

A small bit of the tension on Adam's face relaxes. "That would be fab. Thank you."

Lou takes Mason from my dad and carries him over to where Leo is playing. "Don't worry. We'll be fine."

We enter the small exam room where Sara is lying on a bed with her eyes closed. A nurse is at her bedside looking at the monitor. "Looks like someone has visitors."

Sara opens her eyes and I see the lingering sedation: her eyes are slow to focus. The nurse didn't say so but I'm sure that she's been given some good medication for the pain she must be having.

She looks at Adam first. That's the way it's always been between them. He's always been her number one. And isn't that the way it's supposed to be between a husband and wife? I think so but that's never the way it was between Mina and me. She always put her family ahead of me.

To have my very own number one. To be someone's number one. That's what I want.

Adam sits on the bed and takes Sara's hand in his, kissing the top, while we observe as spectators. "You scared the shite out of me, mo leannan."

"You scared the shite out of all of us," my dad says.

"I scared myself."

Sara recounts everything she can remember about the accident. From what she says, it sounds as though the rain was the major culprit. And although she doesn't mention it, I'm sure that her heavy foot played a part as well. Sara has never been known for driving slowly, but I bet that changes from here on out.

"I want to see my boys." Her eyes widen. "Who's watching them?"

"They're in the waiting room with Max's friend."

"What friend?"

"Her name is Lou."

Sara smiles. "A woman?"

"Aye, Lou is a woman."

"A very pretty American woman," my mum says.

"How long have you known this very pretty American woman?"

"A couple of months."

"You've not mentioned a word about her?"

I've said all that I want to say about Lou for now. "I think you mentioned something about seeing the boys?"

"Yes. Someone bring my babies to me."

"Stay, Adam. Max and I will go out and get them," Mum says.

Mason is sitting on Lou's lap and Leo is tucked beneath her arm. She looks like a mother hen with her wing wrapped around her baby chick. She's reading a children's book to them and has the full attention of both boys. I'm not sure that I've ever seen either of them be so still and quiet. The two of them can be quite the pair of wee shite stirrers.

My mum stops as we enter the waiting room and places her hand on my lower arm. "Lou is a beauty. And she seems like a sweet lass."

"She is."

"The boys are certainly taken by her."

"No more than Ava Rose."

"Introducing a woman to your daughter is a big step."

"It wasn't like that, Mum."

"Then what was it like?"

"The on-duty nanny became ill during her shift and I couldn't get a replacement. Lou stepped in and took care of Ava Rose for me. She saved my arse."

"You are fully capable of raising your child. I don't know when you're going to see that so many nannies are unnecessary."

I don't want to have the nanny conversation again. "Sara is anxious to see Leo and Mason. She'll be sending Adam out to get them if you don't take them to her."

Mum releases my arm. "I know. You're right."

I dodged that bullet. For now. The nanny conversation is one that Mum brings up on a regular basis, so I know that the argument is only postponed until another time.

"I want you and Lou to stay at the house tonight. The family should be together after going through this close call with your sister."

Lou at my parents' house? Spending time with my family? I'm not sure that's a good idea.

"We already have a room for the weekend." Fuck. I think I just admitted to my mum that Lou and I are sleeping together.

"Yes, you do, and it's called your old bedroom at your parents' house."

Maybe Mum does want the family together, but that isn't solely what this is about. I smell ulterior motive. "You want to spend time with Lou."

"Is that so wrong?"

My mum has no idea that our relationship is a paid arrangement. An arrangement that will end in a few weeks. It seems cruel to let her pointlessly become acquainted with Lou. "I don't want you to make more of our relationship than it is. We're just having a wee bit of fun together. It's not serious."

My mum smiles. "Your father and I were just having a wee bit of fun together too. And here we are, thirty-six years and three children later, still having fun."

True. But neither of my parents ever married into the Lochridge family.

29

CAITRIONA LOUDEN

CALVIN DRIVES THROUGH A VILLAGE AND STOPS THE CAR IN front of a large honey-colored stone house settled in the middle of a golf club. Although the property is beautiful, it's not the sprawling renovated castle on top of a hill that I was expecting. "This is where you grew up?"

"Aye."

"It's very modern-looking compared to your house."

Hutch laughs. "It was built in 1877, but there have been a few renovations since, the latest only a few years ago."

"I wouldn't have guessed it to be that old."

"It didn't look this way when I grew up here. Mum and Dad are constantly doing something to improve it."

Hutch's parents are obviously well off. This is at least a million-pound home, but I assumed that they were ultra-rich like Hutch. After seeing their home, I don't think that's the case.

Hutch takes our bags from the car and I follow him up the walkway to the front door. "How is this going to go?"

He chuckles. "If I'm being honest, it's going to go any way Clarissa Hutcheson wants it to go."

He doesn't understand my question. "Are we sleeping in the same room or will I be in the guest room?"

"They don't have a guest room. They have a guest-house. But you'll sleep in my bedroom with me."

"Will that be all right with your parents?"

"Aye."

"How do you know it's okay?"

"Lou, I'm thirty-four years old. That's how I know."

"I don't think parents care how old you are if you aren't married." Although mine wouldn't give two shits what I did.

"My mum doesn't expect us to sleep in separate bedrooms when we were obviously going to share a bed at the hotel."

I didn't think about that. "I still feel funny about it."

Hutch stops and places a quick kiss against my lips. "I don't, so you shouldn't either."

He opens the front door and we enter the foyer.

"Mum," he calls out.

"In the living room."

"We're going to put our things in my bedroom, and then we'll come down."

I follow Hutch up the stairs, and he leads me into a large bedroom. Gray walls. Dark linens. Furniture with clean lines. It's clearly been remodeled since he left home. No teenage boy or young man would have a bedroom that looked like this. "Part of the improvements?"

"Aye. It definitely didn't look like this when I lived here."

"I didn't think so."

We go downstairs to the living room and join Hutch's parents, brother, and nephews. His mother is rocking her younger grandson while the older one sits in his grandfather's lap, watching a children's show on the television. It's a picture-perfect image.

I see the love and affection and connection between these people and know that this is what family looks like. And while it makes me happy to see them this way, it also makes me sad because I've never had this in my life. And I'm terrified that I never will.

"I'd like for you and Lou to stay the rest of the weekend if possible."

Hutch looks at me. "I think we can manage that if Lou doesn't have to go back to Edinburgh for anything."

Is he asking my permission? Or hoping that I'll speak up and say that I need to return? I don't know; I can't read him. I only know that I want to stay.

"I don't have anything pressing to do."

"Wonderful. Will you send for Ava Rose in the morning? I want the whole family together this weekend."

"I'll have Mrs. McVey bring her in the morning."

"Did you hear that, Leo and Mason? You'll get to see your baby cousin tomorrow."

I'm only beginning to enjoy my time with Hutch's family when we all go our separate ways for bedtime. But we have the rest of the weekend to spend time together. And I'm looking forward to it.

I come out of the bathroom wearing one of Hutch's T-shirts, leaving off the lingerie I packed for our weekend getaway. It feels all kinds of wrong to wear crotchless panties in his parents' house.

Hutch is lying shirtless in bed with his hands folded behind his head, and I sigh with pure pleasure as I behold the sight of him. God, he's just so beautiful.

I crawl into bed beside him and pull the covers over my chest. I turn over, facing him, and smile.

He reaches out and caresses my arm, igniting chills over my body. "What are you thinking?"

Our arrangement has changed and none of the guidelines in our contract outline how we should treat this unanticipated situation. "You've been very clear about what you want, need, and expect from me, but meeting your family has thrown me for a loop. I'm not sure what my role is while we're here."

"Aye, our previous agreement will need a wee bit of a revision for the weekend."

"Your mother already knew about me prior to tonight. She said she had seen pictures of me." And I need to know what that means before I get my hopes up.

"She was looking at photographs on my mobile and flipped too far. She saw a photo of us together."

The only photos Hutch has of us on his mobile are the ones in bed together. Great. "I can't wait to hear how you explained that one to her."

"I didn't have to explain anything."

"Right. Because the picture was self-explanatory."

I wonder which one she saw. Guess it doesn't matter. I was basically naked, covered only by a sheet, in all of them. "Was she upset?"

"Not at all. She told me that I was the only person who could know when it's time to move on with another woman and if I felt ready, then it was time."

I'm not surprised; Hutch's family seems very reasonable. "You must be relieved."

"My family has never been the ones I was worried about."

Right. Mina's family is Hutch's problem. But they aren't here.

"Who am I supposed to be to you this weekend?"

His fingertips glide down my arm. "You're the woman

in my life. Let's leave it at that and not put a label on it. Giving our relationship a name will only complicate things with my family."

"Fair enough."

Hutch reaches for the lamp and turns off the light before reaching out and pulling me against him. "I know you aren't a cuddler and you like your space in bed, but I want to fall asleep holding you."

And that's exactly what he does.

30

MAXWELL HUTCHESON

Lou is still asleep when I wake. No surprise there. I've come to understand that her body requires more sleep than mine. Actually, I've come to understand her body in a lot of ways.

I was born into a family of early risers, but I'm the first one up this morning. Probably because bedtime came later than usual for everyone. That means I get to have my coffee in peace. At least until Leo and Mason get up. The peace will be over for all of us when that happens.

I'm reading the paper and drinking my coffee when Mum comes into the kitchen. "Good morning."

"Morning, Mum."

She pours a cup of coffee from the pot I brewed. She and Dad still like it the old-fashioned way. The single-cup brewer never appealed to them. "I made it strong."

"Just the way we like it."

Mum takes the seat next to me and picks up the sections of newspaper that I've already read. "Did you and Lou sleep all right?"

"I had a hard time falling asleep. I couldn't stop thinking about Sara and what could have happened to her."

"Her accident opened old wounds for you?"

"Aye."

"I think that's to be expected. I don't see how you couldn't be reminded of Mina's accident."

"Lou helped me hold it together last night." I recall how reassuring she was before we arrived at the hospital. She was full of optimism. "I can't say exactly what it is, but she has a special way about her."

"Lou's personality is soothing. I see the calming effect she has over you. It's nice."

I don't usually have one-on-one moments like this with my mum. And I don't know when I might get another. "From the outside, I may look like I have everything together, but I don't. I'm failing at life."

"Son, you are very successful. You aren't even remotely failing at life."

"I am, Mum. At least where Ava Rose is concerned."

My mum smiles. "You're a new father who's learning how to be a single parent to a newborn after the loss of his wife. No one expects you to know how to do it perfectly. There's going to be some trial and error. You're going to make mistakes and that's all right."

I feel like all I ever do with Ava Rose is make mistakes.

"Lou has an unhealthy relationship with her father. He's had a very negative impact upon her life, and her pain has been the driving force responsible for making me see how important I am in Ava Rose's life. I never want to hurt that sweet girl."

"I know you could never hurt Ava Rose."

My mum doesn't understand. I would never intentionally make any decision that would hurt my daughter. It's my unconscious decisions that could bring her pain.

My daughter. I've never thought of Ava Rose that way before. But I do more and more each day. Because of Lou.

"It's clear to see that Lou has a large influence in your life. A positive one. She's good for you."

"I've never known anyone like her." She's been knocked down so many times that she should be shattered into a million pieces, and yet she's the one who's putting me back together. "She's so strong, Mum. She doesn't think so, but she is."

"Are you falling in love with her?"

Falling in love? "There isn't a place for that in my life."

"You deserve to love again, and it would be a tragedy to deprive yourself of happiness because Mina's family makes you feel like it's wrong. They've controlled your life for too long."

"Good morning."

I turn at the sound of Lou's voice, completely surprised to see her awake. "Good morning."

My mum gets up and moves toward the coffee maker. "Would you care for some coffee?"

"None for me. I'm not a coffee drinker."

"Tea?" Mum says.

"Lou prefers juice."

Mum goes to the refrigerator. "We have apple juice."

"Apple works for me."

"You're up early this morning."

Lou smiles. "Ava Rose is coming. I didn't want to be in bed when she gets here. I'm ready to see her."

Ava Rose and Lou are becoming attached to each other. I see it happening right before my eyes. And I don't know what that means for either of them when we go our separate ways in a few weeks.

A few weeks. The end of us. The time is arriving much sooner than I ever expected it to.

"I'm ready to see my sweet granddaughter. It's been too long."

Work. The hour-long drive. My own selfish desires. I allow too many things to get in the way of seeing my family. "I'm going to work harder on bringing her to see you more often. I promise."

"I know you're busy with work, but family comes first. Always. You've allowed yourself to forget that in the past. Don't let it keep happening."

"I won't, Mum."

Sara is discharged from the hospital and the entire family is present at my parents' house by early afternoon. Sara didn't need a lot of convincing that the next few days would be easier for her if Mum and Dad could help Adam with caring for her and the boys during her recovery.

Mum and Dad have always spoiled her. They still do.

Lou has only spent a few hours with my family, but she has already found a comfortable place among them. I watch her sitting on the floor with Ava Rose and the boys, and the way she interacts with them comes so naturally. All three have taken a special liking to her.

I'm not the only one who has noticed Lou's ease with the children. My mum watches her, smiling as she looks on. "The boys never connect like that with someone new."

"She's good with kids."

"They sense her nurturing quality and it naturally puts them at ease. People either have it or they don't, and Lou definitely has it."

"It must come naturally because Lou didn't learn that from her parents. They've treated her very poorly."

My mum frowns. "Does the poor lass have anyone?"

"Only one person—her best friend."

"And she has you."

She does but only for a few more weeks. I'm not looking forward to saying goodbye. I already know what my life without her in it looks like and I don't care for it.

Maybe we could talk about extending our arrangement? I wonder if that would be something she'd consider?

The doorbell rings, and my mum sits taller on the sofa beside me, looking at my dad. "Are you expecting someone?"

"Not that I can recall."

My mum gets up and disappears into the foyer, returning a moment later with a guest. Not one that I want to see, especially at my parents' house while Lou is here. And I am pissed off.

Fuck my life.

"What are you doing here?" My words are rude, and I don't give a fuck.

This is my parents' home. The place where I should be able to escape my life in Edinburgh and retreat to my family home. This is where I should feel at ease with zero chance of my life with the Lochridge family colliding with my world that includes Lou. And here comes my sister-in-law Blair, sending all of that into a tailspin.

"I came as soon as I heard about your sister's accident. Is she all right?"

This is ridiculous. Blair hardly knows Sara. Why wouldn't she call instead of driving up from Edinburgh?

"She has some broken ribs but otherwise she's all right."

"Thank God for that."

Nothing about this visit feels right.

"I see that the whole family has come together to rally around her." Blair's eyes widen when she notices Lou sitting on the floor with the children. "And the help apparently."

Damn.

Confusion is etched in the growing lines over my mum's face. Thanks a lot, Blair.

I have to do something before this situation spins further out of control. I need to separate Blair and my family before she says something that I won't be able to explain.

"Come have a cup of tea with me, and I'll catch you up on everything."

We go into the kitchen and my back is turned to Blair as I pour fresh water into the kettle. "Sara was very lucky. It could have been so much worse."

"Your housekeeper is here?"

"Aye. Lou has come to help with the children." That sounds legit, right? Until you recall that I have four nannies on staff.

"Your entire family is here. Why do you need her help with the children?"

"I wasn't certain about Sara's condition when I got the call about her accident. Lou volunteered to come stay with the children at the house so we could be at the hospital with Sara."

Blair crosses her arms. "Lou has a way of inserting herself into situations in which she isn't invited."

No, Blair. It's you who has a way of inserting yourself into situations where you aren't invited.

"I don't know what you mean by that. I've not had any problems with her."

"I found her taking a bath in your tub—in your bathroom—while you were away."

I wondered when Blair was going to bring that up.

I have to make that situation look as transparent as

possible. "She told me about that. And she apologized for overstepping her boundaries. It won't happen again."

"Are you having an affair with your housekeeper?"

"No." That's technically not a lie because Lou is definitely not my housekeeper.

Blair shakes her head. "I knew you wouldn't stoop to the level of sleeping with the hired help, but I had to ask."

I hate the way she refers to Lou as the hired help. But I can't correct her.

"You should be careful with that one. She's looking to sink her claws into you."

"I'm sure you're mistaken."

Blair laughs. "You really don't see it, do you?"

"See what?"

"You're perfect, Max. And everything that every woman dreams of having for herself."

I'm suddenly more uncomfortable than I've ever been in my life. Blair's statement isn't something that a married woman is supposed to say to another man, especially her dead sister's widower.

She moves into my personal space and places her hands on my upper arms. "You're going to be ready to move on at some point, and I want you to know that you have my full support when that time comes."

Fuck, that's unexpected. And out of the clear blue.

Does she mean that? Is she being sincere?

I don't know what Blair's MO is or what her words mean, but there's no way I'd confide in her about any part of my personal life. "There's only room for one girl in my life right now and that's Ava Rose."

Her smile is wide. "That's exactly what I expected you to say."

Nothing about my sister-in-law's numerous unannounced appearances into my life feels right. She never showed up without notice when Mina was alive. I'm not sure what to make of her surprise visits except that I don't like them. Each one increases the risk of her figuring out what Lou and I are doing. And that's a clusterfuck that I don't wish to tame.

31

CAITRIONA LOUDEN

Calvin is driving us back to Edinburgh, and I'm thinking about how much I've enjoyed the last three days with Hutch's family. The label that we weren't supposed to place on our relationship somehow affixed itself to us like a magnet to steel. I became his girlfriend.

Girlfriend. That's what his brother called me, and Hutch didn't correct him. It felt wonderful, like we haven't been pretending to play roles for the last ten weeks.

Hutch reaches for my hand across Ava Rose's car seat and rubs his thumb over the top. "You're quiet."

I can't tell him what's swirling around in my head. "I'm just thinking about how great your family is and how glad I am that I got to meet them."

"They think you're pretty great too. Especially my mum. She's a wee bit taken with you."

"Your mom is great. You don't know how lucky you are to have her. I wish with all of my heart that I'd had someone like her in my life when I was growing up." Or even now.

Who would I be today if I'd had someone like Clarissa

Hutcheson raising me instead of a mother who chose alcohol and drugs over her child?

We stayed the entire day at the Hutchesons, so it's late when we arrive at the house. I get Ava Rose down for the night and meet Hutch in the bedroom. He wraps his arms around me from behind. "I finally get to have you to myself."

His hand slides into the front of my shorts and goes straight for the kill, his fingers diving into my slit and finding my clit.

"You're wasting no time."

"I can't help myself when it's been a week since I've had you," he groans in my ear, teasing me with his fingers.

A week, my ass.

"It's only been three days," I correct him.

"No way."

I lean into him and press the back of my head against his chest. "True story."

Three days or three minutes. Doesn't matter. I'll always want him again and again.

But I won't always be able to have him.

He slips a single finger inside me and then a second. "It feels like forever since I've been inside you."

His rock-hard erection grinds against my bottom while he slides his fingers in and out of me. The way his hand is wrapped around my body and in that particular position feels sensational. His fingers are rubbing my sweet spot in the most delectable way, each stroke bringing me closer to orgasm.

"Come for me, Lou, and say my name when you do."

I grind harder against his hand, chasing that powerful orgasm that is almost within my reach. Just a little more.

Hutch. Hutch. Hutch. I say his name in my head, ready to scream it when I fall over the edge into that pure oblivion that only he has ever given me. And then it happens. "Hutch… I'm coming."

"Tell me what I want to hear."

Yes. I know exactly what the possessive bastard wants to hear.

"I'm yours." Quick breath.

"All yours." Quick breath.

"Only yours." Quick breath.

The spasms that this man gives me deep within my core… I've come to love them so.

I recognize the sound of tearing foil wrapper, and then he pushes down on the waistband of my panties and shorts, dragging them down my legs. "Bend over the bed."

He's going to take me hard and fast from behind. And I say bring it.

Stretching my upper body across the bed, I grip the linens. His hand cups the back of my thigh and he lifts, placing one of my knees on the mattress. Spreading me apart. Opening me to take him in.

I feel the tip of his erection against my wet core and then he pushes inside me with a force that demonstrates his frustration of not having me for the last three days. The sudden invasion wrenches a cry from my throat, and he stills. "Too rough?"

The sharp stab fades and my body adjusts to the fullness of him inside of me. "No, don't stop."

I rock against him, wanting more, and the rhythm of our rocking bodies finds the perfect synchronization. He grips my hips, pounding into me over and over.

"Lou." My name is only a soft whisper on his lips but it's my cue, the indicator that he is slipping over the edge.

He stills and places a soft kiss against the bare skin of my shoulder. "You are precious to me."

The words are barely there but I hear them. And I covet them.

~

I WAKE AT TWO IN THE MORNING WITH A STORY RUNNING through my head. A love story. A modern-day fairy tale. It's our story, mine with Hutch, and the ending is beautiful.

I get out of bed and grab my laptop. I return to my place beside Hutch and put down the ideas in my head. I can't stand the thought of forgetting a single detail or losing one minute that I could be next to him.

After Hutch has gone to work for the day, I go to the covered raised deck at the back of the house, taking my laptop and fresh ideas with me. I tap upon my keyboard, forming the outline of my new fairy tale based upon us and everything I feel in this moment.

I secretly love this man.

I secretly long for him to ask me to stay.

I secretly dream of a happily ever after with him.

The door leading from the house to the deck opens and I'm slightly irritated by the interruption. Expecting to see one of the staff members—and praying to not see Blair—I'm surprised when it's someone quite unexpected.

Clarissa Hutcheson.

My pulse, which is already racing from the excitement of the story in my head, speeds faster. Why has she come? "Mrs. Hutcheson?"

"No worries, Lou. All is well. I'm only here to visit."

After we just spent the entire weekend together? This seems odd.

"Hutch is at work." Which I'm sure she already knows. "Should I call him?"

"No, lass. I didn't come to see him."

Clarissa Hutcheson is here to see me? That's exciting and scary.

"Would you like to sit out here, or would you prefer to go inside?"

"I'll join you out here. I could stand a wee bit of sunshine and fresh air." She sits on the lounger next to me, her legs extended and head resting against the back of the chair. "I sometimes forget how beautiful this property is."

"It is gorgeous."

"Have you enjoyed living here with my son?"

Shit.

Double shit.

I don't know how to answer that question.

Clarissa laughs. "Don't look so frightened, Lou. I'm not the firing squad."

Maybe not but I still don't know what to say.

"It's all right. I've known for a while that you've been living here with Max."

She knows the truth. I see no reason to insult her by lying. "Yes, ma'am."

"Max and I aren't as close as we once were, but I still know my son well. And he loves you. I see it in the way he looks at you."

I wasn't expecting to hear that.

Is she right? Does Hutch love me? Or is she seeing an extension of the lust he feels for me and is mistaking it for love?

"It's the same with Ava Rose. That wee lass is attached to you. Now you may think me a shameless, meddling mum, but I'm going to ask anyway. Do you love my son and granddaughter?"

I don't have to search my head or my heart for the answer. "I love both of them very much."

And I don't know how in the world I'll ever be able to

walk away from either of them. If the first step doesn't shatter my heart into a million pieces, then the next most assuredly will.

Clarissa Hutcheson slings her legs around and sits sideways on the lounger, facing me. "Max once loved Mina, but something happened between them. He's never told me what it was, but I watched him fall out of love with her. For him, their marriage was over long before she died. Her family didn't see it happening, but I watched all of it unfold before my eyes. And I believe that my son is ready to move on. In fact, I know he is. And I think he could be ready to do that with you."

"He believes that moving on will ruin him in everyone's eyes."

"It's true. Moving on will ruin him in the eyes of some, mostly Mina's family, and they'll see it as a betrayal, but it won't be the end of the world."

"They are deeply rooted within his life."

"Like a weed you can't get rid of."

It's clear that Clarissa sees things as I do.

"He's concerned about his position at the firm."

"And with good reason. Thomas Lochridge will probably fire him and do everything within his power to make sure no one in Edinburgh hires him. I personally believe that would be a blessing. It's time for Max to see that there is life outside of his career and it's passing him by." Clarissa sighs. "What good is all of his money if he doesn't have someone to love? And someone to love him back?"

I already thought that Clarissa Hutcheson was delightful, but now I think she's phenomenal and I adore her.

"We share the same opinion."

"Max is going to be stubborn. He isn't going to want to put his career on the line, and that's where you must do some of the heavy lifting in your relationship. You have to show him that a life outside of that investment firm is a life worth living. A life where happiness means everything and wealth and power and success are minor details."

"He's a money-minded man. That could be hard to do."

She reaches out and takes my hand, squeezing it. "Show him love and everything else will fall into place. I promise."

What she's saying sounds good in theory. Everything could have the potential to fall into place… if our relationship was real. But it isn't.

32

MAXWELL HUTCHESON

Only seven days until my time with Lou is over. A week is too soon to say goodbye. I want more time with her.

I've had hell to pay with Thomas for neglecting some of the firm's most important clients, but I can't help myself. I'm desperate to spend every minute with Lou. I simply can't get enough of her. And that's why I've returned to the house to see her after only being at work for an hour.

Thomas is going to give me shite when I get back to the office.

Fuck, I may not even go back. I might take the whole day off and spend it with Lou.

I open the bedroom door, hoping to find her still in bed. No such luck but I hear the shower running. That could be just as much fun.

I slip out of my jacket and I'm loosening the knot of my tie when I hear Lou's mobile ring. I admit that I'm prying by walking over to see who is calling, but I can't help myself. She knows every aspect about my life, and there are still so many missing pieces to the puzzle of Lou.

Cameron Stewart. It's that name again and this time it's not a notification about a missed call. The personalized ringtone is 'Love Me Harder" and the photo on the screen is of a shorter-haired Lou and a man who looks like he's around her age. The fucker's arms are wrapped around her from behind, and his lips are pressed to the side of her neck right over that spot that drives her crazy.

They look happy. They look like a young couple in love. And I fucking hate it.

The mobile has been ringing for several seconds, so it'll go to voicemail soon. Do I let that happen? Or do I answer Lou's phone and finally find out who he is to her and why he's calling again?

My drive to find out gets the better of me, and I slide the bar across the screen, answering Lou's mobile. And I immediately go blank because I don't know what to say.

"Cait?" a man's voice says.

Cait? That's Lou's real name?

"Are you there, Cait? Can you hear me?"

I remain silent, waiting to hear what other kind of information I might be able to collect before Cameron Stewart realizes that it isn't Cait who has answered her mobile.

"Please listen to me, Cait. I want to tell you how sorry I am. That woman was a mistake and I see that now. Can you ever forgive me?"

I see that I'm not the only one who's been cheated on.

"Damn, I've missed you, baby. And I was hoping that we could get together and talk about how we can make this work. I'm not ready to give up on us."

No, Cameron Stewart. You and Cait won't be getting together to discuss anything.

"Will you at least say something?"

"Sorry, but Cait can't take your call right now."

Silence.

"Are you still there? Did you hear me?"

"Who is this?"

"Cait's boyfriend." Let's see what he has to say to that.

"Is it safe for me to assume that you won't be giving her a message to call me?"

"What do you think?"

"Are you that insecure in your relationship with her?"

I actually am but I'll never admit that to this dick.

"She's with me now. Don't call her again."

I press the end button and return Lou's mobile to its charger on the nightstand. I sit on her side of the bed waiting to see if he'll call back. One minute passes and then another. Nothing. Because he knows that he'll get me again and I'm not who he wants to speak to.

The water stops and Lou comes into the bedroom a few moments later. She's naked with a towel wrapped around her freshly shampooed hair, bringing my cock to attention.

She jolts and a soft squeal escapes when she sees me. "Shit, Hutch. Have you been here all this time?"

"No, I went to work after I kissed you goodbye this morning. I couldn't concentrate so I came back."

She comes to me and wraps her arms around my shoulders. "To see me?"

"Aye."

Her eyes divert to my jacket lying on the bed. "Were you about to take off your clothes and come into the shower with me?"

"I was." My eyes are locked on hers. "Until Cameron Stewart called you."

Her brows tense and a deep V forms between them. "What?"

"He called while you were in the shower. I needed to

know who he is and what he wants with you, so I answered your mobile."

"Why do you need to know these things?"

"Because you're mine. Because the thought of you being with another man makes me crazy. Because I needed to know if he's from your past or present. Because I wanted to tell him to fuck off. Take your pick."

Fuck, I sound obsessed with her.

Because I am.

"I am yours. I'm not with Cameron and I haven't been for a while. He's my past and I've already told him to fuck off. More than once."

"Is he the man that you thought you loved?"

"Stupidly, yes."

"What happened?"

"Before Inamorata, I waited tables at a bar. Cameron was the bartender there and he did what all asshole bartenders do at some point: he went home with a customer. That would have been fine except he was dating me at the time."

He cheated on Lou. He hurt her. And while it pisses me off to know that he did that to her, it also makes me feel relief.

"How long ago?"

"It happened right before Christmas."

Has it been long enough for her to get over this bastard? It isn't possible to guess without knowing the other important variable of their relationship. "How long were you with him?"

"Six months." Twice as long as she's been with me. Not what I wanted to hear.

"Do you still love him?"

"I loved a version of Cameron, but that version turned out to be a fraud. I loved a lie," she says.

"That isn't a no."

"I don't love Cameron. Because I can't love something based upon a lie."

I can't love something based upon a lie. Fuck, those words are poignant. Sobering. Pragmatic.

A lie. That's what I paid her to be.

She looks away when our eyes meet and that's when I see the truth: we are a lie. And she can never love something based upon a lie.

But I don't want to be a lie anymore.

33

CAITRIONA LOUDEN

HUTCH GRIPS MY HIPS AND PULLS ME FORWARD, PRESSING his forehead against my upper stomach. His warm breath against my still-damp skin sends chills over my entire body. "I'm sorry, Lou."

Sorry for what Cameron did to me? I don't think so. "What do you have to be sorry for?"

"I paid you to be my lie."

I watch my fingers twirl through the top of his hair, but it becomes a blur because of the wet lens forming over my eyes. "Please don't say things like that." I don't want this to be a lie.

"I'm sorry for the secrecy. Sorry for making you pretend. Sorry for fucking you when I should have been making love to you."

I realize that the wet lenses over my eyes have become tears rolling down my face when they drip from my jaw.

"It kills me to see you cry."

Lifting his face, he stretches upward and kisses both of my wet cheeks. And I die a little on the inside.

His lips move from my cheek to my mouth and he

presses a kiss there. When I open my mouth, his tongue slips inside and the two come together for a familiar yet new sensual waltz.

We've shared countless kisses but this one is different. It's new. It's telling. And I taste the words that he can't or won't say.

His touch has changed. It's tender yet possessive, as though he's handling his most precious, delicate treasure.

Hutch cares for me. I feel it.

His mouth feathers kisses lightly down my chin and throat. It slowly travels lower, tasting my skin, until it reaches my breast and closes around it. I lace my fingers through his hair when the wet glide of his tongue over my sensitive nipple prompts something between a moan and the sound of his name.

He looks up at me. And I see something more than lust in those pale blue eyes.

Is it love?

Please, please, please let it be.

I want so desperately for him to love me.

I shake my head and the towel wrapped around my wet hair falls. Wet strands fall forward, and he reaches up, pushing them away from my face. "Such a beauty. My beauty," he whispers.

Taking my time, I undress him. And when he's as bare as I am, I climb on top of him.

His flesh against my flesh—there's nothing in the world like it. The sensation it creates sends a wave of tingles directly between my legs. And I'm no longer wet because I just took a shower.

He slides off the edge of the bed and stands, taking me with him. Our bodies turn and he gently lowers my back to the bed. My mouth, my neck, my chest, my belly, my hipbones, and everything in between—that's the path that his mouth takes on its way down.

He kisses the inside of my right knee and then the inside of my thigh. Closing my eyes and breathing deeply, I wait for what I know he's going to do. And then it happens—his wet tongue moves smoothly up my center.

I lift my head from the bed and watch the top of his head moving between my legs. Reaching out, I push my fingers into his hair and scrape my nails against his scalp.

A young rosebud slowly opening until it's in full bloom.

A snowball rolling down a hill, growing in size, and coming apart when it crashes into a tree.

A tub filling with water until the excess flows over the edge on to the floor.

That's how my orgasm happens.

When the more powerful contractions in my womb stop, I relax against the bed and breathe, savoring the final little post-orgasmic quivers. And my brain is empty. Total mush.

Hutch scales my body, kissing his way up until he's hovering above me. His eyes bore into mine and I know it sounds crazy, but it feels like something within us links. Like we mesh to become one.

Bending my knees, I wrap my legs around Hutch. I tilt my hips upward and the tip of his erection presses against my opening. With my hands splayed on each of his cheeks, I cradle his face and watch his eyes as I use my feet to coax him inside of me. Unsheathed.

His bare erection enters me, and we are entwined. Joined. Fused.

One.

He closes his eyes and whispers a word that I don't quite understand, but I'd swear that it's my name. My real name.

"Say it again."

"Cait."

Watching Hutch's beautiful face dancing over me, I revel in the sensation of feeling him, skin on skin, inside of me for the first time. All that I can taste is this moment, and I know that I'd give up everything I have to stay like this with him forever.

The affection I feel for him squeezes my heart like a thousand pounds sitting on my chest. Hot tears roll down the sides of my face as I finally own the feelings that I have for this man.

I love Maxwell Hutcheson with every beat of my heart, with every breath in my lungs.

"I want to come inside you."

My head spins with the ecstasy of his words and I forget who he is, who I am, and what our arrangement has been. "Yes. I want you to."

Mark me. Fill me with a part of yourself. Make me yours.

Tightening my legs around him, I use my feet to squeeze his body against mine. He groans and thrusts deeply, stilling when he spasms inside of me.

With his forehead pressed against mine, I look at his eyes and whisper, "I love you."

There. I said those three words.

And I regret saying them when I see the expression on his face. I have made a mistake.

I don't know what I see in his eyes, but it isn't love. And why should it be? He paid for my companionship. Not my love.

Oh my God. I feel so stupid.

I need to get up. I need to get away from him.

"Get off of me."

I push at his shoulders and he rolls away from me. I

stumble, narrowly evading a fall, as I make a mad dash for the bathroom. Cupping my hands over my mouth, I look at the woman in the mirror with tears streaming down her face.

You want his love so badly that you've allowed yourself to see and feel something that isn't there. It was never there. And it'll never be there.

Your love for him. It's the very weapon that will wound you the deepest.

I swore that I would never make the same mistakes as my mother. I said I'd never love a man who didn't love me in return. I vowed to stop it before it went that far. And I still let it happen.

It isn't wanton flesh but love that brings me shame.

34

MAXWELL HUTCHESON

Her name is Cait. But she'll always be Lou to me.

My NOLA girl.

Lying on my back, I stare at the ceiling and attempt to sort out the thoughts in my head and emotions in my heart. I'm so fucking confused by the happiness and fear that I feel. The two are battling one another inside of me, and I'm not sure which is stronger.

Lou means something to me. There's no denying that. But being with her openly will change everything. There's no denying that either.

Part of me wants Lou to leave so I can go back to my life before her. That life was lonely, but it was easy. And then there's this other piece of me that exploded when she said that she loved me. That part longs for her to stay with me forever.

I leave the bed and go to the bathroom door. Of course, it's locked. "Lou?"

No reply.

"Please come out so we can talk."

"You should just go back to work."

That isn't Lou's normal voice. It's nasally and congested because my sweet lass is crying. And it's more than I can stand.

"Please, Lou."

Another minute passes, and she opens the door. Her body is wrapped in another towel and her eyes are downcast—she's hiding both her nude body and eyes from me.

"Please don't do that, Lou."

Her eyes still don't meet mine. "Don't do what?"

"Hide from me."

I reach out, tilting her chin upward so I can see her eyes, but she closes her lids and locks me out. "Please look at me."

A moment later, she does. The whites of her eyes are red and inflamed, confirming what I already knew, and the hurt I see beneath her beautiful hazel orbs wrecks me.

I love her.

I love her and I can't admit it.

"Come here."

Taking her hand in mine, I pull her to the bed. I untuck the towel under her arms and she grips it in the center between her breasts. "Let it go."

She releases her grip and lets the towel fall to the floor. And again, we're flesh against flesh.

"Lie down."

When she's on her back, I creep over her on my all fours. She blinks and it forces some tears to roll down her temples and into her hair.

She's drenched with my come and I glide into her with ease. "Close your eyes. Close your mind. Just feel me moving inside of you. Only feel us in this moment and you'll know how important you are to me. I won't have to say it."

I study her face, paying particular attention to her

mouth. Her lips part and the pace of her breath moving in and out of her chest is in sync with the rhythm of my body moving in and out of her.

Slow. Deep. Steady.

I love you, Lou. Even if I don't say the words, can't you feel how much I love you? Can't you sense it in the way that I touch you? See it in the way that I look at you?

Her walls contract around my cock, and it pushes me over the edge. I come deep inside her again, giving her every drop that I have to give.

Lowering my head, I press my forehead to hers. "I need you to tell me that we're okay."

She blinks rapidly. "We're okay."

I'm not sure I believe her. "Do you swear?"

"I swear."

I stay that way for a while, my cock softening inside of her. "I wish I could stay with you, but I have to go back to the office."

"I know."

She watches me put on my suit and then crawls behind me, sliding her arms around my waist when I sit on the edge of the bed to put on my shoes. "I'm never going to make it back to work at this rate. I'll probably get fired."

"I don't think that would be so bad."

"Losing my job wouldn't be bad? In what world?"

She presses the side of her face to my back. "Wealth and success don't equate to happiness."

I turn my face, looking at her over my shoulder. "What does that mean?"

"There are other things in life that can make you happier than praise and money."

I turn around and push her down on the bed, pinning her hands over her head. "What kind of things would make me happier?"

"Only you know the answer to that."

Lou's words are a spark that ignites a flame. And that flame burns hot in my mind.

Lou has given me something to think about.

35

CAITRIONA LOUDEN

TOMORROW IS THE LAST DAY OF THE MONTH. AUGUST 31. My final day with Hutch.

It took twenty-three years to find love and only eighty-one days to lose it. Is it possible that life is actually that cruel?

How will we say goodbye? Will he hug me before he leaves for work and tell me that it's been a blast? Will he hold me in his arms and savor our final moments together? I don't know. And I don't want to think about it. I only know that even after I'm gone, he'll still have a piece of me.

My heart.

He's sleeping beside me in the dark and I listen to his breathing. It's a predictable cycle: a slow deep breath in, his lips stick together, and the breath he exhales makes a "puh" sound on the way out. I've been hearing it since the first night I slept in his bed. It annoyed the shit out of me in the beginning, but I'm used to hearing it now. I expect it. I love it. And I'm going to miss it.

Lying on my side, I face him, and I cry. I cry like a damn baby. I cup my hands over my mouth, muffling the deep gasps when I feel like I'm losing my breath. He tosses in the bed and I cup my hands tighter, hoping that he won't hear my sobbing.

"Lou?"

I don't answer, hoping he'll assume that I'm asleep.

"Lou?"

"Hmm?"

"Are you crying?

I take a deep breath and my chest makes that betraying sound only associated with crying. "No."

God, that didn't sound even a little bit convincing.

"Come here."

I slide across the bed and place my head on his chest. He wraps his arm around me and rubs it up and down from my shoulder to my elbow. "Everything okay?"

"Yeah." I lie because it's easier than telling him what's killing me inside.

"You don't sound okay."

No. Nothing about losing the man that I love is okay. But I can't tell him that, so I do the one thing that makes me feel closest to him. The thing that makes me feel like he loves me back even if it's not true. Because it's a lie that I've come to love.

My beautiful illusion.

I move to my all fours and hitch one of my legs across him, straddling his body. My hands are palm side down against the mattress, one on each side of his head. I bend my elbows, lowering my still-naked body down on top of his, and I press my mouth to his for a kiss.

I roll my hips, moving my wet slit up and down the length of his swelling erection. I move a little higher than intended and hook the tip of his cock at my entrance. The angle is perfect for sliding inside of me. So I let it.

He grips my hips, squeezing them and pulling me

downward. I rise up and sit back, sinking his remaining length inside me until it can go no farther.

"I feel things with you that I've never felt before," Hutch whispers.

"It's the same for me."

He flexes his hips up every time I slide down and a deep groan vibrates from his chest. The sound is so male. Such a turn-on. And I would do this with him every day if it were up to me, but it's not my choice. It's his. And he isn't asking me to stay.

He has my heart.

And I haven't a chance.

"Fuck, Lou." His fingertips dig into the fleshy part of my hips. "I'm going to come inside you."

His cock twitches inside me and he makes a deep growling sound. And I know that he has just filled me with a part of himself, just like every other time we've been together this week.

I collapse against his chest, his arms wrapping around me. I don't know how long I listen to his heartbeat, memorizing the sound.

"I have to get up, mo maise."

He kisses the top of my head and slides out of bed, walking naked to the bathroom. That perfect ass… it's another thing that I'm going to miss.

When he's ready to leave for work, Hutch comes over just to kiss me goodbye as he has every morning since I moved in with him. "I'll try to leave early so we can do something special tonight."

"What kind of special?"

"Anything you want. Your choice."

"You might regret giving me that kind of leeway."

"Never." He places a closed-mouth kiss against my lips. "See you this afternoon."

~

"Everyone may call you a redhead but you, my sweet Ava Rose, are a carrot top. Your food is the same color as your hair."

Ava Rose smiles and a little baby giggle fills the kitchen. "You think that's funny, huh?"

She opens her mouth and I spoon another bite of smashed carrots into her mouth. "Mmm… mmm… that's good stuff, right?"

Ava Rose finishes her lunch and we go into the living room. We sit on the sofa and I begin reading her favorite book. How do I know it's her favorite book? She always becomes very still and quiet when I read it to her.

Lunch. Book. Nap. It's become our daily routine. And I'm going to miss it terribly.

"The wee bunny hopped…" I stop midsentence when I see movement in my peripheral vision. Dammit. The snobby sister-in-law is back.

"This must feel very gratifying for you."

Gratification is the last thing I feel right now.

I've had two interactions with this nosy woman, and everything out of her mouth on both occasions was insults and violations of Hutch's privacy.

"Oh, look, Ava Rose. Aunt Blair is here." Auntie monster is more like it.

"It's amusing that you think you can come into my sister's house and fill her shoes."

From what Hutch has told me, Mina was a bitch. I wouldn't want to fill her shoes. "I'm not trying to fill anyone's shoes."

"Speaking of shoes… since when does a housekeeper wear Louboutins?"

Well, shit. She's got me there. "I don't owe you an explanation about my shoes."

"It's funny that you mention explanations. Let's talk about those." She takes a folder out of her purse and opens it. "Caitriona Brooke Louden. Born July 8, 1996. Does that person ring a bell for you at all, LOU?"

Shit. How does she know my full name and birthdate?

"It should since it's me. Lou… short for Louden. Do you have a problem with my nickname?"

"Your nickname? No. But I have plenty of other problems with you so let's keep going. Your mum, Rebecca Louden, died when you were sixteen. Overdose. But before that, she worked in a bar on Bourbon Street. Not exactly mother material."

"I can't argue with that." I'll save her the time of reading my dad's history aloud. "My father, Arran Watson, he's not parenting material either. At least where I'm concerned. Is this supposed to be going somewhere?"

"It looks as though we have a case of like mother, like daughter. You followed in her footsteps by waiting tables at The Last Drop."

"Unfortunately."

"Where did you go to work after you left your waitressing position at the bar?"

"I became a housekeeper for Mr. Hutcheson."

"You mean after you were trained at Inamorata to be an escort?" she says.

Every little detail in her report has been spot-on so far, but I neither confirm nor deny her allegation.

"There's one thing that the private investigator hasn't been able to prove. Did Max hire you to be his live-in whore, or did you come to work for him with the intention of weaseling your way into his life and then his bed?"

Nothing I say at this point is going to redeem myself

with her, and I don't really care to, but I can at least save Hutch's image. "Mr. Hutcheson hired me to clean the house. I thought I could seduce him, but my efforts were useless."

"I hope you realize that you can't continue working here."

Who the hell does she think she is, coming in here telling me I no longer work here? "My employment is between Mr. Hutcheson and myself."

"Listen to me carefully, Caitriona. You're going to take Ava Rose to her nanny, and then you're going to pack your things and leave. Today. Now. I want you out of Max's life. Out of Ava Rose's life. Out of my life."

"I'm not walking out on Mr. Hutcheson."

"You are because if you don't, I'm going to tell my father everything that Max has been doing with you."

"There's nothing to tell."

She opens the file and takes out a photograph, holding it up for me to see. It's Hutch and me. We're in his bed. Naked. Kissing. Having sex from the looks of it. It looks like the photo was taken outside through his bedroom window.

We were being photographed in bed? What a fucking invasion of privacy. Hutch won't be happy about this at all.

"I know everything about you and Max. Your friend Chambers was very forthcoming about you and your employment at Inamorata."

Well, damn. Chambers managed to fuck me after all.

"If you know everything, then what was the point of asking me about Hutch?"

"I wanted to see for myself how you'd react. And now that I know you care about Max, I'm going to use that to my advantage. Leave and never contact him again. Say one word to him about any of this and life as he knows it is over. I will ruin him."

I love Hutch. And I can't allow his life to be ruined because of me. Especially when our arrangement is almost over anyway.

He doesn't love me. If he did, he would have said so by now. And he isn't going to ask me to stay. If he were, he would have done it already. God knows that I've given him every opportunity this week short of begging.

"All right. I'll go."

She smiles and she should. She's getting her way. "I look forward to never seeing you again."

Tear rolls down my face as I take Ava Rose to the nursery. I don't want to give up this little girl. I don't want to walk away and never see her again. I love her.

Mrs. McVey has stepped out of the nursery so it's only Ava Rose and me. I sit in the glider and she wraps her arms around me, her head on my shoulder. Ready for her nap but I have things to say to her.

"Your daddy loves you. Don't ever think for one second that he doesn't." I rock back and forth with her, sobbing like a baby myself. "This hasn't been easy for him, but he's changing. He's changing for you. He's not where he needs to be yet, but he's going to get there. He just needs a little more time."

Ava Rose falls asleep in my arms, and I hold her against my chest. Against my heart. "You'll always have a place in my heart. I won't ever forget you or the time we've spent together."

I get up and place Ava Rose in her crib. I kiss my fingertips and press them to her soft, chubby cheek. "Goodbye, sweet girl."

36

MAXWELL HUTCHESON

Today has been one of the more miserable days of my life. That's saying a lot after everything I've gone through during the last few years.

The life I've had with Lou for the last three months is coming to an end. I've put it off for as long as possible, but it's time for me to make some hard decisions.

I see three options:

One—I let Lou go. Allow our contract to expire at midnight and never see her again.

Two—ask her to extend the contract and continue our relationship with the same terms.

Three—allow our contract to expire and ask her to continue our relationship without terms. No contract. No arrangement. No exchange of money.

Option one is a no. I can't never see Lou again.

Option two is a possibility but not what I really want. I've tired of the secrecy. And I want more.

Option three is the only choice where I get what I really want.

Decision made. This arrangement is ending and not

only because our time is up. I want a real relationship with Lou.

I have my family's approval. And Ava Rose's. Neither are necessary for Lou and me to be together, but I'm happy to have their acceptance. It means a lot because they're the most important people in my life.

And everyone else… to hell with what they're going to think or say. And that goes double for the Lochridges. They're done dictating what I should and shouldn't do with my life.

I feel good about this decision. Very good. And I can't wait to talk it over with Lou.

I tap on Thomas's office door. "I'm leaving for the day."

"You've been doing that a lot lately, haven't you? Leaving early?"

"I don't think four-thirty is considered all that early by most people's standards."

"Perhaps not, but we have different standards at this firm, don't we?"

I've always worked seventy to eighty hours a week for Thomas. I earn more money than any other employee at Lochridge Investments. I'm quite certain that he isn't a fan of my decreased hours.

Wealth and success don't equate to happiness. There are other things in life that can make you happier than praise and money.

What kind of things would make me happier?

Only you know the answer to that question.

I haven't stopped thinking about that conversation with Lou. I want to find the happiness that she was talking about and claim it as mine.

"I'll see you tomorrow, Thomas."

HUTCH: I'm leaving the office. Can't wait to see what you have planned for tonight.

I look at my mobile every few minutes, eager to see what Lou's reply will be. Nothing. And still nothing by the time I arrive home.

It's not like her to not respond within a few minutes. Maybe she's running late and is in the shower? Or maybe she's busy tending to the details of something she has planned for tonight?

I enter the house and I'm surprised to find Sonny still here. Guess we're having dinner at home. And why wouldn't we? Lou has no idea that I'm ready to take this relationship public. She wouldn't have planned on us going out for dinner.

"Something smells good. Did Lou request something special for tonight?"

"I haven't seen Miss Lou today. I chose salmon for tonight. I hope that's all right."

How odd. I would have expected her to choose the menu for tonight.

"Aye, salmon sounds delicious."

I go to the bedroom and no Lou, which contradicts my theory about her not replying to my text because she was in the shower.

Perhaps she's in the nursery? She's been spending a lot of time with Ava Rose.

"Good evening, Mr. Hutcheson. Come to visit the wee lass?"

She isn't in the nursery either. "I'm actually looking for Lou. I thought that she might be visiting Ava Rose."

The corner of Mrs. McVey's mouth tugs downward. "You've not spoken with her?"

You've not spoken with her? Something about that sounds ominous.

"Not since this morning."

"Oh… Mr. Hutcheson."

"Has something happened?"

My first thought goes directly to Cameron Stewart. Did he call again? Find a way to get to her?

My next thought is of her father. Has that bastard done something else to cause her pain?

Or Chambers?

"Miss Lou brought Ava Rose to me just after lunch and she was in tears. Completely beside herself."

"About what?"

"She didn't say. I only know that it happened after Miss Blair's visit."

Oh, great. Another visit from my nosy, overbearing sister-in-law.

"Where is Lou?"

"She's gone."

"What do you mean gone?"

"She said her goodbyes to Ava Rose and me and left."

"Did she say when she was coming back?"

"She isn't coming back, Mr. Hutcheson."

"What time did she leave?"

"One-thirty. Maybe two."

Fuck, that was three hours ago, and she didn't call me? What is going on?

"You don't know where she went?"

"No, sir."

I don't understand what is happening. We had plans for tonight. Surely, she wouldn't have left me without so much as a goodbye.

Except that she has.

I call her mobile as I return to the bedroom, and it

goes straight to voicemail. I immediately end the call and message her.

HUTCH: I don't understand. What happened?
HUTCH: Where are you?
HUTCH: We need to talk.

I search the bedroom while I wait for her reply. Her purse is gone. No laptop in its usual place or its charger plugged into the wall. But what causes me the most anguish is that her birth control pills are gone. She has left with no intentions of coming back.

Why have you done this, Lou?

HUTCH: Why have you left me?
HUTCH: We aren't finished. I have so many things to say to you.

Mrs. McVey said that Lou was upset after Blair's visit. That bitch did this. She knows what happened. I'm certain of it and she's going to tell me.

The drive to Doug and Blair's house takes far longer than I'd like. Traffic is always a killer this time of day. It's always been one of the reasons that I often stayed late at work. That and my lack of desire to go home to Mina. But it's been different with Lou. I wanted to leave work sooner so I could spend the evenings with her.

Doug and Blair have no staff members in their home so it's Doug who answers the door when I knock. "Max. This is a surprise."

I'm guessing that it's a surprise for him but not his wife.

"I've come to see Blair. Is she home?"

"Aye, we were just sitting down to dinner. Come in and join us."

I enter the house and follow my brother-in-law to the dining room. Blair smiles when she sees me as though she didn't just turn my world upside down. "Hello, Max. I wish that you'd called. I would have set a place for you."

She wishes that I'd called before showing up at her door? That's rich coming from her.

"What happened with Lou when you came to my house today?"

Blair places her hand on her chest. "Oh dear. Is everything all right?"

"No. I came home from work and she was gone."

"Well, you know how those kinds of people can be. They find other positions and move on without any notice at all. They're an unreliable lot of people."

"Mrs. McVey said that she was crying after your visit."

"I'm sorry, Max. I don't know what to tell you."

"Did you have words with her?" Again.

"We spoke briefly but the conversation was friendly."

Fucking liar. How do I know? Blair is never friendly.

I don't know why I came here. Blair is never going to admit to anything that might have prompted Lou's desertion. She's made it very clear that she doesn't want her around.

"I'm sorry to have interrupted your dinner."

Blair gets up from the table and follows me. "Don't go, Max."

I stop when I reach the front door. "I have to find her."

"You shouldn't worry about her. She's just a housekeeper. You won't have a problem finding another one."

Every word out of Blair's mouth is wrong. "You shouldn't make statements about things you know nothing about."

Five steps. "Max."

Five more steps and her voice isn't quite so soft. "Max..."

Five more steps and she screams my name the same way Mina did when she didn't get her way. The sound sends a chill down my spine.

Ignoring Blair's shouts, I stalk toward the car. Once inside, I punch the back of the passenger seat in front of me. "Fuck!"

Calvin looks ahead and is silent.

"I'm sorry."

"No worries, sir. We've all been there."

I already hated that bitch, but my previous feelings were nothing compared to the rage I feel toward her right now. She's the reason Lou is gone. I know it without a bit of doubt.

Think, think, think. Where would Lou have gone?

Home. It's the only reasonable answer.

"You drove Lou to her flat once?"

"Yes, sir."

"Do you remember where?"

"It's been a while, but I think I could manage to find it again. Would you like me to take you there?"

"Aye."

A wee bit of the panic that I was feeling subsides during the drive to Lou's flat. I'm confident that this is going to be all right. We'll talk it out, and I'll make right whatever way Blair wronged Lou.

"This is it, sir."

Damn. It's a large building with many floors. "I don't suppose that she would have indicated which flat is hers?" It's a stupid question but I have to ask.

"She didn't, sir. I'm sorry."

"It's all right."

I get out and go to the front entrance. As expected, it's locked.

What the fuck do I do now?

Wait. I wait for someone to come out or enter. There's no other choice.

Five, ten, fifteen minutes pass and a tenant finally comes out of the building. Thank fuck.

"Excuse me, sir. I'm looking for a tenant in this building. A woman. Twenty-three years old, small frame, long brown hair and hazel eyes. A real stunner."

"You just described at least a dozen women in this building."

"Her name is Cait."

The man shrugs. "I'm sorry. The only Cait that I know in this building doesn't match your description."

"What about two roommates? Cait and Rachel?"

He nods. "Aye. I know who you mean. They stopped coming around. I think they moved out."

"Are you sure?"

"No. I only know that I used to see them a lot, and now I don't anymore."

"Thank you, sir."

All right. This has turned out to be a dead end, but Inamorata won't be. Cora will be my saving grace. She knows everything about Lou's real life.

"No luck, sir?"

"No, but Inamorata is our next stop. I'll get the answers I need there."

The young woman sitting at the front desk of Inamorata is a new face. "I'm here to see Cora."

"Do you have an appointment?"

"No, but tell her that Maxwell Hutcheson is here to see her."

"All right. Please have a seat while you wait. You're welcome to help yourself to a whisky if you like."

Aye, I could stand a wee bit of the water of life.

"You can go in, Mr. Hutcheson. Cora will see you now."

Finally. Something is going my way.

"What a lovely surprise, Mr. Hutcheson. What may I do to help you?"

"I'm here about Lou."

"Aye, your contract is ending at midnight. You're here to talk about extending it?"

No. I'm done with that nonsense. "I'm here to get Lou's contact information."

Cora's head tilts and her brows tense. "Why would you need that information? Are you not presently in contact with her?"

"She left today, and I don't know how to reach her."

"You don't have her mobile number?"

"Aye, but she isn't answering."

"She's still in contract with you. Why would she not be taking your calls?"

"I'm not sure."

"You've not had any problems prior to today?"

"None."

"Do you think that she's in any kind of danger?"

"No, I don't think it's anything like that."

"That's strange. Give me a moment and let me see if I can find out what's going on."

Cora places her glasses on her face and watches her computer screen as she types on her keyword. No doubt, she's opening Lou's file—Lou's file that contains all of her personal data. Fuck, what I wouldn't give to have a look at that information.

Cora picks up the phone and enters a number. "Lou,

this is Cora. I have Mr. Hutcheson in my office and he's very upset. What is going on?"

Cora nods as she listens to Lou talk. Fuck, I want to reach over her desk and swipe the phone out of her hand. This is between Lou and me. Cora really has no part in it.

"I understand. I'll take care of it."

Cora ends the call. "All right. She explained everything and this problem is easily solved."

Thank fuck.

Cora takes out a leather binder and writes down Lou's information.

"This should take care of it."

She tears the paper along the perforated line, and I look at the check she's handing to me. "What is that supposed to be?"

"You're short a day of the contracted time frame. It's a refund."

"I don't want a fucking refund. I. Want. Lou."

"I'm sorry, Mr. Hutcheson. That isn't possible."

"Why the fuck not?"

Cora places the check on her desk and pushes it toward me. "Your refund, Mr. Hutcheson."

"I told you. I want Lou. Not a refund."

"Take the refund or don't." She shrugs. "Makes no difference to me."

"I need you to tell me where Lou lives."

"I'm not going to do that."

She wants money. "How much?"

"How much what?"

"How much money is it going to cost me to get her address?"

"I'm not withholding Lou's information because I want your money. I run a business that is based upon trust and privacy. I'm obligated to keep all personal information private. I can't give that kind of information to clients. Surely, you understand why."

"I'm not just any client."

"No, you certainly are not. I'll give you that."

"I'm not here because I want to stalk Lou. I'm here because I love her."

"I believe you, Mr. Hutcheson, but it changes nothing. I can't disclose her private information."

What the fuck do I do now?

This isn't happening. The woman I love didn't just walk out of my life without a trace. I didn't just hit another roadblock in my only real lead.

"I can't let her go."

"I appreciate your attachment to Lou. I do. And I'd love nothing more than to see you find her and work this out. But it can't be with any information from me. You'll have to find her on your own."

"And how do I do that when I don't even know her real name?"

"You're a wealthy man who always gets what he wants. I'm sure that you'll come up with something."

I leave Cora's office, walking like a zombie to the car. I get inside and sit there. Thinking. Thinking. Thinking.

Fuck, I'm such a wanker.

Lou told me that she loved me. I had the perfect opportunity to tell her how I felt, and I let it slip through my fingers.

It's no wonder she left. Why would she stay?

Lou entered my life and became my world. I fell in love with her and now she's gone. But this isn't over. I'm not letting her go like that. At least not without telling her how I feel.

I phone Brady. Damn, I'm lucky that conniving son of a bitch is my best mate. He'll know what to do next.

37

CAITRIONA LOUDEN

I don't understand. What happened? Where are you? We need to talk. Why have you left me? We aren't finished. I have so many things to say to you.

Hutch's texts wrecked me. Wrecked. Me. And it was the hardest thing I've ever done, but I blocked him. I had no choice—I can't bear to read any more of his messages when I already know that I can't respond.

"I'm so sorry about this, Rachel. I don't mean to intrude on you and Claud, but I have nowhere else to go."

I could have gotten a hotel room. I have plenty of money, but the truth is that I couldn't stand the thought of being alone tonight. I need Rachel. She's the only constant in my life. The only support I have.

"Don't worry about it for a second, Cait. Claud and I don't mind. You can stay here as long as you like."

Claud's house is enormous. I could stay in one of the wings and never run into either of them, but I still feel like I'm intruding.

"I'll start looking for a place tomorrow."

"Tomorrow is a wee bit soon. I think you need time to

decompress before you jump into something as stressful as looking for a place to live."

"Claud's being very kind by letting me stay here. I don't want to interrupt his life. Or yours."

"You won't be interrupting anything. He's going out of town tomorrow for a week. You and I can catch up on our girl time."

As much as I love being with Hutch, I've missed Rachel. "I would love that."

"You didn't bring a bag. What do you need?"

I ran out of Hutch's house without packing a thing. I grabbed what I couldn't live without and ran like someone fleeing a house fire. "I can get by tonight if you'll give me something to sleep in. Any old thing will do."

Rachel laughs. "I think you know that Claud has seen to it that I don't have *any old thing*."

"Right." Just like Hutch saw to it that I didn't have *any old thing*.

"We'll go shopping tomorrow and get everything you need."

"A fresh start sounds like a good idea."

"Do you want something to help you sleep?"

"You know what? I think I do."

I'm not sure what kind of medicine Rachel gives me. And I don't care. I want to turn off my mind and not think about Hutch and me.

I stare at the ceiling in the dark, waiting for my sleep aid to kick in, and I'm reunited with an old familiar feeling —the ache of heartbreak. I can't believe that I'm in this place again, and what's worse is that it's my own fault. I did this to myself.

I didn't want to see the truth because doing so would mean that my beautiful illusion would be destroyed. I believed the voices in my head telling me that I was worthy of love, that I was deserving of good things, that I was good enough for Hutch. And I believed the lie. Because I'm a foolish woman.

Truth hurts. But it always wins. And the truth is that Maxwell Hutcheson may not always be in my life, but he'll always be in my heart.

Hutch and Lou's story will conclude in
Beautiful Ever After: Beautiful Illusions Duet Book 2

ABOUT THE AUTHOR

Georgia Cates is the New York Times, USA Today, and Wall Street Journal Best-Selling Author. She resides in rural Mississippi with her wonderful husband, Jeff, and their two beautiful daughters. She spent fourteen years as a labor and delivery nurse before she decided to pursue her dream of becoming an author and hasn't looked back yet.

Sign-up for Georgia's newsletter at
www.georgiacates.com.
Get the latest news, first look at teasers,
and giveaways just for subscribers.

Stay connected with Georgia at:
Twitter, Facebook, Tumblr, Instagram,
Goodreads and Pinterest.

ALSO BY GEORGIA CATES

BEAUTIFUL ILLUSIONS DUET

Eight-One Nights

Beautiful Ever After

STANDALONES

Dear Agony

Indulge

Sweet Torment

THE SIN TRILOGY

A Necessary Sin

The Next Sin

One Last Sin

The Sin Trilogy Bundle

SIN SERIES STANDALONE NOVELS

Endurance

Unintended

Redemption

THE BEAUTY SERIES

Beauty from Pain

Beauty from Surrender

Beauty from Love

The Beauty Series Bundle

MEN OF LOVIBOND

Tap

Stout

Porter

Men of Lovibond Collection

GOING UNDER SERIES

Going Under

Shallow

Going Under Complete Duo

THE VAMPIRE AGAPE SERIES

Blood of Anteros

Blood Jewel

Blood Doll

The Complete Vampire Agape Series

Made in the USA
San Bernardino, CA
10 May 2019